DARK WATERS

DARK WATERS

Peter von Bleichert

4249-VONB

ISBN #: Softcover 0-7388-2132-2

This is a work of fiction. Names, characters, places and incidents either are the product of the author's imagination or are used fictitiously, and any resemblance to any actual persons, living or dead, events, or locales is entirely coincidental.

This book was printed in the United States of America.

To order additional copies of this book, contact:
Xlibris Corporation
1-888-7-XLIBRIS
www.Xlibris.com
Orders@Xlibris.com

CONTENTS

1

2

3

For Jennifer A.

1

Prologue: Relics

1.

The back wheels of the mud caked Land Rover skidded slightly, its headlights bouncing momentarily on the twisted thickets and prickles that lined the dirt and gravel road. Here, four hundred miles from the sea amid the arid wilderness of the Australian interior, the sun was setting later and the land held onto the last trickle of day light that escaped the veil of night.

"'Ere, mate, have a beah."

"Thanks. Nice and cold, eh?"

The orange wisps of the sky silhouetted the two bouncing passengers inside the speeding vehicle. Rocks and dust scattered in a cloud that further colorized the dusk; the Rover sped up.

"There they arrre, mate." The larger of the two men from the nearby town of Richmond, population: one thousand four hundred, pointed. Two pick up trucks in the now gray distance were parked perpendicular to one another; their bright head and roof lights illuminating a small grass covered embankment. The seat springs squeaked as the truck hit another violent bump. The taller slender man who drove reached up to steady his fedora that was already indented from hitting the roof of the cabin.

The day finally surrendered to night behind the craggy peaks on the horizon, raising a curtain of stars across the huge sky. The Land Rover pulled up to the other two trucks and the commotion next to the illuminated area. Its occupants threw open their doors, exited the vehicle and slammed them in unison. Shapes stood hunched over an area as a cry came from the huddle.

"Eh, Rob, Johnny. Took yah two lawng enough mates! Christ. Look 'ere, we got's a treasure for yah."

"Yeah, and it would eat you for breakfast." A woman's voice came from beyond the huddle of people. The two men pierced the crowd and saw the brownish fossilized bone of a tooth-laden skull. It's long jaw holding rows of well preserved long, thin spike-like teeth. The woman, her long brown braided hair descending from beneath her hat and finally resting on her round hips, gently brushed the dry caked earth from an eye socket and the cap of the fossilized brain cavity. Her wooden handled camel hairbrush gently removed fine pieces of stone and dirt from the folds of the bone. "There is minah damage to the hid section 'ere. Note how you can see the primary hard palate and the outline of what used to be the posterior soft palate. The nasopharynx and piglottis have also left an imprint in the surrounding soil. Hey John, how are yah?"

"Fine, Bridgett. Whatcha got?"

"Looks like the big one. An intact specimen. Congrats. I want photos of the trachea area before further excavation. There are some juicy anatomical details. Can't wait to get the whole lot back to Sydney." John tipped his hat and kicked the ground. "After you get your commish of course. You can pull your team off anyway, an' I'll get mine in."

2.

Yoshikazu Miyamoto looked out over the Ishikari Mountains of Hokkaidō and started down the pebble path to the lake's shore. As with every morning, fog began to cascade down the surrounding foothills and settle into a thick blanket on the lakes mithril surface; it would again retreat in late morning when the sun moved higher into the clear sky. Yoshikazu was an Ainu, an aboriginal people that differed from and were often persecuted by the Korean descendant mainstream Japanese. At forty-three he was fit from years of manual labor. He thought of the smooth warm skin of his wife and the lovemaking they had shared in the chill air of the new day. A humble man, Yoshikazu was unaware he would help begin the unfolding of far off events.

Residing on the northernmost of the Home Islands, the Ainu held tightly to the traditions and mores of the ancient culture; so often discarded by the materialistic modern Japan. Having reached the smooth stones at the shore of Lake Kussharo, he clapped his hands three times and bowed to the rising sun as it peaked from between the jagged peaks in the eastern distance. The homes nestled amongst the trees of the town Teshikaga, the wood and paper houses of his family and friends, glowed in the golden light of the dawn.

After repeating honors to each of the still dark remaining compass points, Yoshikazu turned for the handful of small wooden docks that jutted out from the shore. At the end of the shortest one, his wooden skiff was tied. Though modest, she was proudly cared for. Named after Yoshikazu's wife, Miki, the skiff sat abreast of his friend Akira's smaller, older vessel. Her freshly painted white hull stood out in the grayness of the morning at the end of the planked dock. Yoshikazu strode to her and, like a gymnast on the vault, boarded.

He removed the small opaque bottle of sake he had filled the prior evening and carried in a leather pouch at his side. Sprinkling the line and hooks with the rice wine, he then raised the bottle to the misty lake and drank a mouthful on its behalf giving it a symbolic taste. The traditional meeting of the first day of the fishing season continued when Yoshi bellowed, "Chinkara!" to the lake. A swan answered somewhere in the distance. He moved for the back of the boat where, from the transom hung an outboard motor. Like Yoshikazu, it too began to show the years.

After being gently lowered into the cold, fresh water and with a puff of blue smoke, the seventy-five horsepower Yamaha kicked over. Pushing the red button on the silver throttle that hung off the side of the small center console, Yoshi nudged the engine out of neutral. The skiff accelerated and the bow began to rise as the dock was left behind. Once the front had risen enough to obscure his forward view, Yoshi toggled a switch and, with the whine of a small hydraulic pump, the trim planes nursed the bow down slightly to achieve a near perfect planing of the hull on the glass-like surface of the lake.

The skiff's wake barely disturbed the vast body of water and was quickly reabsorbed by the overall calmness.

The short, stout, slightly hunched over shadow of Yoshikazu disappeared into the misty veil. The hum of the outboard diminished as he throttled back and slowed the boat.

3.

"Look 'ere, see the way the rib cage is blown outwards. Bet 'er gut bust. That's why she sank. Whatcha reckon?"

"Could be, could be. She's a beaut' awl-right." The men stepped back to admire their work, removing hats to wipe down their dripping faces with dusty sleeves. Now brightly lit by an insect swarm-encircled spotlight, the clearing revealed far more than anticipated. A small Honda generator chugged away somewhere in the shadows behind the lights.

"Rob, my mate, I'd say we've got an intact skeleton 'ere."

"Cam-on, wait till we clear around the edges before we get everyone a dancin'. Get to it boys." Pointing to his aboriginal helpers to finish up clearing of the protruding bone and the now obvious outline of a large slender creature, he reached for two large cans of Fosters that sat on the front seat of his truck. "Still got ah bit a chill to 'em. Eh, mate, bettah start your engine, your lights are dim. Battery's a-dyin'!"

When the men had cleared the rest of the loose dry soil away from the skeleton, a long neck of individual bone disks was revealed, a thick powerful skull at its end. A short tail protruded from the mess of bones that was obviously the abdominal area. At either of its sides was a five-fingered armature.

"That's enough, leave some for the paleontologists. The university likes to get a little diggin' for its money," Bridgett offered, hating every second amateur mercenary hands touched any find. The sixteen-foot skeleton lay amongst the small fossilized snails and plant life that had inhabited this Cretaceous sea floor with it. A small lizard scurried across the sandy ground, its minuscule footprints disappearing as sand grains settled again over the imprint of a fossilized Sea Urchin.

Bridgett removed a small pocket tape recorder from her deep right hip pocket and pushed its cheap red record button that protruded from the black plastic case. After smacking the device twice with the flat of her palm, she again began to speak. "We have what looks like a holotype specimen of *Plesiosaurus dolichoderius*; moderately sized, probably young adult exposed in dorsal aspect. Only the dorsal and posterior cervical vertebral series are disrupted in what is otherwise a complete and articulated skeleton". Bridgett hopped about the dig site, touching bone and then gritting sandy rock between her callused fingertips as she pondered the find.

4.

Yoshikazu began the long ritual of baiting and setting his half-mile of hand-woven line after dropping a pyramid shaped sea anchor. It would roughly hold the skiff's position on the lake surface. As the last of the line was lowered into the inky lake waters, he prayed silently for a prosperous season. Remembering how scant past years' catches had become and how what little he did catch became smaller and smaller, he opened a small porcelain container his wife had prepared and given him.

Yoshikazu scooped up its contents: two small rice balls wrapped in dried seaweed. A piece of Unagi, a smoked fresh water eel, and some Wasabe would complete the nourishment. He nipped once again at the sake and reached for a red, balsa marker buoy and attached it to the eye at the end of his line before hurling it over board. Moving for the small center console of the skiff, he briefly spied the marker buoy bob up and down out of the corner of his eye. Turning to look, it disappeared altogether for a moment beneath the water. He smiled. Surely, Yoshikazu thought, this is a good omen. He took his hand off the ignition switch of the outboard and reached for an oar instead, having decided he would check the line now instead of waiting until the afternoon. After all, he thought, the way that buoy is moving I must have dropped my line right into a feeding school and filled a third of the hooks.

Yoshikazu removed one of two oars from a rack on the skiff hull and set it in the brass eye on the starboard gunwale. He gently rowed with a proficient 'J' stroke, like a Venetian gondolier, toward the buoy. Rings moved across the silvery surface of the water, the bobbing marker at the center. Reaching for his gloves, Yoshi moved slowly and silently, as if a noise might free whatever had impaled itself onto the shiny steel barbed hooks.

Stretching his arm over the gunwale, beyond the safety of his boat, he sprawled for the fiberglass pole that extended from the top of the erratic buoy. He grabbed it momentarily and then, dipping away, it escaped him. Yoshikazu cursed under his breath and reached again. Once the buoy was aboard and the fishing line unhooked, he dropped the buoy to the skiff's deck and wound the first few feet around the barrel-like spool that sat on the skiffs starboard gunwale. Opening a small hatch in the deck of the skiff, he removed a stainless steel handle, attached it to the large spool and braced his body in preparation for the hard work of bringing in the long line.

He grunted for that hardest first turn of the spool and found it would not budge at all. Could the hook be on the bottom? Impossible, he thought. The half-mile of line dangled between the two surface buoys; sagging to a depth of around two hundred feet—depending on how far apart the fisherman had set them. Regretting having not bought the electric motor to power his spool as well as having foolishly refused the services of the teenage boy at the dock the prior day, he better braced himself and again pushed against the shiny handle. It gave slightly, paused and then slowly began to come around. Yoshi bellowed again to the lake this time not in thanks or asking for strength, but under the strain of the task. After several revolutions of the spool, the glimmer of the first hook pierced the darkness of the depths and entered the brownish surface waters, causing the refracted light to appear yellow to him. Bait is still on, he observed with a grunt. The spool creaked but continued to turn reluctantly. The second baited hook appeared. The line now visibly danced in the murky water from the movement of whatever lay farther below. Yoshikazu's back ached and a sweat broke on his brow. The skiff listed another degree under the weight; the sake bottle rolled across her beam.

Yoshikazu stopped for a moment to ease the acid-like burning of his arms. The taught line seemed to sense his moment of rest and immediately tugged in the opposite direction. He braced the steel handle and reached for a small lock on the spool side and slipped it into a toothed gear, locking it in position. His skiff leaned again under the weight, water lapping against her side with a sucking sound.

In hope of breaking the surrealistic scene Yoshi looked around into the enveloping fog for another fisherman and then closed his eyes for a moment to muster more strength. He loosened the drag on the spool and released the lock. Mumbling a chant he began again to mechanically reel in the line.

5.

Bridgett knelt, small sharp stones digging into her bare knees.

"The skull is difficult to interpret. It is dorsoventrally crushed and somewhat distorted by virtue of its preservation in a dewatered marine sedimentary layer." She tossed her head back and inflated her cheeks like a chipmunk as she always did when thinking. " The orbital margins are difficult to distinguish. A key hole-shaped extension to the anterior corner of the orbit possibly represents the prefontals position. Rob, John, have you boys got a cee-bee with yah?"

"Sure do, love," Rob answered, swatting away one of the valleys notorious blood sucking desert flies. "My truck is over theah."

"Thanks, hon'. There are a few people I need on this one. I want to get a call in to Dr. Wright in America as well as soon as possible. Whatcha yah think is the best way?"

"Well we could stop at Wally's Watering Hole. He's got a phone and the operator should be able to get you an international line within a half houah."

"Great. Lets get the site covered and ready for night. Organize a first watch until we can get back with tents and provisions."

6.

At first, Yoshikazu did not discern the shape from the surrounding water. Then, as he made out its almost grotesque form, he momentarily stopped turning the spool. Focusing on the strange outline he thought, both at the same moment: this will feed my family for weeks and there is nothing this big in the lake. For one of the first times in Yoshikazu's life he felt fear. Grinning at his stupidity he continued to struggle the oddity to the surface. The brass gear of the spool squeaked in protest of the strain. Yoshikazu trusted his knowledge of both indigenous Japanese and other fish worldwide.

The line and hook protruded from the lamprey-like, tooth-lined sucker mouth. He said to the cataract-shrouded white eye of the peculiarity that squirmed but a foot under the surface, "What the hell are you then?"

Chapter 1: Aide-Memoire

1.

Sir Christopher Dunham looked at his wrinkled and spotted hands rubbed his eyes and sighed. He scanned the large wood paneled office and reached for a small remote control, looking briefly at a model Oberon class fast attack submarine that sat between a green glass banker's light and a personal computer on the intricately carved oak desk. He raised the remote to the room and turned on the television that sat flush in the rich wood of the far wall.

Chris raised his aged body from the brass rivet-studded soft black leather chair and moved for the large tinted plate window that extended upwards from the carpeted floor. Wanting to see the fog of his breath Chris approached to within inches of the glass and looked upon a gray depressing morning; as it seemed to be more and more as the years slipped by, he thought.

From high in the Canary Wharf Financial Center building, Chris surveyed the Thames and the mud flats she exposed at low tide. He watched the red Lite Rail train squirm its way from Tower Bridge and then looked to the East End of London, with its squat brown row houses and old quays. Looking west, barely visible in the foggy blanket tucked over the city, was Parliament and the top of Big Ben. The sound of the television drifted into his thoughts.

"This is Naomi McAllen in Atlanta. Next on World News: American forces clash with Serbian regulars as President Clinton orders Tomahawk cruise missile attacks on Serbian power, water and communications facilities. The increased tensions come in the wake of the massacre of two hundred thirty Kosovo Albanians in a cave near the Albanian frontier." Chris turned in time to see blue helmeted British and American soldiers burying the rigid bodies of women and children. He closed his eyes for a moment and then moved for a pot of tea that sat on a warm plate at a small service. As he filled a Wedgwood cup, he thought of retirement in a year and how he might fill his time.

"Also tonight: a Japanese fisherman stuns the world by catching an ancient fish in a mountain lake that was long thought extinct," the beautiful American newswoman smiled to her colleague who listened with interest. Chris again aimed the television remote control and increased the volume. "Experts around the world are baffled at the news. Also, Australian farmers find the worlds finest marine reptile fossil on the bottom of what was once a warm shallow prehistoric sea; now a dusty plain the size of the State of Massachusetts. These stories and more tonight on World News. Please stay with CNN International."

Chris slowly sat down again behind his desk and opened a silver cigar case. Reaching for one of the Havana's, he sat back in his chair and let the memory the news story had triggered surface even more. He clipped a small triangle hole at the end of the cigar with a golden tool and placed the bit in a crystal ashtray. He wrapped his fingers around a small marble lighter and spun its wheel, focusing on the flame. Twirling the cigar in the dancing blue and yellow fire while drawing gentle puffs, he thought back to the War as the blue smoke wisps reached for the ceiling . . .

2.

Commander Christopher Dunham dropped his cigarette butt, crushed it into the moist concrete and adjusted his white cap to keep the drizzle out of his face.

"Tighten up on the number two line," he barked. Chris had spent years on various ships taking the best the winter Atlantic could throw at him, making the cold Vermont morning feel like a touch of spring.

"Damn it, watch your drift, lads!" The cylindrical, white submersible swayed in the breeze. The steel cable that suspended the submersible from a yellow crane over the icy waters groaned under its weight. Three young men dressed in white and green-striped winter camouflage pulled on their respective lines attempting to keep the submersible centered over the semi-circular cradle at the stern of the ship.

"Easy. That's several million quid worth of equipment." Chris Dunham had learned not to question orders. As an officer of the *Special Boat Squadron*, he was always prepared for the out of the ordinary. The courier had arrived at his home in Edgemond, a quaint town in Shropshire near Wales. Chris barely blinked an eye when he read he was to report to an American Colonel for immediate reassignment to the United States. "We need your expertise on this one, Chris," his superior at Whitehall had told him. "If we are going to knock Gerry off the Continent, new toys will be necessary." Chris knew toys meant anything that was very expensive and essential to the plethora of missions his group of men was expected to accomplish against Axis forces.

Chris had flown to the United States via Greenland on a series of both British and American transports. On the first leg of his flight he had thumbed through the red-covered handbook marked *UTV-5: SECRET* he had been given in England. The second leg of his journey, on an American DC-3 transport, was too nauseating to contemplate reading.

"Dunham? Pleashah. How was your flight?" General Melshen had asked in what Chris assumed was a New England accent. The stocky general jutted out a hand the size of a bear paw. Chris reached for it.

"Fine, sir. Thank you, sir."

"What we have heah is basically a mud crawlah. She can hold an assault squad of ten souls for three houahs. She is designed to be launched at sea, submerge to the bottom and begin to crawl to the beach on these two tank treads heah," the general said pointing to a poor black and white photograph. "We figah when our men finally hit the beaches, we are gonna want to get our own Special Forces ashore in conjunction with airborne drops to secure vital strategic areas and to protect the flanks of a landing from any immediate countah-attack. General Dynamics in New London put this baby together to do just that."

"Her displacement, sir?"

"Foah tons."

"And speed?"

"She ain't no screamah. She'll do foah, maybe five knot's tops on the treads and maybe one or two moah on the prop. You ain't gonna run from a sub or destroyah at that speed so the trick is to stay undetected. If that doesn't work, there will be a self destruct system on boahd," General Melshen said as he carefully examined the face of the tall, thin British officer standing before him. He saw no reaction to his last statement. "When's the last time you slept, Commandah?" Chris could only smile in response. "The orderly outside will fix you up. Be in Operations at 0345 for further briefing." General Melshen bit the end off a cigar. "Dismissed, Dunham."

"Aye, sir. Thank you, sir." Chris saluted and spun to face the door.

3.

Chris awakened to a tap on his door.

"Sir?"

"Yes," Chris answered, chewing the foul taste that filled his mouth.

"Sir, it's 0330."

"Cheers."

"Excuse me sir?"

"Thank you."

"My pleasure, sir. Call if you need anything," the voice

mumbled through the pressed wood door. Chris scanned the small quarters through puffy eyes and tried to clear the haze in his mind; his disrupted Circadian Rhythm fought back. He slowly rose and moved towards the small shower stall and wash basin in the corner of his Spartan quarters.

4.

"Okay, listen up!" A hush replaced the mumbling that had filled the small briefing room full of tired looking soldiers. "This is Commandah Christophah Dunham on loan from Britain. He will be in charge of this test." Chris stood from his gray folding, metal chair and surveyed the room. "This man heah is James Attwater from General Dynamics. He's a civilian so no salutin' will be necessary," General Melshen scanned the young faces. "Chris, you wanna take it from heah."

"Good morning, gentlemen," Chris said as he moved toward the podium and its hissing, snake-like microphone. "Although I have yet to go through the specs, it looks as if the engineers in New London have delivered us a fine toy. Our dive today will test the effectiveness of the UTV-5s propeller and tread propulsion, pressurization, sonar and environmental systems. We will do a dead dive to the lake floor, maneuver on the treads for four hundred yards, beach the vessel, carry out an assault on a mock German pill box your engineers were kind enough to build and then retreat to the lake for a propeller return at one hundred feet to the mother ship. Any questions?" Chris asked the now attentive room. "All right then, oh-four hundred at dock two. Hope you did not eat too much for breakfast." Chris walked out into the still dark morning and motioned to his driver that he was ready.

"The docks please, lad," he said as he rested his highly polished shoes on the Jeep's dashboard.

"Aye, sir." The young, freckle-faced boy shifted the reluctant gears of the Jeep and sped off down the cliff road to the shore of the lake.

"Starting to drizzle, sir. Want me to put up the top?"

"No thanks," Chris said smiling. If only this kid knew how much ankle deep mud, blood and guts he had crawled through; how many rainy mornings he had stayed in his fox hole making sure Gerry did not sneak into the perimeter around Dunkirk.

After emerging from the thick woods, the road curved around a rock outcropping and then revealed the white research vessel that had been 'drafted' by the military for this test. Chris knew it had been dismantled and shipped from the coast of Massachusetts by rail and then truck. Chris saw her through the fence that lined and separated the shore road from the lake. The parasite submersible, any vessel that depended on another to get it someplace, sat covered on a heavily guarded flatbed next to her. The Jeep skidded to a halt at a small weathered shingle guard post. The sign on the rusted wire fence said *Ronkonkoma Fisheries.*

"Eye-dee." The husky Marine guard said with an impatient tone. The young Corporal presented identification for both himself and Commander Dunham. The Marine straightened up and gave his best dress salute. "Thank you, sir. Please proceed, sir." The gate creaked as it opened hesitantly on its rusting track. The Jeep jumped as the Corporal let the clutch out too fast and sped towards Dock Two, passing piles of tattered nets and old traps. As they neared, Chris read the proudly stenciled name of the vessel from her bow, "Halcyon."

5.

"I said tighten up on line two! You bloody deaf?" Chris abandoned his cordial tone for his battlefield bark. The effect on the younger, inexperienced soldiers was noticeable. He could have sworn he heard sphincter's tightening. "Easy." The Marines carefully maneuvered the submersible over the stern deck of the Halcyon, the ships yellow crane straining under the workload.

"Mister . . . Commander Dunham?" James Attwater Ph.D.,

the young, desk-pudgy General Dynamics engineer, asked through rain-spotted wire rim glasses.

"Yes."

"Sir, here is your start up checklist. She, the UTV-5, has had her batteries charged and environmental is in the green. You will have an umbilical to the Halcyon's systems until you are free of her. That will top off any battery or oh-two loss on the trip out to Point Alpha." Point Alpha, Chris knew, was in the middle of the lake at its deepest point.

"What's her maximum depth, James?" Chris asked as he continued to supervise the loading of the submersible with his peripheral vision.

"That's need to know sir. I can tell you she will be fine on this lakes —"

"Easy, damn it!" Chris yelled to a nervous Marine, cutting off James' answer. The noise assured Chris that the precious cargo was now safely aboard the Halcyon. The hydraulics of the stern crane hissed in relief and its operator jumped from the small control booth.

"All right, lads, let's get her secured and ready to ship out." The Marines answered him with a synchronous grunt as they continued to hold their lines as if the precious contraption was still dangling in the air.

"You can let go now son. That's not your girl's bum, you know." The brawny Marine chuckled. Chris suspected that the chuckle was directed more at his accent than his joke. "Get those lines around cleats. Good work."

6.

"Clear the bow line," the bearded Captain mumbled into a telephone, his face immersed in the green glow emanating from the radarscope. Besides the echo of the Captain's deep voice, the bridge of the Halcyon was silent.

"Clear, sir." A distorted voice responded through a speaker.

"Clear the stern line."

"Stern line clear, sir."

"Clear the starboard spring line."

"Spring clear, sir."

"Reverse one third on port and ahead one third on the starboard screw." The left and right propellers began to spin on their brass shafts. The Captain adjusted his hat and breathed the chilly air the crew complied with his orders.

The Halcyon gently came about sending small dancing vortexes through the calm black water of the lake. The smell of diesel fumes and rain permeated the surrounding still air.

"Set course to two hundred thirty degrees, ahead half both engines."

Chris finished his visual inspection of the thick rubber tank-like treads that ran down the axis of the submersible, a formality since they had been thoroughly checked by General Dynamics. The UTV-5s web-like structure of buoyancy piping and electrical conduit on the pressure hull interior had also been checked inch-by-inch. Chris adjusted his black wool jacket and moved towards the bridge of the Halcyon.

"Captain? Commander Dunham," Chris said offering his hand. "How long to alpha?"

"About twenty minutes, Commander," the Captain answered; his eyes never leaving the large, liquid filled compass.

"Sir, we are at course two three zero. Both engines read ahead half," the wheelman informed.

"Increase to three quarters. Steady as she goes," the Captain almost whispered. Chris gazed out over the somber, foggy lake, and then turned to the ranking Marine.

"Have your men ready in ten minutes. I want to go down the checklist."

"Aye-aye, sir," the officer answered in a thick, Southeastern American accent.

"One aye is enough, Marine." Chris looked for a sign of intimidation in the steel-blue eyes of the wiry soldier that stood before him but saw none. Good, he thought. The Marine turned and went out the bridge door. Chris removed another cigarette from the silver holder he had in his breast pocket and tapped it on his watch face. While keeping his face nestled in the rubber skirt of the radar scope, the hunched over Captain reached into his jacket and then extended his arm to offer a cigar clutched in his unnaturally positioned hand. He mumbled, "Here, smoke this. Those'll kill yah." Chris reached for the cigar and smiled.

"Thanks." He put it in his pocket and tapped the ash of his cigarette onto the steel floor of the bridge. It stayed for a moment and then disintegrated when a door opened.

The Captain looked up for a moment to check the revolutions on the port engine and said, "Black as molasses out there this morning," then his face disappeared into the rubber skirt of the crudely installed radarscope once again. Chris answered with a groan as he pulled deeply on his cigarette and twisted his mouth to guide the exhaled smoke out a small brass-rimmed portal.

7.

"Okay, lads," Chris said to the team assembled on the stern of the Halcyon, "stow those rifles." He adjusted the last of the straps of his black diving fatigues, having abandoned the formal suit of the Royal Navy in one of the cabins below. "Since the Captain seems to be able to work that bloody radar, we should arrive at the Alpha reflector buoy shortly. Sergeant, prepare to embark."

"All right, you heard the man. One by one up the ladder. Immediately secure your weapon and strap in tight," the Marine Sergeant ordered. As the last of the squad climbed up the ladder and then through the snug hatch at the top of the submersible, Chris himself began to climb. He paused at the hatch opening and peered through at the shuffling men below. Their green fatigues were a sickly purple in the red light of the submersible's cramped cabin.

Surveying the horizon of the black lake and the mist that danced across its glassy surface, Chris swung a foot onto an interior foothold.

8.

Chris moved towards the two forward facing seats at the bow of the main pressure hull, and passing the ten strapped in Marines. They faced one another in two rows of five, their rifles pointing skyward. They carefully watched the British officer. Chris could feel the stress of the young Americans, forced to entrust their lives to him without say.

"Not to worry, gentlemen. I piloted a craft just like this, mind you she was a bit smaller, when we did the raids into Norway," Chris said jovially, hoping to dilute the thickening tension. He sat in the right seat and was immediately encircled by a myriad of dials, gauges and controls.

"This is the simplified version," James Attwater chuckled and snorted as he traversed the familiar ladder down into the submersible's pressure hull. "You should have seen the first version. I will handle all buoyancy, environmental and general navigation. You will pilot her with that joystick there," he said with an engineer's enthusiasm, pointing, as he landed on the steel floor with a muffled thump.

"See, I told you there was nothing to worry about." Chris strained to turn and show his relaxed but rehearsed smile to the human cargo.

"I ran all the checklist except navigational surfaces." James motioned to a radio that had obviously been hurriedly installed. Chris reached for the small microphone at the end of a coiled insulated wire.

"MOTHER, this is BABY, radio check."

"Loud and clear, BABY," the voice echoed through the hull.

"Please check my bottle, MOTHER."

"Roger, BABY, proceed." Chris gently moved the joystick to the left.

"Rudder to port. Check." And then right. "Rudder to starboard. Check." Chris then pulled back and then pushed forward on the hand grip-shaped joystick to test the pitch and yaw surfaces of the machine. The radio speaker crackled again. "Pitch and yaw surfaces: check." James stood, moved towards the ladder and stretched his arm to reach the hatch, closing it with a resonating metallic thump. He spun the wheel at its center until sealed and locked.

"Remember, Commander, she has a bit more power than you are used to so be ginger with that throttle," James said, squinting both to point and to coax his glasses higher onto his nose. "Okay, we have green across the boards, Commander." He coaxed his plump body into the small seat and strapped in.

"All right then," Chris sighed. "MOTHER, BABY ready to leave home."

"Roger, BABY." The jerk of the Halcyon's stern crane caused the UTV-5 to swing slightly. After some jerky maneuvering and lowering, the submersible settled into a meandering swing. "Feet wet," Chris recognized this to mean the submersible was now over the freeboard and had nothing but water under her.

"Prepare to release on my mark, MOTHER. Three, two, one, mark." A shudder moved through the steel craft as the Halcyon's crane released the lifting hook and the submersible fell two feet to the lake surface.

Chris scanned the men behind him, making sure all were well.

"MOTHER, commencing dead dive." James opened two of four valves. Water rushed all around the submersibles pressure hull as the ballast tanks began to fill with the cold lake water. "Planes are at minus fifteen degrees," Chris mumbled to the control panel.

9.

"Switching to low frequency radio. MOTHER, come in, this is BABY," Chris said as he turned an over-sized dial.

"MOTHER here BABY," the speaker crackled. The voice sounded far-off.

"We are in dead dive, all lights are green," Chris said smiling to the engineer at his side.

"Roger, BABY. Radio silence until egress from beach."

"Understood MOTHER, you won't hear from us until we are done or done for." His comment met with muffled noise behind him. Chris winked at James whom half smiled and said, "Activating sound navigation and ranging." A high pitched ping filled the water around the submersible. "I have the lake floor at six hundred seventy-two feet. Solid return on sonar. Depth gauge agrees." The submersible silently glided through the water on its way to the bottom. "Heater one coming on," Chris said as his body shivered and he activated a red toggle switch.

"We are at three hundred," James announced. The metal hull popped and groaned as it adjusted to the increased weight of the lake outside. The submersible's cargo of Marines shuffled nervously. "Coming up on four hundred feet."

"Bringing dive planes to minus ten. Slowing decent. James, call depth under the keel."

"One fiver zero."

"Roger, one five zero feet to the bottom. Planes to minus five. Rate of decent at forty feet per minute."

"One hundred feet."

"Planes to minus three, we have slowed to a thirty foot per minute descent."

"Fifty, five zero feet."

"Roger. Fiver zero."

"Four zero."

"Roger, four zero, planes to zero angle, straight and level," Chris said as he gently nudged the joystick to the position marked with a fluorescent 0°.

"Three zero, sinking fifteen feet per minute."

"Roger."

"Two zero."

249-VONB

"Planes level. Fifteen per."

"Ten feet. Activating terminal sonar." Several pings fired in succession as James verified the submersible's distance to the lake floor.

"Five, four, three, two—."

The treads gracefully met the lake's floor and the UTV-5 settled slightly into the soft gray silt wasteland at the bed of Lake Champlain.

10.

"Okay, we are on the bottom. Unlocking tread mechanism. Switch motor to tread position and disengage the propeller." Chris said as he motioned to James to pull the red handle on his right.

"Treads enga-" The submersible jumped forward from the mud, stealing the last syllables of James' sentence. "We are on our way. Four hundred yards to the beach. We should start to climb in about one hundred yards," Chris said as he surveyed the small navigational chart of the lake with a course laid out in red ink.

The Marine Sergeant began to review the mock assault mission with his men as the UTV-5s treads bumped it along the bottom. "Eddie, you lay down the grazing fire. Team One will move towards Pillbox A while Team Two protects the flanks here and here," the Marine said pointing to a small tablet attached to his thigh. "For this test we will take this beast right onto the beach but next time or in the real thing, we would deploy about fifty yards from the beach through the wet hatch." he said pointing astern to a large unpainted hatch that had *Experimental* hastily stenciled on it in white dripping letters.

"Commander, I put us at ninety yards from our landing point, two hundred and ten from the beach," James said as he pushed up his glasses and wiped some moisture from the glass face of a gauge with the sleeve of his brown wool sweater. He then logged that cabin humidity control needed adjustment.

"Roger, we should start to climb soon." Chris answered matter-of-factly.

"BABY, this is MOTHER, come in please." Chris picked up the radio microphone and answered, "Go ahead," with a questioning glance to James. Chris waited for the response through the static and asked, "Breaking radio silence?"

"BABY, we are showing a contact. Bearing: one eight zero. Range: five hundred yards from your present. Depth: two make that three zero three."

"Got a speed, MOTHER?" Chris said smugly as he whispered to James. "Look's like they want to expand the test a little."

"Roger, seven knots. Recommend you go to internal for a better track." Chris nodded to James who immediately started the submersibles passive sonar.

"Commander, I have the contact. No machinery noise, something else."

"Must be divers. Okay, cut the engine. Let's stop dead and see if they can spot us or not in this murky water. Probably an Underwater Demolition Team."

"Contact has increased speed to nine knots, same bearing. Range: four hundred and ten yards." James looked to Chris for reassurance.

"Don't worry, it's just an unscheduled test. Guess they want to make this as realistic as possible by giving us a welcoming committee. You sure there is no machinery noise? They must be using scooters at that speed."

"Negative, no machinery noise." James replied. "Three hundred ninety yards." Chris again reached for the radio.

"MOTHER, BABY."

"Roger BABY, MOTHER here."

"MOTHER, we have your contact on sonar. Please confirm, is this part of the test?" The radio crackled as he released the small switch on the side of the radio microphone.

"Negative BABY, not our surprise."

"James, go to active sonar." Chris ordered. James cleared his throat in response and a bead of sweat formed on his large forehead. "Sonar is active." The successive pings radiated from the submersible like ripples on a pond. The atmosphere inside the cramped cylinder became serious and silent.

"Contact. Range: three hundred, same bearing. Speed: twelve knots!" James said looking wide-eyed at Chris.

"Twelve? You sure there, James old boy?" Chris' voice was monotone and calm.

"Ya-yes."

"Okay, get me ten feet of the bottom and engage the propeller. Let us see what we can find." Chris' voice trailed off as he concentrated on his maneuvers.

"Can we deviate from the test?"

"We can now. Do as I say." Chris' frustration at having his order questioned showed through the pleasant tone he had tried to use.

"Roger, we are off the bottom, engaging propeller." The submersible succumbed to the suction of the mud for a moment and then quickly rose to ten feet off the featureless lake floor.

"Commander?" James asked, his voice trembling.

"Yes, what is it?"

"Sir, I am reading at least thirty feet in length on whatever is out there."

"What? Better run diagnostics on your equipment man."

"I did. Speed increasing to fifteen knots. Range: two four three."

"MOTHER, this is BABY. Looks like we definitely have company down here."

"Roger BABY. From what we can see I would guess we have a net caught in the current."

"Negative MOTHER, we are getting solid returns from sonar."

"Your call, BABY."

"We are aborting test, MOTHER. Surfacing now. Please rendezvous with us at grid five mark two."

"Roger, BABY. Aborting test."

"James, prepare to surf—. What is it?"

"Just lost contact. There is a ridge of rock about one hundred yards at zero fiver zero. The target must have moved behind it."

"Blow tanks one and two, James. I'm putting fifteen up on the planes."

"Commander! I have contact at one eight zero. Range: twenty yards!"

"How the hell?"

The first impact on the submersible hull knocked James from his chair. Chris heard the Sergeant calm his men as he grabbed for the radio microphone.

"MOTHER, we have impacted with something. Please confirm: are we clear of underwater obstacles?"

"Roger, BABY, the nearest snag is an old barge about seven hundred yards away at zero two three." Chris reached to help a shaken James back into his seat. He then stood and turned to the submersible's cargo of Marines.

"Gentlemen, there is no need to worry. When we hit Trondheim, we must have snagged on at least three unmarked obstacles. Just like day sailing, I tell you." The second impact knocked Chris to the cold, steel floor and the air from his lungs.

"Damn, what could it be? My kingdom for one bloody window in this can!" Chris said through clenched teeth as he rose to his feet with the aid of an overhead pipe.

"James, emergency surface!" James was already holding the valve with the red paper tag marked: *Emergency Surface.*

"Blowing all tanks. Ballast away. Damn it. Reading rate of accent at ninety feet per minute!"

"James! Ascent rate warning!" An alarm interrupted the cascade of bubbles that seemed to surround the submersible. "The pressurization system cannot keep up with the-" A Marine screamed in agony behind him. Others began to hold their hands to their ears in a futile attempt to relieve the pressure. The Marine screamed again.

"Sergeant, your man must have an air bubble lodged behind

his ear drum. Find something sharp and puncture it!" Chris watched the ascent rate meter and the screaming Marine in his outlying field of vision. The Sergeant reached for his Infantry Rifleman pin that he wore proudly on his lapel, unhooked and drove it into the ear canal of the soldier. The shriek confirmed the eardrum had been punctured and that the trapped air was allowed to escape.

"Damn it, James, slow our ascent."

"Slowing ascent. Feet per minute at seventy, sixty, fifty —." Chris grimaced, feeling his ears would explode momentarily, and watched the ascent rate meter move to under forty feet per minute.

"Good work, James. Everyone okay?" Chris did not wait for an answer and immediately went back to nursing the new machine.

"Planes at plus twenty degrees. Rudder seems to be sticking a bit. Call our depth, James."

"Two hundred and ten. Two hundred. One ninety."

"Hammer the sonar again, James."

"Active sonar has a red light, switching to passive."

"I have a faint contact at one eight zero degrees. Range: forty yards. Sounds like bubbles."

"Bubbles? Okay, when whatever it is is within twenty yards, I want you to start shooting pictures with the aft camera."

"The camera's will not be installed until the UTV-5 goes into production." James answered as he listened intently to the sonar speaker.

"Wonderful."

"Commander, we are at one hundred feet."

"MOTHER?"

"Go ahead, BABY."

"We are at one hundred feet. Please confirm."

"Roger, BABY. We have you at one hundred feet and rising at thirty-three per."

"Roger."

11.

The Captain of the Halcyon ordered all engines to stop and began surveying the surface of the lake with a pair of brown binoculars. The sun slowly began to peek through the ground hugging mist on the distant shore.

"Expect surface break in a couple of minutes," the Captain said to the bosons mate. "I want a diver in the water to assist in case they are damaged."

"Aye, sir," the boson said as he snapped a salute.

"Surface break in twenty seconds," the Captain of the Halcyon almost whispered to his bridge crew.

"Gentlemen, brace yourselves," Chris said to the UTV-5s frightened human cargo.

The bow of the submersible cleared the water's surface and came crashing down in a boil of white foam. "All right. We have sky over us. James, the hatch if you would." Chris ran his fingers through his black hair and let out a sigh.

"Hatch open and clear, sir." James said still stretching and bracing the weight of the hatch. The cold morning air flooded the stuffy cabin.

"Sergeant, start getting your men out. Halcyon will be coming along side of us in a minute," Chris mumbled as he stood.

"MOTHER, BABY. We have breached."

"Roger, BABY, we have a visual on you. Looks like you took a beating down there."

"Roger, MOTHER, got thrown around a bit. Might have been safer to do this in the Atlantic after all. Any idea what we hit?"

We hit? No. It hit us, Chris thought.

"Negative."

Commander Dunham's head pierced the top of the hatch and, as the cargo of Marines moved onto the aft deck of the Halcyon, he slowly surveyed the lake.

"Okay hustle. Sun'll be up soon. Let's get off this lake before awla Colchester wakes up." A voice came from the deck of the Halcyon.

12.

Sir Christopher Dunham snubbed out the last of his cigar in the crystal ashtray on his desk and lifted the telephone receiver. "Claire-love, please come into my office for a moment."

Chapter 2: Catalyst

1.

Jorgé adjusted the cloth napkin that covered the basket of oven fresh, blue and cranberry muffins. A metal cover kept a plate of Eggs Benedict and red skinned potato's warm next to a cellophane covered glass of ice-cold grapefruit juice. The cart skipped over a carpet edge and Jorgé once again made small corrective adjustments to make the tray appear perfect. He passed Edna Kay, the boss' secretary, and the highly polished golden letters that spelled out *The Explorer Channel* across the green marble wall.

Jorgé knocked after Edna had announced him, opened the tall double doors to the executive suite and mechanically mumbled, "Good morning, Mr. Johnson," to the floor. He quietly prepared the tray near the large leather chair across from the large desk so as not to disturb the phone call the boss, Chip Johnson, was in the middle of.

"Hey, Marty, what's up? Really? I see. Five million pound sterling!" Jorgé twitched involuntarily in the background. "I definitely see! This guy one beer short of a six? Yes. Ship building tycoon. War hero. Knighted! Guess not."

Jorgé adjusted the already perfectly placed plates in a desperate attempt to appear busy during the long pause that followed the boss' last word.

"Well, Marty ol' buddy, you can count my company and I in. I will begin to put together a team immediately. My channel gets full rights to air whatever we find, even if it's nothing? Great! Lets get our bloodsuckers together to work out the details. What about the mercenaries? Well, that kinda money's bound to bring up all sorts. Yep. Okay. Thanks, Marty! Love to Amy. Okay ol' bud, see-. Huh? Oh yeah, thanks. See you."

The boss inhaled deeply to sample the wonderful smells that had drifted over from the tray Jorgé had set and arose from his desk. He lit a cigarette, grasped the Washington Post and moved for the chair where Jorgé's gloved hands gestured. Jorgé added an ashtray to the silver serving tray.

"Get me pen and paper please," the boss asked as he unfurled the first section of the paper and eyed the Hollandaise covered poached eggs that sat atop a generous slice of Canadian bacon and lightly browned English muffins.

"Of course, sir," Jorgé replied getting both from a nearby table in a fast, efficient manner. "Anything else, sir?" From the corner of his eye, he watched the boss write down on the small pad he had provided—*Ian, Wright, lake guru, BOAT!*—as he awaited an answer. The boss glanced at Jorgé and, recognizing his expectant look, said, "No. Thanks. That will be all George."

The boss began to cut into the steaming eggs. Jorgé backed out of the suite as if leaving the presence of a Caesar and closed the tall double doors behind him.

2.

Ian loved the rush of the hunt. He moved stealthily through the tall, dry savanna grass towards the strolling lion. As he reached for the rifle butt slung across his back, Ian's eyes momentarily met the scanning gaze of the young lion. Ian knew lions and recognized that this adolescent was pretending not to have seen him as he further scanned the grasses for other shapes or movement. Seeing none, his gaze quickly shifted back to Ian.

"Shit," Ian's whisper blended into the rustling of the gentle tidal sway of the dry savanna grass. Ian slowly raised the wooden rifle butt into the air of the hot, dusty day. With a low growl and a brief transience through trotting, the lion began a galloping charge towards Ian.

"Shit!" He pulled the trigger and turned to run. "Mafume!"

"Yes, Mr. Ian." The panting native fired his rifle, splitting the silence of the oppressive heat and nearly knocking Ian to the ground. The lion stopped in a violent braking of its charging mass. He paused, looking confused at the thunderous sound and, surprised to still be alive, he turned to run. This lion has heard a gun before, Ian thought.

Ian leaned against the small trunk of the tree, angling his body to maximize the use of the shade. He lifted his canvas hat and wiped the sweat from his brow with the sleeve of his sweat soaked tan shirt. As he adjusted the beige cloth covered plastic snakebite guards that encircled his ankles; he grabbed for the camera that lay on the parched earth of the grasslands. Ian had mounted the camera and it's bulky zoom lens on the wooden stock and barrel seat from an old Winchester for rapid and accurate aiming. The picture of the charging lion he had just taken was certain to be a good one. I'm pretty sure I had him focused right, Ian thought as he sipped from a cloth-covered canteen.

"He can't be more than two bloody miles away!" Ian exclaimed to the exhausted looking native. "Yes, Mr. Ian, no more than two miles," the tracker was able to get out between gasps for air. Ian Chelsea was not one to lose his trophy. This summer in Ethiopia had brought him many. This beast, however, was giving him a run for his money. He had first picked up the lion's tracks a day ago and had lost them the previous night. Spotting them again in the pink light of the morning he followed them to a small, rapidly evaporating drinking hole. At thirty-one, Ian was one of the worlds best known and highest paid free-lance photographers. He slung his camera over his shoulder, winked at his tracker that it was time to go and set out for a small cluster of hills in the distance. "He can't be much more than two miles away."

Ian knelt and then went down on all fours. The sharp stones pressed into his callused hand as he peered through the tall swaying grass and the water hole that lay at the foot of a small knoll. There, in a cloud of dust at the far side, Ian witnessed the latest skirmish between old adversaries.

"Let me have the sixteen mill' my friend," he asked, his eyes locked on the cantering male lion. His tracker hurriedly complied, handing Ian the Panaflex and its top-mounted film magazine. In exchange, Ian handed Mafume his canvas hat over and got on one knee to steady his body. Deciding to film the large male's attack in slow motion, Ian flipped a small metal switch on the cameras black body.

The lionesses began to move their cubs from the shelter of a bent lone tree to the core of the pride's territory when the first hyena approached. The largest scarred lioness gently lifted a cub in her mouth and saw there was now three hyenas squealing and jumping about. The hyena's knew they were still too few in numbers to risk an attack, Ian noted. Quickly their numbers grew and closer they came to the now surrounded tree. The lionesses began to crouch in fear, growling at the nipping hyena clan. The cubs knew to stay still and silent as the hyenas probed the perimeter of lionesses.

The approaching lion's mane pulsated as he went from a canter to a gallop, breaking from the flank-high sea of grass. The frightened and pain-filled cries of the pride females seemed to make him move faster. This was also no fight over a kill, but one of territory, Ian thought. Noticing no males accompanied the lionesses and this years litter, the matriarch of the hyena clan, ever the opportunist sought to alter the long established border between these two savanna predators.

The lion burst from the brush, immediately sending the hyenas into a panicked retreat. He pinned a large male hyena and snapped at another. The lionesses retreated even closer to the tree that harbored their cubs; their bodies low to the ground like crawling soldiers. Ian zoomed in closer as the lion quickly slaughtered the squealing animal under foot and pounced at another that had mistakenly passed too close in the panic. It died quickly.

Ian released the trigger of the humming camera and brought the rubber eyepiece away from his sweaty eye.

"Excellent."

3.

Andrew Wright looked down at his clay-caked hands and crusted fingernails and asked himself, Is this this what I am? He drifted for a moment in the blinding day. The sting of sweat on his eyeball brought him back to the dust choked moment. He thought of his wife as he reached for the camel hair brush that lay on the dry, tormented earth. He felt the loneliness she must have felt before dying alone. A tear traveled a moment and then disappeared, surrendering to the dust on his cheek and the heat of the air. A breeze danced across his face causing him to blink. The silence around Andrew did not betray the thirty or more eyes that watched his every move.

"See, look at the architecture of this flipper," Andrew said brushing gently and precisely across the beige and red bones. Moans of understanding replied. "Plesiosaurs' flipper was like a present day penguin, suggesting they may have been capable of high speed under water," he said to the enveloping mass in his best teacher's voice.

Andrew traced the outline of the large paddle-like limb that protruded from the surrounding rock. "Look how nicely this Cretaceous layer is defined, this reddish layer."

"Dr. Wright, what species is it?" Came calling from somewhere behind Andrew.

"You tell me," Andrew responded before the student's query disappeared on the breeze; stealing a quick glance over his shoulder.

"Well, um, the flipper is elongated, more than a Muraeonosaurus. It's pretty hard to tell without seeing its girth and neck but I would say we have an Elasmosaurus here."

"Excellent," Andrew said flatly and sneered.

"As we said, they were fast, probably the fastest of the large marine reptiles." Scurrying pens greeted his voice. The zealous students scribed his every word as if fearing they would forget what they heard.

"Now, in the early Cretaceous, about a hundred million years ago—the tail end of the Mesozoic—a shallow sea stretched across the Great Plains. Basically the Mississippi is the very bottom of that old sea, the Rockies, the old shore. Hell, in Boulder you can see the rippled sand flipped up on end. Much of our coastal regions were also submerged, up to the Sierra's and Appalachians." Andrew continued to gently remove particles from between the fossilized hand-like flipper. "You know, Elasmo here probably flapped these up and down for propulsion, much like modern sea turtles, humpback whales and, as before, penguins."

Andrew blinked, keeping his eyes closed just a bit longer than a normal blink, as if in slow motion. Only one perceptive dark-eyed woman in the crowd that surrounded Andrew noticed. In that extra second of darkness, or pinkness—you can't really block out completely the desert sun with your eyelids—Andrew relived the horror of finding her.

"Does anyone know what Elasmosaurus means?" Andrew's voice wavered slightly. He stood and faced the students. His wood handled camel hairbrush fell to his side. Andrew's limestone-blue eyes surveyed the nervous looking perimeter of the crowd of students. The 'nerd line,' he thought. Behind this outer layer of kiss-asses were his better minds. The ones he felt were truly worth his time. A hand reached for the blue sky. "I believe in the Socratic method, speak!" Andrew's impatience startled some. I am tired, he thought.

"Plated, uh, thin plated lizard," the young woman in the middle of the crowd said, her confidence growing with every syllable of her sentence.

"Your name miss?"

"Molly," the young brunette seemed to grow taller as she

slipped her shoulders back and her small breasts forward. Her eyes seemed to smile.

"Molly, tell us about this thin plated lizard please," his politeness forced.

"Well, it was the longest of the Plesiosaurs, and over half of its fifty foot length was neck. It probably used this long, muscular neck like a snake to strike at fish. Late Cretaceous. Primarily North America and Asia. Had to surface to breathe," she smiled as her sentence tapered off.

"Thanks, Molly." Andrew wanted the shade of his trailer and a cold drink from its small refrigerator. "Okay, everyone take a few then get to your assigned grids. I want the upper torso and neck located and started on by lunch. Remember, carefully. You're paleontologists not brick layers!"

4.

Rebecca squinted under the blinding mountain sun, shaded her eyes with her left hand and reached for her plastic identification badge with the right. She inserted the card in a slot under the bronze *National Oceanic and Atmospheric Administration—Oceanographic Modeling/3-D Bathymetrics* sign. The glass door slid open on its tracks blasting her with the cold, conditioned air of the dark computer center.

"Morning Rebecca," came in different voices from the shadows as she strode gracefully to her office.

"Morning guys," she mumbled to the *Dr. Rebecca McClintock—Director* that hung on her office door. Rebecca entered her cluttered office, flicked the red switch on her Mister Coffee machine and sat down at her desk. The mounds of files and computer printouts seemed to surround her like an enveloping army.

"Eric? You there?" Rebecca spoke into the white intercom that protruded from under a sonar map of the mid-Atlantic ridge.

"Yeah, morning, Rebecca. What can I do you for?"

"Bring me the latest thermo read on El Niño please."

"You got it," the voice mumbled through the intercom. Rebecca sat back and reached for the now brewed black gold. She ran her fingers through her long, brown hair and poured the coffee into her green Cousteau Society mug. Rebecca caressed the mug and drew a long sip as a rap at the door woke her from her trance.

"Come on in, Eric!"

"Hey Rebecca, how was Mexico?"

"Okay. Got to do a great dive off the Yucatan. How has everything been here?"

"Pretty quiet," Eric said as he thumbed through the file he held, pulling the report that Rebecca had requested.

"Thanks."

"Pro noblem," he answered as he moved for the door, and then paused. "Remember, you've got a three o'clock lecture." Rebecca groaned. She took another sip of coffee and finally felt as if she was beginning to wake. From the still open door a voice squealed, "Hey ho, nice freakin' tan bitch!"

"Hi, Elaine," Rebecca said to her coffee cup, her head still hung low.

"Let's get togetha for lunch, 'kay? Oh, Eric said to put on channel ten. Then, take a nap. That tan ain't hiding those eye bags sweetheart." With her infamous devilish grin, Elaine glanced at Rebecca momentarily and then disappeared behind the wall.

"Thanks," Rebecca said sarcastically and smiled. "See you, hon'." She yawned and reached for the mouse that sat on a blue mouse pad, the NOAA shield embossed in white in its center. The alternating green, red and blue fractal screen saver prompted her for her password and then let her back in the system when she complied. Clicking on a small television icon launched the video program; Cable TV came up in a window in the corner of her screen. She selected channel ten from a pop-up menu and turned on her computers external speakers. They crackled to life as she tweaked a failing green bulb on the computer's tower body with her slender finger.

"The lake, fifty kilometers south-east of the city of Kitami, high in the mountains of Hokkaidō, the northern-most of the four main islands that comprise Japan, is four hundred twenty feet deep at its deepest point and is similar to other glacial lakes." Rebecca watched as a computer animated glacial cap receded towards the North Pole, leaving deep lakes in Asia, North America, and Europe. "For another theory on how the once-thought extinct fish could get in an isolated lake we go to Mike LeBeau at the Museum of Natural History in New York. Mike."

"Thanks, Natalie. You can see here a fossil of an ancient fish that is very similar to the one caught in Japan. This globe here shows how shallow and deep seas once covered many landmasses. As these waters receded and the plates shifted large inland seas developed and themselves flourished. When they also eventually receded, species could be stranded, land-locked if you will." Rebecca's mouth slowly opened as she moved the cursor and made the television window fill her entire screen. Rebecca grinned and said, "Cool."

5.

Ian watched the last of the days sun cling to the sky in pink hues. The lonely silhouette of a large twisted tree occasionally broke the otherwise flat and stark horizon. He handed his small metal plate to his tracker and said, "Excellent antelope steak Mafume. Thanks." Ian reached for the blue metal pot that sat on a small grill suspended over the fire his tracker had put together and poured a cup of the herb and flower tea it contained. Its tart taste was tolerable and almost had the tang of a nice cup of Earl Grey. Lord, he thought, if you think this tastes like Earl Grey, you have been in the bloody bush too damn long. He added some crystallized honey lumps from a small tin set on a nearby rock. Ian swirled the tea in its barely clean clay cup and turned for the olden canvas tent his tracker had expertly erected in minutes.

He first pushed aside the mosquito mesh that was so often necessary in this part of the world; his own fight with malaria was proof of that. The second heavy canvas flap was also necessary for the violent thunder and dust storms that could shred even the best of nylon tents. He entered to see his sleeping bag invitingly unrolled and his equipment bag neatly placed in the corner. The tracker's sleeping mat and cover was still rolled up and wrapped in a tattered leather strap. He would most likely sleep outside, keeping the fire alive and hyenas at bay, unless the night was unexpectedly cold or if the weather went foul.

Ian opened an aluminum case and removed his lap top computer that sat in the custom fit blue foam interior. A second case contained a small satellite dish with three telescoping legs.

He pulled a few small airplane bottles of Cutty Sark from his rucksack and opened one of their plastic caps with a seal breaking snap. Ian emptied half the bottle into his mouth and swallowed.

"Mafume," he coughed.

"Mister?" Came from beyond the closed tent flap.

"Take this outside." An inquiring head pierced the tent door opening then an arm. "Point this at the sky. When this flashing light stops flashing," Ian said pointing to the green LED on the dish's armature, "put it down on these legs here."

"Yes sir, Mr. Ian." The tracker took the cone shaped satellite dish, trailing a thin black wire that connected to one of the laptops serial ports. Ian turned the lap top on and heard the hard drive spin-up, then the RAM check clicked off. He saw the solar charged battery indicated three hours of power. Ian took out his toothbrush and a small tray from his pack and glanced at the screen – the operating system was building his file structure. He removed a deflated plastic pillow from its cotton case, pulled out the small, clear plastic nipple and began to fill it with air. When he heard the machine-like male voice announce, "*You have mail*," he knew it was done booting up and had launched his communication software. He reached for the small track ball at the bottom of the keyboard and moved to select the first E-mail in his inbox; the one he recognized as from his wife: patc@aol.com. The second, from cjohnson@explorer.dir.com, was far more intriguing:

Ian, You are needed in Bethesda immediately! Drop everything. All I can say is you get $50k up front! Enough said? Get here ASAP! As in now!! PS—why are you still reading this? Move!

"Mafume." He drew the last of the alcohol and threw the small bottle onto the dusty earth.

"Yes, Mr. Ian?" The wide-eyed face again pierced the tent flap.

"Pack our things when you wake in the morn. I want to set out for Addis Ababa at first light. Get on the radio now and have one of your men meet us with transport tomorrow at the road. Understand?"

"Yes, Mr. Ian. Mafume understand." Ian smiled at him and clicked on the *Reply to Mail* icon. He typed: *On my way geezer!* and pressed the [Enter] button on his keyboard to send his response. After the simulated voice confirmed his mail had been sent, he went to a prompt and typed: */sysdown*. When the laptop had shut down and been put back in its protective case, Ian crawled to the soft sleeping bag atop a foam-sleeping pad.

He slipped into the cool material; seeing blurry through slit eyes the satellite dish wire snaking along the ground and out of the tent. Ian's last thought as he drifted off into sleep was I would put it away in the morning.

6.

Andrew went for the small refrigerator first thing after throwing open the light, sheet metal door of the dirt caked trailer. From its frosty-cold interior he pulled a Cherry Cola and popped its seal with a hiss. He looked around the trailer—his notes at the desk, the better fossils from this dig perched on a small wooden shelf, the tiny kitchenette, the old striped couch for the occasional nap, and a library of reference books. Everything a man—a paleontologist—could ever need in the field. He took a long, deep draw on the cold, sparkling cola and gasped at its bite on his throat. Andrew moved for the small desk and sat down in its rickety chair. He shuffled the scattered notes and found what he had last been working on—the notes for his opening lectures for his new class at CU/Boulder: Introduction to Paleontology. He twirled his 1922 silver Parker and began to scribble.

PA101 Dr. Andrew Wright. Andrew could only laugh out loud at how formal that sounded and how messed up he felt inside. *I. What is a fossil?; II. Location and excavation; III. Learning from the fossil.*

I. What is a fossil? A fossil, literally meaning 'dug up', is the remains of an animal or plant that lived millions of years ago. After death, the soft tissue was eaten by other animals or rotted away, or the wood of plants was submerged and buried in layers of sand or mud before they could decompose. Over time, the water receded and the sediment turned into rock. The hard remains of the animal could change chemically and become stone. Sometimes, they were preserved essentially unchanged. The rock layer then folded and became exposed to wind and water at the earth's surface. Millions of years later, the rock eroded away, exposing the fossil.

He shivered when he saw her. Molly. He could only see her silhouette with the sun behind her in the trailer doorway, but, still, he recognized her.

"Dr. Wright," she groaned. Andrew swallowed, stood and instinctively stepped forward.

"Yes, Molly."

"I have a question," she smiled. Andrew had to close his eyes momentarily.

"Yes, Molly?"

"Well, Andrew—. Can I call you Andrew?"

"Of course." What a face. Her eyes remind me of Annie. Her brain too, he thought.

"If an Elasmosaur has such a voluminous rib cage, you assume its lungs were equally large?"

"Mmm."

"Well, even though it would allow Elasmo to hold his breath for a long time, wouldn't he just float up to the surface filled with all that air?" Andrew's dust caked solemn but handsome face cracked into a large grin.

"You are a bright woman, Molly. You know a zoologist, I think his name was Matt Rinds, from Australia, watched a big ol' crocodile swallowing small, smooth river stones and then diving more easily. I think Najda in St. Petersburg, Russia not Florida, put two and two together and theorized that most Plesiosaurs probably relied on this method as well to counter-act their natural buoyancy—for deep dives." Molly cocked her head ever so slightly, mesmerized by his voice, sad eyes, and what he was teaching her. "One of the skeletons at this site in fact contained a cluster of around thirty, three inch diameter smooth river stones in the base of the stomach cavity. Almost looked like a small appendix-like ante-stomach held the ballast; perhaps aiding digestion as well with the bacteria colony it most likely contained. I assume they would be able to regurgitate or excrete these stones at some point, which explains the strange deposits we've found among fossils of the sea fauna." Andrew smiled as seductively as he could without being obvious. God, he thought, I want this beauty. A quick rap on the screen door of the trailer broke the locking of their eyes that had accompanied the silence when Andrew had stopped speaking. The door creaked open and the brilliant day intruded into the shadows of the trailer. Andrew saw the Site Director's head pop inside, looking disapprovingly at Andrew and then at Molly. Andrew's eyes adjusted to the daylight and began to water from the dusty dry air. That worm, Andrew thought. He thinks every professor is doing the horizontal mambo with the students. Wish it were true in this case. He winked at the Site Director as his beet-red face was eclipsed by a letter carrier holding a red, white and blue cardboard envelope.

"Come on in" Andrew said to the carrier who pushed past the director.

"Dr. Wright?"

"Yes."

"Overnight letter for you. Sign here please." He handed a

clipboard to Andrew and stood smiling at Molly, hands behind his back.

"Thanks." The letter carrier spun for the door.

"We'll probably see that guy on the news with an AK-47," Molly joked. Andrew giggled and pulled the perforated strip to open the US Mail Priority Letter.

Explorer Channel
Chip Johnson
101 Connecticut Avenue
Bethesda, MD. 20906-2379
August 17, 1998
Dear Dr. Wright:

Enclosed please find a first class ticket for United flight 1810 departing Denver International Airport 5:30 p.m. Monday, November 17, arriving Baltimore-Washington International Airport at 8:30 p.m. local time. Expect limousine transport to the Four Seasons Hotel and again to our main office on Connecticut Avenue the next morning at 10:30 a.m. Please enjoy all amenities of the hotel.

"What the hell?" Andrew said, inviting Molly to take a peak. Molly leaned closer to the letter Andrew held and squinted to focus. She gently rested her hand on his shoulder. He felt the subtle pressure of her thigh against his arm. "What is this about?"

Note a wire transfer of $5,000 has been made to your checking account for travel expenses. Your fee and the project can be discussed upon arrival. Full arrangements have been made with the university to ensure a substitute is available to lecture in your absence.

Thank you for your time and cooperation Doctor.

Best regards, Chip

7.

Jorgé began transferring the piping hot coffee from the commercial percolator to the large silver serving pot. He arranged five fine white cups in a semi-circle around the pot that sat in the middle of a serving cart. A three level silver tray held coffee, cinnamon and other assorted sweet cakes.

Jorgé took a final glance at his latest creation making sure all was perfect, and opened the louvered French doors into the main conference room.

He first saw the boss in the large black leather, high-backed chair at the head of the table surrounded by a rather multifarious looking crew.

Jorgé moved his tray closer to the table and began to pour the coffee into the cups.

"Dr. Wright, this is Dr. Rebecca McClintock," the boss said to the tan young man with the short hair cut and sun lines on his face.

"Pleasure, ma'am," Andrew tipped an invisible hat to Rebecca who sat leaning on one elbow across the large conference table. Rebecca smiled back and then looked to Ian.

"And this is Ian Chelsea," the boss said pointing to the man with the long blonde hair. He actually stood, stretched awkwardly across the wide table and offered Rebecca his hand. "You will team up with one of our standard camera and specialist crews for a program of this sort. We have a vessel waiting for you in Colchester, Vermont."

"Vermont?" Andrew turned back to Chip Johnson.

"You guys are going to hunt for a monster. And because some mad Brit.', who happens to be one of my dearest friends, thinks he once had a run in with it, he is offering a large reward for evidence. Thus, other people are willing to back our little expedition. A high risk investment but a high potential rate of return."

"Monster, eh?" Ian said sarcastically.

"Yes, Ian. And you my friend are going to help film it."

Jorgé approached each of the people arrayed around the table from over their left shoulder. First the lady, then the boss, then the two men would get a steaming cup of coffee, as well as a pastry plate with a stirring spoon and a small fork wrapped in a lace napkin in its middle. Jorgé then reached for the three-tiered server and offered each a delicacy.

Each of the people, despite the near frantic conversation, paused to sample one of the inviting cakes he had prepared the night before. Jorgé was learning to be a chef and, one day, hoped to own a restaurant.

As was customary for meetings, Jorgé placed the sugar and cream within easy reach of all. Otherwise he would have put two cubes of brown sugar and poured half-and-half for one second into the boss' cup.

"What's our access to equipment like?" Rebecca asked Chip Johnson.

"Whatever you need. The Navy even sold us two obsolete Sound Surveillance System hydrophones."

"Cool, SOSUS sonobuoys! That's the Ffq-10 sensor station, right?"

"Correct, doctor."

Jorgé retrieved his tray and retreated through the French doors for the small prep room. He had honey Dijon glazed chicken breast, Gruyere and bacon on croissant sandwiches and leek soup to make for a twenty-plate luncheon conference that afternoon. He stowed the tray until later for when he went to refill any cups that needed it and to retrieve the pastry plates and scrape up the crumbs.

"You each get fifty thousand US currency up front, fifty more if we discover something. There is also a bonus of twenty thou' if you can capture a, well, specimen."

"Come on, Chip. Gimme a break. What we will be looking for is impossible—cannot exist. But hey, I will take your fifty grand if you want. It will help finance a few digs," the voice of the short hair, good-looking man filtered through the ajar door. Jorgé laughed quietly. This gringo has cohones he thought as he pushed open the louvered doors and again entered the room.

"And you bums get to be on television," the boss proclaimed, ignoring Andrew. You will each of course get the rights to any research on the expedition, but my channel gets exclusive to the footage. Any objections?" Ian only held up a flat hand to Jorgé when he offered more coffee and then let the uniformed Spaniard clear the setting. The others only stared back blankly at Chip. "Good. Provide the project manager with a list of all your needs tonight please. We have you booked on a flight from National to J.F.K. in New York. From there to Burlington, Vermont. That's in two days. In the meantime, please enjoy D.C. and your hotels. I look forward to, well, whatever happens."

With that the boss stood. Jorgé immediately opened the main doors to the conference room named *Darwin*, allowing the boss' guests escape to the hallway. The boss was the last to leave, patting Jorgé on the back but not making eye contact. Maintaining the authority, Jorgé thought. Eh, this job is only a stepping stone, he reminded himself. Anyway, this gringo boss was not all that bad, not like the last cabron he had worked for. Jorgé smiled as the boss and his guests strolled down the marble hallway to the nearest elevator bank.

8.

Miko Hakinen, a Finn by blood, closed the door behind him and entered the cold, dark, silent morning. He walked down the narrow cobble stone street past the clapboard homes, the snow compacting under his heavy winter boots with a crunching sound. The fishing port of TromsÆ, his home and the home of his family for generations, sat nestled in a deep fjord on the northeastern strip of Norway between the islands of RingvassÆy and Senja. He reached the stone sea wall and the thin, single plank dock that jutted out into the blackness. His slush-covered boat sat moored near its end.

Miko sighed, having little desire to work this dreary morning. He began down the dock; balancing carefully and stepping foot in front of foot. Reaching its end, he uncovered a small dinghy and cautiously stepped in. With a deep breath of the cold morning, Miko began to paddle lazily for his moored boat some thirty feet away.

The diesel engine of Miko's boat gurgled and burped from its exhaust pipe on the stern. The rhythmic sound of the pistons almost sounded like his father's old steam driven pump. He expertly stayed in the narrow channel as he rounded a first turn and then another. After negotiating the tight turns and jagged outcropping-lined walls that formed a gauntlet along the first third of the main channel, Miko entered a large protected harbor.

He looked at the surrounding water, momentarily hypnotized by the small bursts of green, blue and red that surrounded his boat. Ever since the War, bunker oil continued to rise from the cold depths, creating a psychedelic display at the surface. Below lay the giant German battleship Tirpitz. The Lancaster bombers of Britain's 617 Squadron, which had been formed to breach the dams of the Ruhr Valley, had finished off the leviathan. These Dambusters as they came to be known, used a twelve thousand-pound Tallboy bomb to finish off the crippled war ship. Miko tipped his cap to honor the fellow mariner's that rested beneath in their cold, black watery grave.

Miko set course for another channel at the other side of the harbor. After a short trip through the wider passage, he would come upon a formation known as Thor's Twins. It was open water to his favorite and luckiest hunting ground from there. The tattered flag of Norway, white outlined blue cross on a red field, snapped and whipped in the furious gusts that resulted from channeling air between the steep fjord walls. When this shearing wind finally reached an opening to the sea it was as if the land itself was exhaling.

Miko flipped a switch on a bracket-mounted black box to activate the autopilot. He tightly tied his windbreaker and lifted a moldy canvas sheet that concealed a small, rust bitten metal box. He removed from it an M79 *Blooper* he had bought in New York. The one armed gun dealer had explained it could lob a grenade out to three hundred and fifty meters and had been developed to fight those, how did he put it, "Nasty little bastards, the Viet Cong." Now it was used to drive pods of the most frequently caught local prey, the Minke whale, to a killing ground. While this would be madness in most industrialized, or at least civilized nations, Norway, along with Japan, continued to openly snub their noses at the international community and it's Whaling Commission moratorium.

Whalers did not have to worry about protest or arrest in these waters. Many a time, he himself had been hired to specifically avoid arrest and illegally provide some of the worlds seediest and most inhumane aqua parks with dolphins, seals, killer whales and sea turtles from supposedly protected waters.

Miko first spotted the small black backs and dorsal fins of the breaching Minke pod off the port bow. He slapped open the M79 and slipped one of the light-blue high explosive grenades into the agape barrel and snapped the breech closed with a quick wrist movement. He then clicked off the safety. Holding the weapon high to the sky, he prepared to arc a grenade in front of the twelve or so mammals. Miko slowed his boat slightly. As its name implied, the M79 made a bloop sound as the grenade hurled out of the barrel and through the sky.

The column of water that erupted twenty feet in front of the Minkes confirmed the grenade had landed where he had wanted it. The explosion caused the lead whale and then the rest of the pod to turn towards the outreached arms of the coast's fjords. A second round exploded behind the now frantically swimming Minkes as they charged for the shallows; the three obviously younger and weaker ones began to tire and lag behind. A female instinctively hung back to lessen the widening gap between the pod and the younger whales. Miko's large gaff hook missed the muscular tail of the young Minke he had come along side of.

"Vittuu," he swore and struck again, driving the hook deeply into the bucking whale. He did not hear the high pitched scream that filled the now red water. A few swift blows on the bulbous skull of the Minke and it would be unconscious; soon to drown as it was towed behind Miko's boat by its tail. Miko stood and saw the larger Minkes now partially beached on the sharp eroded volcanic rock of the fjord. Froth grew on the shallow water as the whales thrashed in panic.

He navigated his boat into the dangerous fjord, carefully studying the colorful display of his depth meter. Grabbing a shotgun from a locker under the console he again eyed the squirming black mass of mammals. Miko wondered if the whales knew death was imminent. Looking into the black eye of the largest one, he suspected they did.

He had moved to the bow of the now stopped boat and began to raise the barrel of the shotgun when the radio hissed and popped to life.

"Miko, come in. Miko Hakinen. Urgent. This is Christian—please come in. Urgent." Miko slowly lowered the shotgun, cursed, "Satana," and moved for the radio in the small cabin opening. He ripped off his red glove with a snarl and grabbed the radio microphone.

"What the hell is it, Christian?"

"Money, my friend. Money."

2

249-VONB

CHAPTER 3: COMMENCEMENT

1.

"Okay. Ready. Annnd action!" The lights flooding the aft deck of the Explorer cast long shadows of the furiously working crew. The glimmering lights of Burlington and Colchester reached out across the black surface of the lake in long, thin reflective bolts.

"Welcome to Explorer Magazine. I stand here afloat on a mysterious lake called Champlain. Named for Samuel de Champlain, the so-called Father of New France and founder of Quebec, he discovered it while exploring as far west as Lake Huron. On July 30, 1609, de Champlain and his recently recruited Huron Indians slaughtered the local Iroquois with gunfire on these very shores; thereafter the Iroquois were bitter enemies of the French."

"Okay, cut. Make-up, get in there. Let's change angles, Chuck."

"Right, Todd." The narrator said between patting's with a powder covered puff. Muffled claps echoed up from the small flotilla of pleasure boats that had surrounded the M/V Explorer.

"Okay people, positions please. Quiet! Ready, Chuck?"

"Bring the TelePrompTer in a little closer please. Okay, perfect. Thanks. Ready!"

"Camera ready. Annnd action!" A tie-dyed member of the film crew stepped in front of the camera and said, "Scene one, take one on angle two." He then snapped shut the black clapboard.

"We are here, however, to explore a side of the lake other than its role in the French and Indian Wars, the American Revolution or the War of 1812. We are here to explore the possibility that a marine reptile, what the Iroquois still call the *Horse of the Water*, is alive and well in this and perhaps other lakes around the world. Like Loch Ness in Scotland, home of the famous Nessie, the waters of Lake Champlain are peat fed, making them opaque and freezing cold. But, instead, like Japan's Lake Ikeda and its inhabitant Isi, Canada's Lake Okanagan and it's Ogopogo or Naitaka, Sweden's Lake Storsjön or Loch Roe in Ireland, Lake Champlain is not well known to the world as being the home to a monster."

The narrator strolled along the deck railing, pausing to look upon the lake before again speaking.

"According to Hector Boyce's 'History of Scotland', in 1527, a Mr. Duncan Campbell reported a *terrible beast* came out of the water early one morning and *did very easily and without any force of straining himself overthrow huge oaks with his tail and killed outright three men that hunted him.* This encounter introduced Scotland and then the world to the possibility that a serpent-like creature could still live. Mr. Hugh Gray of London took the first alleged photograph of such a creature in 1933 at Loch Ness. The most famous of the photographs was of course that taken in 1934 by Dr. Robert K. Wilson, also at Loch Ness, which clearly showed a head and a portion of the neck. Recently however, the photograph was revealed to be an imaginative hoax; a carefully kept secret for over sixty years."

He looked to the deck, shook his head twice and again stared into the camera. He slowly walked towards it while continuing to speak.

"Now we are here at this American lake, a lake that has no ruined Castle Urquhart looking over it but which nevertheless spawned its own legend. We are here at Lake Champlain on the border between Vermont, New York and Quebec, Canada. The legend of a creature in this lake, which some call Champ, reaches far back to the native Iroquois who paid homage to the serpent through ceremony. Sightings in Scotland's Loch Ness reach back even farther to 455 AD. What could this creature really be? A giant fish? An ancient dinosaur from a time long forgotten? Does the creature, if it exists, live alone in the deep, cold waters of Lake Champlain? Some researchers believe that Lake Champlain is inhabited by Plesiosaurs, a marine reptile that dominated the world's oceans as top predator long before sharks and thought to be extinct for millions of years. The theory is that Plesiosaurs entered and then became trapped in the lake during the last ice age when the outlets to the sea disappeared. The answers to these questions remain a mystery, but we have assembled a team to try and answer them. Huge prizes have been promised for proof positive that the beast lives, but, to this day, no one has yet been able to catch one. Incredible legend? Fantastic myth? Or clever hoax. What do you believe?"

"Cut and print. Fan-freakin'-tastic, Chuck!" The congregation of weekend warriors on their boats once again erupted with whistles, clapping and one drunkenly operated air horn. "Okay, that's a wrap for tonight folks." The blinding spotlights of the film crew shut down one by one, leaving the task to the yellowish light of the Explorer's deck lamps.

2.

Andrew watched the film crew pack the last of the equipment into their black, aluminum framed cases, the larger ones being wheeled. Leaning over the freshly painted white railing of the Explorer's upper deck, he gazed out into the star-filled sky and whispered goodnight to the brightest one. Andrew turned for a hatch that led to the warmth of the ship's interior.

Strolling the Explorer's hallways for a while, looking bored and pensive to those he briefly encountered, Andrew passed a door that was no different from the others; he was compelled to stop, turn and face it.

He knocked before even questioning his actions.

"Enter," came muffled through the windowless door. Andrew entered the dimly lit room and saw Dr. McClintock—Rebecca—

intensely fixed on the collection of incomprehensible instrument displays that lined the wall.

"What's up?" Andrew asked the back of Rebecca's head and the skinny assistant that was currently frantically playing his hand-held video game.

"Shhh!" Came back as Rebecca sprung around and both she and the kid gave him the death look.

"Sorry," Andrew smiled and shrugged his shoulders. Rebecca's face went from yelling at him to saying hello.

"Oh. Hello Dr. Wright."

"Andrew," he raised his eyebrows.

"Andrew," Rebecca smiled, "Welcome to the shack."

"The what?"

"The sonar shack."

"Oh. What you up to?"

"Calibrating the sonar and sensors. I also found something."

"Oh?" Andrew used his practiced *tell me more* look.

"A thermal inversion layer at around two hundred feet that is going to make it difficult to penetrate the depths of the lake from the surface. Our sonar will just bounce off the layer like it's a solid bottom. Brent, fire one off please." The assistant pushed the pause button on his game, rolled on his chair with arms and legs flailing and reached for the wall panel. "One ping coming up, Doc'." A resounding sonar wave left the bulbous housing of the Explorers SQS-53 bow sonar at a twenty-degree angle and penetrated the depths.

Rebecca adjusted the brightness of a small instrument display and waited for the return of the sonar and the information it carried. The screen burst into a colorful display of the waters that lay below.

"Here we go," Rebecca said, again adjusting the controls of the display. "Here's the thermocline at two hundred and three feet. We're getting about fifteen feet's worth of data only beyond the layer. We must have a significant temperature variance at this level. This phenomenon is pretty common for glacial lakes of this depth. I have even seen some inversion layer storms."

"What do you mean?" Andrew sat in the chair at the sonar operator station that the assistant had abandoned. His video game sat perched on the knob and dial covered panel. Andrew and Rebecca turned to see the door close behind Brent as she again began to speak.

"Okay. Picture this. A cross section of the lake divided in three. The upper warmer layer, the inversion layer or thermocline and then the lower, colder waters. The wind pushes water of the upper layer to one side of the lake, pushing down on half the inversion layer and storing the energy. This then causes the entire inversion layer to pivot as if on a fulcrum. This seesaw effect creates turbulence on either side of the moving layer. In some cases, the movement is so rapid that the thermocline breaks up and the upper and lower waters mix until the layer can again form when the lake settles." Andrew studied the beautiful, sharp-featured face and Rebecca's long brown hair that was tucked in a pencil pierced bun.

"There is also usually a dead zone."

"A what?"

"An oxygen starved layer, where organic material has fallen to the bottom and is decomposing. The way this lake behaves, I have doubts a zone could form though."

"Wow," he smiled.

"More info. than you needed, huh?"

"No, no, interesting."

"This lake might turn out to be a harder nut to crack than I anticipated. Do me a favor Andrew, turn on that printer behind you." Andrew uncrossed his arms and complied. "Thanks. I want a hard copy of this test." The door exploded open and the skinny assistant, his clothes baggy and hanging practically dove for the still precariously perched game.

"We done for tonight, Doc'?" He asked the startled, green-lit silhouettes.

"Sure Brent, get outta here," Rebecca replied after a moment and forced a smile that was meant to say thanks for your help, goodnight, and see you tomorrow morning all in one. The small laser printer behind them began to hum as the local area network of the ship assigned the print job Rebecca had selected to it.

"Hey, you hungry, Rebecca?" Andrew asked standing and rubbing his stomach.

"It's 11:30 at night. Dr. Wright, how do you expect me to keep this lady-like figure?" Rebecca asked with a cocking of her hips.

"Okay. Come with me anyway. You can keep me company while I raid the refrigerator."

"Deal. I could use a soda anyway," Rebecca answered with a stretch.

3.

Ian spit into the yellow and black US Divers mask that hung around his neck and then rinsed it in a bucket of lake water. "Jack, hand me that regulator." Jack Meder, the chief cinematographer of the Explorer Channel's team, handed Ian the regulator and adjusted the rear strap of his fins. The two large cylindrical shaped SOSUS hydrophones purchased from the US Navy sat upright on the metal, grated swim platform that hung off the Explorer's stern. A small door in the white aluminum transom wall gave access.

"Okay, Ian, buoy two here is on a non-stop ride to the bottom. Buoy one has been rigged to trigger your camera array and will be tethered to the bottom but float at a depth of one hundred feet," the deck hand with the beat up looking clipboard and pen tucked behind his ear said matter-of-factly.

"Right. Jack and I will check on number one at depth. I want to make sure the connections to the cameras are not severed on its trip down." The deck hand's walkie-talkie crackled. He removed it from his belt, adjusted the squelch dial and depressed the transmit button. "Go ahead bridge."

"We are in position."

"That's a roger. Proceeding. Mr. Chelsea, we are in position."

"Okay." After a final check of the airflow to their regulators, first Jack and then Ian rolled backwards off the platform and into the lake's waters. Once the whirlpool of bubbles Ian created when he broke the lake's surface disappeared, he turned the beam of his light towards where Jack should be.

The dark brown, silty waters seemed to allow the light to travel a few feet and then snuffed it out completely. It did not fade slowly or gradually become dimmer but simply stopped. A tap on Ian's back told him Jack was behind him. As planned, Ian and Jack moved aside to allow the Explorer's crew to push the heavy buoys overboard to begin their lonely journey into the deep.

The seabed deployed SOSUS hydrophones had once stood guard between Iceland and the northern coast of the United Kingdom. Their job had been to detect Soviet missile submarines or boomers, running the Greenland-Iceland-UK gap on their way to the Atlantic and the eastern seaboard of the United States. A leather-gloved deck hand maneuvered the first buoy and its concrete block anchor to the edge of the platform. He gently deployed the three whip-like antennas at the cylinders' top. When the Wall fell in 1989, the United States and her North Atlantic Treaty Organization allies decided to cut back on the expensive to maintain SOSUS network in favor of increased American P-3 Orion and British Nimrod anti-submarine warfare aircraft patrols. Lethal assets indeed. To acquire the two buoys, Chip Johnson had to personally bid against both the National Geographic Society and NOAA. They would be useful many times over he had rationalized.

Ian saw the boil of yellowish foam thirty feet above at the surface. The concrete anchor headed for the lake bottom, quickly followed by the buoy. The column of bubbles the rapidly sinking package produced confirmed the buoy was descending at a near perfect ninety-degree angle to the bottom and would land relatively close to the intended touch down point. He gave a thumb up to Jack who floated near the surface. Ian noticed how little sunlight penetrated the inky water and the second concrete anchor burst through the mercury-like surface. This time the buoy did not immediately follow the anchor. Ian watched as hundreds of feet of cable unfurled, then the buoy entered the water, this time ringed by a large yellow inflated flotation collar. This would compensate for the weight of the anchor wire and the camera package Ian had added.

This hydrophones descent was more erratic and, as Ian looked to Jack and again began to penetrate the deep, he hoped the violence of the trip did not disturb the carefully arrayed photography equipment.

As Jack and Ian descended through the freezing blackness they stayed as close to the column of bubbles as possible, both for guidance to the buoy, which now hopefully was coming to a rest at a depth of one hundred feet, as well as for orientation. The rising bubbles became the only way to tell which way was up. Ian looked at his depth gauge that read ninety-two feet and then spotted the bright yellow, which looked more like a dark brown down here, flotation collar of the buoy. Jack sped up and passed Ian as he swam for the base of the hydrophone buoy, momentarily disappearing behind the fully inflated flotation collar.

Ian made for the small pallet of cameras. He immediately noticed one loose wire connection but easily tightened its self-purging connector. Jack appeared again from behind the buoys main metallic cylinder and began inspecting the three whip antennas that would deliver the hydrophone data back to the Explorer via Very Low Frequency radio, operating in the 3-30 kHz range. Floating either side of the buoy, which looked to Ian like a donut with a breadstick pushed through it, Ian and Jack gave one another a thumbs up and slowly began to ascend from the dive.

4.

"Okay, I am getting good readings from both. The one on the bottom is a little faint but that is understandable with the thermocline being where it is. At least we now have sensors in both halves of the lake. Andrew what does that temperature gauge read on hydrophone two?"

"Thirty four degrees. Damn, that's freezing. Well, almost."

"And hydrophone one?"

"Forty seven Fahrenheit. How far off the bottom is number one, Rebecca?"

"Five hundred fifty feet. And about one hundred feet below the surface. Brent, how's battery power on two?"

"Uh, looks good. Nineteen twentieths on the meter." Ian entered the sonar shack, a glass of Black Label in hand. The three cringed like vampires as if the hall light would burn them.

"You guys sure make me feel welcome."

"Sorry, pull up a chair."

"Thanks, Andy."

"Andrew."

"Hi beautiful. What you and Andy doing here?" Andrew shook his head and Ian rattled the ice in his glass, the oily whiskey clinging to the sides of the wavy crystal.

"Monitoring the hydrophones you set. So, please keep it down. If you must stay, sit in that corner there out of the way," Rebecca said pointing with a *don't mess with me* look on her face. Andrew leaned over to Ian and whispered, "Don't worry, I had a similar reception the first time." Ian grinned, again clanked the now smaller ice cubes against the glass and then sipped the alcohol.

"Hey, Doc', buoy two is picking up something on passive sonar. We are getting good reflection off the inversion layer above it," Brent said adjusting his red, white and blue New England Patriots cap.

"Talk to me, kiddo," Rebecca straightened up from the slouch boredom had set in and looked at the blinking light on Brent's panel.

"I dunno yet." Brent put on his headphones and listened intently for a moment. "Schoolafish maybe. Whatever it is, it's pretty close to the thermocline. We may be able to get something off the Explorer's active sonar—especially if the contact moves into the upper layer."

"Spin up the system, Brent. Let's have it ready." Rebecca was really animated now. "Andrew, please flip that red lever to bridge the circuit to ships power."

"Sounds like rushing water or bubbles or something. It's rising, approaching the thermocline. I've lost it, lost it in the inversion layer. Come on baby!"

"When you pick it up again above the inversion layer, hammer the active sonar."

"Okay, Doc'. Should be just a few more seconds." Brent's sneakers shook with excitement.

"Rebecca, how thick is the layer?"

"About twenty five to thirty feet Andrew. Brent, anything yet?"

"Nope. Must be loitering in the thermocline."

"You guys actually believe you might have something here? Doctor, surely-."

"Getting something again," Brent cut short Andrew. "Just piercing the thermocline. Ready on active, green light on the array."

"Steady, give it a few more seconds." The passive sonar data that arrived from hydrophone two, suspended seven feet above the gray, powdery mud of the lake floor, lost contact, while hydrophone one, floating in the upper half of the lake, began to display a solid green bar among the clutter of other lake noise.

"I'm getting a solid contact on one."

"Hammer the active."

"Okay, Doc', here goes." The loud ping echoed through the steel plates of Explorers bulkheads and hull.

"Damn, there are two!" Brent looked wide-eyed at Dr.

McClintock and then panned to see Dr. Wright and Mr. Chelsea huddled in the corner of the shack. Andrew's face emerged into the dim green glow given off by the equipment and smirked, "Two what boy? What do you think you have here, huh?" Brent looked back at the two small dots that blinked on his display.

"Do it by the book, Brent," Rebecca interjected supportively.

"Right, two contacts. Depth: one hundred ninety six feet. Speed, range and bearing: unknown 'til we triangulate."

"Roger, hammer it again." A second ping filled the surrounding water and sounded like a wrench striking an iron pipe. The screen of the sonar unit updated with the fresh data.

"Here we go. Depth: one hundred ninety six feet. Bearing: oh eleven. Range: about a thousand feet of the port forward quarter. Speed: about two knots, maybe three. Contacts are running parallel to each other and one looks bigger than the other." Ian stood, stumbled slightly and announced, "Well, I am dry. Going for a refill. Have fun chasing your fishies."

"Such open minds," Rebecca rolled her eyes but did not look back at the departing Ian.

"Going below the layer again. Hydrophone one has lost 'em. Checking two. Faint contact. Fading." Andrew stood, stretched and looked briefly at Rebecca's profile, her skin glowing in a green aura. "Fading." Focused on the fresh data, she did not notice him slip out the door. "Gone."

5.

Ian observed Andrew sneaking out of the sonar room as if he was a boy leaving to meet his girlfriend and afraid to wake his parents. Ian decided to speak a little louder. "Hey, Andy!" Andrew almost jumped out his skin like in a cartoon.

"How 'bout some shore leave, ol' boy. Nowhere in my contract does it say I have to be booored to death." Ian laughed, swung his arm around Andrew, a half-empty bottle of Black Label clutched in a white knuckled hand. "Think we can find a bloody cab in this part of town?" Ian erupted in laughter and Andrew, despite his mood, began to chuckle as well. Andrew slowly began to support more and more of Ian's weight as they moved down the side of the Explorer towards the stern. Andrew was fighting gravity and gravity was winning.

"Damn, your heavy. You sure you can make it to town."

"You baaahstard! You wouldn't leave me on this bloody barge now would you?" Ian's eyes and head rolled from side to side. Arriving at the transom, Andrew carefully propped Ian against the side and unclipped a rope that blocked the way to a wooden ramp. "Okay my friend, carefully or you will end up in the drink." Andrew grasped the sleeve of Ian's sweater, "and put that bottle down."

They both proceeded down the planked, rope lined ramp to the small floating platform that sat tied to the Explorer near her water line. Ian sprawled out onto the platform and gaped at the sky. Scanning the lake from the Explorer's anchorage off Burlington's Municipal Beach, his eyes immediately drawn to the lights of Battery Street, Andrew reached for a canned air horn that sat lashed to a small cleat and sounded four blasts to call for the launch.

The gurgling sound of the approaching launch echoed off the lakeshore. He then saw the red and green navigational lights on her bow. Andrew made out the warmly dressed launch operator and the blue launch he piloted: the Flow. With a quick adjustment of the steering column and the whine of the diesel engine reversing to slow her momentum, the Flow gracefully met the gently rocking floating platform. Her operator lassoed the nearest cleat and backed off the reverse throttle. "Evening. Please watch your step when you come aboard." Andrew offered Ian his hand and grunted to lift his practically dead weight. Ian stumbled onto the launch and fell onto one of her benches.

"Where you headed?" The launch operator whipped the rope free of the cleat and engaged the engine.

"What are our choices?" Well, there is Mariners Inn restaurant over towards the beach, the Yacht Club, same area. Both have private docks; and then there is always town dock. That's where the Keeseville Ferry docks. Yah know, on Battery between Main 'n' Maple."

"Town dock then please." Andrew looked back at the Explorer and the bubble of light that seemed to surround her in the rays of the now setting sun. From the stern platform and her small hydraulic crane to that Godforsaken *Explorer Channel—Lake Champlain Expedition* banner that hung along practically the entire length of the superstructure; then the orange covered lifeboat and the high proud bow. Her glossy white paint made the Explorer glow, almost gave her an aura and thus a soul. Her length must total about seventy-five feet, Andrew thought. He then remembered reading exactly that number on the brass *Avondale Shipyard, Louisiana* plaque that hung on the bridge and in the lounge. Behind the Explorer and obscured, betrayed only by the light that bounced off the low, thick clouds, was Plattsburg, New York. Andrew looked at the now stoic looking Ian and asked, "Feeling better?"

"The air is nice," Ian's response was barely audible above the engine. As the launch neared the other shore of the long, thin, deep lake, the Explorer receded. Andrew spotted the main dock ahead, with its gauntlet of lights and strolling couples oohing and aahing the sail and powerboats that were tied along side. Ian stood, swayed slightly and propped himself on the gunwale. "You my friend are suffering from premature intoxication," Andrew observed. The launch operator slowed the momentum of the heavy wood boat. Ian smiled.

"Mate, they just seem to go down so easy after a dive." The launch idled and approached the public dock that announced on a sign in red letters: Maximum Dock Time—Twenty Minutes. No Fishing. B.P.D.

"Three fifty each sirs." Andrew dug for his wallet in one of the side pockets of his weathered leather jacket.

"Here, this looks good, Ian," Andrew pointed at a rustic sign that proclaimed *Schooner's Food and Drink.*

"Hope it is not one of those Yank yuppie bars."

"After you, *Your Highness.*" Andrew threw open the door and bowed deeply. Ian groaned and proceeded in. The noise of the crowded bar spilled out into the street, drawing the curious looks of passerby's. They made for an opening in the crowd that led directly to a man cleaning a glass.

"What'll it be?"

"Well, my esteemed colleague here will have scotch neat." The bartender glanced over at Ian, rolled his eyes and asked, "And you?"

"Hmm, let's see, I'll have a Cape Cod—use Absolut." Andrew turned and scanned the crowded, smoky bar room and then beyond the divider to the rather comfortable looking eating area. "Got any eats at the bar?"

"Nope. That'll be eight bucks," the chubby bartender said placing the drinks on the dark stained oak bar. "Wanna table?"

"No, tha-."

"This will be on me doctor . . . Dr. Wright, is it not?" Both Ian and Andrew turned to see the tall, blond man with the piercing; almost lifeless ice blue eyes place a new twenty-dollar bill on the bar.

"And you would be?" Andrew asked with a touch of attitude. Ian just stared at the towering man.

"A fellow adventurer." His shoulders went back and chest came out as if presenting himself for inspection.

"You working for Explorer as well?" Andrew swallowed two gulps of the strong drink while Ian simply noisily tumbled the cubes in his glass and eyed the stranger with suspicion.

"Hah! No, no. I am, how do you say, free lance."

"That's how you say it. I wasn't aware we had competition."

"Oh no, no competition. Different, how you say, ob-, ob-."

"Objective?"

"Yes, different objective."

"I see," Andrew said with a questioning glance to Ian who sat transfixed by the latest beautiful woman to cross his field of vision. "Well, thanks for the drink, uh, I don't think I caught your name?"

"Miko. Miko Hakinen. See you on the lake."

6.

"Rebecca, can you pass me that bag please."

"Here you go," Rebecca passed Ian the mesh bag that contained his flippers and snorkel.

"Thanks." Ian first stretched and then snapped the rubber flippers on. He turned on the small forehead lamps both he and Rebecca had donned. "Okay. All set then?"

"All set. You sure you feel up to it, Ian?"

"Yeah, yeah, let's get on with it then."

Rebecca cleared her regulator and, holding her long brown hair up in a tail, slipped the transparent mask over her head. Her neon yellow wet suit stood out in the cold, gray, drizzly morning. Both Rebecca and Ian swung their legs in unison over the dark lake water. They sat for a moment and, after a quick glance of assurance to each other, tumbled into the lake headfirst. Despite being an experienced night diver, the blackness of the lake was unexpected, catching Rebecca by surprise and momentarily disorienting her. Perhaps sensing Rebecca's confusion, Ian gently touched her arm and waited for the expression on her face to subside. He then winked at her, his face squeezed into an almost comical expression by the tight black flange of his mask. She laughed nervously in a cascade of bubbles. Ian jackknifed his body and began to descend into the dark, looking back to make sure Rebecca was close behind. She was.

Ian removed what appeared to be a hand-held megaphone from his weight belt, the kind protesters are always barking through, and held it out in front of him. He paused in the darkness and aimed the device into the deep. Rebecca checked her depth gauge that read fifty-seven feet. Ian tapped her on her wrist and pointed to the barely legible LED readout on the hand-held sonar unit that said their quarry lay about forty feet below them and slightly to the northwest. Rebecca held up a hand to tell Ian to wait and then removed a small, glass sample container, which she opened, let fill with lake water and then closed. Her thumbs down told Ian to continue their descent.

Rebecca equalized the pressure in her ears and shivered as the thin water layer between her skin and the polypropylene suit began to get colder. Ian adjusted their course and angle of decent as he held the instrument in front of him. He then slowed, turned and pointed. There in the gloom, Rebecca first saw the dark brown hydrophone gently swaying on its tether in the slight current. As they approached the hydrophone, its color changed from brown to its true yellow. Ian stopped, turned to Rebecca and pointed at the large dive watch on his left wrist. He flashed five fingers and then two. Rebecca signaled she understood they had seven minutes at depth.

She turned the register ring on her own Citizen dive watch to mark the position of the minute hand at the beginning of the seven minute countdown and reached for her belt pack. Finding her small test kit, she glanced up to see Ian taking a small ratchet to a stubborn bolt that held the camera array to the sonobuoy. She suspected the burst of bubbles he released yielded profanity once finally at the surface and then went back to the task at hand.

Rebecca hovered about ten feet from Ian and the buoy. Her near perfect balance between her weight belt and the small amount of air in her buoyancy control device meant her flippers barely had to move to maintain her position. She removed the small test kit from its protective cover and pulled the white tab marked *Pull Here* to allow water to enter the instrument. A small bubble exited the hole in the small silver box as lake water rushed into its sensor. The back lit, touch sensitive plasma screen began to spit back data.

Ian felt Rebecca bump into his back. He quickly looked over his shoulder, angry he was interrupted from disconnecting the spaghetti of wiring to his cameras and their strobes. Not seeing her, he then turned to where he thought she had been taking readings. Nothing. He again turned to look behind him and then swam into the surrounding darkness to try and spot Rebecca. He wondered if she was in distress or simply mucking about. His training told him to assume the former.

Rebecca saved the readings and looked to Ian but saw only the dark brown silhouette of the buoy now some twenty feet away. I must have drifted, she thought. The current is so subtle you barely take head of its effects. She turned, looked to her belt in order to replace the instrument in its case and then paused. The feeling that came over her could only be described as similar to the one she felt every time she entered the dark musty attic at her grandmother's house; the feeling she was being carefully watched from the darkness. She slowly scanned the black hole they called a lake but saw only shadows within shadows. Rebecca noticed her breaths were becoming more frequent and shallow and, like any good diver, reminded herself to calm down and think logically. As she knew well, panic was usually deadly to divers. Pushing on the last Velcro strap and, certain the expensive gadget was secured, she slowly began to swim back towards the buoy and Ian. *Ian you pompous, womanizing, booze swilling limy bastard—where are you when I need you?*

The buoy grew larger as she approached and turned first from dark brown in color to a coffee then a muddy yellow. Come on. Closer. Rebecca refused to kick faster even though the feeling she was being circled could not be shaken. *Ian you jerk, if you are playing some stupid joke?* The roar of her bubbles reminded her again to stay cool and take slow, deep breaths. The buoy now filled her field of vision but Rebecca still could not see Ian. *I knew it*; Rebecca almost screamed and circled the hydrophone to where he had been working. Checking the minute hand of her watch, now six past the red dot on the register ring she had set earlier, Rebecca scanned the water and began to worry.

Hugging the buoy for safety, its antennae rasping on the rough steel of her tank, a sudden burst of light filled the surrounding murkiness. Illuminating the silt that floated in the soupy water, the flash seemed like underwater lightning. She expected a thunderclap to follow but, instead, another flash.

Ian found the thin steel wire tether that anchored hydrophone one to the lake floor some ninety-two fathoms below and began to ascend along it. Rebecca saw they had been at depth over eight minutes when she felt the buoy jerk slightly, bubbles began rising around her. She looked down between her legs and her frog-like flippers and saw the silhouette of Ian rising along the anchor cable. He rose next to her, stopped and glared into her eyes. Held in his gloved hands was a 35mm still camera, its clear Plexiglas housing and trailing cables that had been connected to the hydrophone sensors and central processing unit. Ian pushed Rebecca aside, attached a yellow balloon to the camera pallet and inflated it by pulling on a stainless cotter pin on the seal to a small carbon dioxide cartridge.

The balloon and pallet began to rapidly rise towards the surface to be spotted and collected by a team in a Zodiac. Ian again turned to Rebecca who gave him a questioning look. The lens on her mask magnified her green eyes slightly and betrayed the fear behind her calm facade. He pointed upwards and stared back blankly in response.

Ian began to ascend, kicking gently and sending a wash of water over the exposed bluish skin of Rebecca's face. Realizing she was again momentarily alone in the dark, she began to nervously follow.

7.

Just down the hill from where Tyrannosaurus Rex and Velociraptor's threatened crowds at the new Universal Studios Jurassic Park ride, a series of massive tunnels were being dug for the Los Angeles subway system. Ninety feet below the asphalt maze, back hoes scratched away at the rock and soil. Mark Guttier was chief engineer for the Metropolitan Transportation Authority's northern expansion of the Red Line, the spur that ran under Vermont Avenue and then skirted Griffith Park on its way to North Hollywood. The MTA had been building Los Angeles' nearly six billion-dollar subway system for the past ten years and, despite being hundreds of millions of dollars over budget and a political minefield for the mayor, work continued.

"Damn it, another one. Stop the hoe, stop the damn hoe" Mark carefully pulled the small fragment of bone from between the jagged steel teeth of the excavation machine and wiggled it free of the earth. "Get Gunther over here." Gunther Landers, normally hard at work cleaning the asphalt-coated bones of Giant Ground Sloths, American Lion, Saber Toothed Tiger, Dire Wolves and Mastodon's that the gooey La Brea Tar Pits entombed, had taken a leave. Postponing his duties as Research Associate at the Tar Pit Discovery Museum, he would assist UCLA with its excavation and cataloging of the Red Line Subway fossils. He would supervise the cataloging of the now frequent discoveries from here under the worlds most congested and over developed desert.

"Nice," Gunther said as he emerged from the darkness and shone his hard-hat-mounted lamp on the shard of yellowed bone Mark held in his gloved hands. Gunther's pale plump face squinted to better examine the fossil.

"Hmm, I'd say you have a mastodon tooth there Mark." Gunther adjusted the beam of the lamp that illuminated this latest find. "Looks like we have some pollen caked on here as well," he mumbled to himself, taking the shard and heading back into the tunnel towards his makeshift laboratory.

Mark removed his hard hat, wiped the sweat from his brow and made a circular motion in the air to signal the operator of the beastly backhoe machine to again awaken its diesel engine. It sprang to life with a cloud of black smoke that was quickly inhaled by the tunnels temporary ventilation system.

Gunther arrived at the small sheet metal shed that had been erected for him out of the way of the frequent construction traffic. The smaller, perpendicular tunnel it occupied would eventually house an electrical substation. He pawed at the brass Master padlock and then unlocked it with a small brass key that dangled from a string around his neck. The corrugated metal door resisted for a moment and then yielded, digging an arc shaped trench in the soft ground as it swung open.

Gunther turned on the single over head fluorescent light and gently placed the fossil on to a small Formica counter next to an expensive looking Bausch & Lomb microscope. After planting his weight on a wobbly three-legged stool, Gunther glanced at the fossil through a magnifying glass and reached for a compact pocket tape recorder that was perched on a small wooden shelf above him. He ran his fingers through his curly black hair, pushed the record button and began to speak after a hearty sigh.

"Item one twenty two," he said as he carefully placed a small numeric tag on the fossil. "Unconfirmed mastodon tooth—probably left upper incisor—crusted with what appears to be redwood tree pollen. Suggests probable age of item at two hundred eighty thousand years old. Third Red Line fossil found to contain this pollen. Likely that Los Angeles region was much colder and damper than it is today if it supported redwood groves, which are now found only in the cooler climes of Northern California and Oregon. Considering the several desert pollens we found with the younger Red Line fossils, I would conclude that the Los Angeles basin became much drier and warmer about nine thousand years ago."

Gunther pressed the pause button of his small video recorder and placed a small round red sticker on the fossil. It would distinguish it for further examination by electron microscope at a later date. He reached for a small beige starfish that he gently pinched between two pudgy fingers and released the pause button. The small motor of the tape recorder once again hummed subtly as he spoke again. "Perhaps most fascinating and puzzling of all," he reflected twirling one of the five spiny legs that radiated from the long dead creature's body, "is the dozens of fish fossils we have discovered here below LA. Many of the specimens are the first of their kind recorded in North America. Some are also the oldest, dating back as far as fifteen million years. These fish fossils show that much of Los Angeles was at least a half-mile underwater seven to eight million years ago."

A rap at the metal door reverberated through the hastily assembled structure startling Gunther, who again pushed the small silver button on the black plastic recorder and then let it dangle by it's wrist strap.

"Got another one for yah, Landers," Mark said, opening the door and looking fed-up.

"Mark, you look like you want to blame these little critters for your subway being a few hundred mill in the red." Gunther gave a friendly wink from behind glasses that magnified his eyes unnaturally and reached for the bone. "You know in Athens Greece it took 'em a month to go three feet on their new subway cause they kept finding remains of the ancient city." He smiled at Mike; proud to offer the *it could be worse* factoid.

"Well, stopping every two feet ain't freakin' helpin'. I can see stopping for a vase but fish bones? Why don't you just visit my trash after dinner tonight."

"Hey, the law is the law."

"Yeah, yeah," Mark gave a dismissive wave and started back down the tunnel.

"Oh, and please let me remove the fossils when they are found. I need to log-" Mark turned and, at first, gave a *don't push your luck* look. He then cordially said, "Sure," and walked away. Gunther looked at the red clay caked crescent shaped fossil and carefully pried apart the gray shale that sandwiched the petrified bone. "Nice," Gunther mumbled and blindly pawed at the ordered mess of the counter until he felt the imitation leather cover of his walkie-talkie. "Mark, Gunther here. Please respond." Gunther adjusted the squelch on the Motorola radio.

"Go ahead." The sound of the giant excavator that first clawed at the earth and then reinforced the walls with pre-fabricated concrete liners distorted the small speaker of the radio and almost drowned out Mark's response.

"Mark, sorry to interrupt you but at what height did you find the piece you just brought me?" Gunther released the transmit button and put his ear to the small speaker.

"About one foot, in that layer of shale you said was the old sea floor; right below the clay band."

"Thanks." Gunther reached for a phone that hung on the wall and pressed the autodial and then button one.

"Page Museum—Research. Sue speaking."

"Sue? Hi. Gunther."

"Hey."

"Listen, on my desk is a fax number for Andrew Wright. Could you get it for me please? It's on a yellow Post-It."

"Hold on." Gunther wedged the phone between his head and shoulder and reached for a box under the counter. He had just finished unpacking the fax machine when Susan came back on the line. "Got it. Ready? Area code eight-zero-two, the number is: 555-2683. It says *temporary* next to it though."

"Right, that's the one. Thanks." Gunther hastily scribbled a note to Andrew on a yellow legal pad and attempted to sketch the outline of the fossil as best he could. Critiquing the likeness, he decided to snap a Polaroid and hoped the image Andrew would receive would reveal at least some detail. He suspected the facsimile of the gray shale encrusted black fossil would be too dark when received by the machine at the other end of the line.

Encumbered by his pudgy fingers, he fumbled the phone wire that ran up one of the metal walls and out the roof. It eventually connected with the rest of the massive engineering projects wiring on its way to the surface. Gunther found the small clear plastic jack at the top back of the telephone base and disconnected it with one lucky squeeze. Finding the hole on the back of the fax machine labeled *Line*, he inserted the jack with a click and gave it a gentle tug to verify it had seated properly. He placed face down in the fax machine tray the yellow legal paper with the photograph of the fossil carefully attached with tape. Gunther pressed the blue dial button and entered the phone number Sue had provided. After two rings and the terrible noises the fax machine made as it 'shook hands', or synchronized, with the recipient, the paper began to be pulled in as the transmission began. After a minute, and the letter being spat out the bottom, the display confirmed one page had been successfully sent.

8.

After popping into his mouth the last of the toasted bagel, cream cheese and smoked salmon he had rustled up from the galley for breakfast, Andrew started towards the wheelhouse of the Explorer. As he made his way down the twisting halls, an arm reached out, almost choking him as he swallowed the last of his meal.

"Dr. Wright?" Andrew coughed in acknowledgment. "Fax coming in for yah."

"Tha-uh-thanks." Andrew occupied the warm chair the crewmember had vacated and watched the fax machine slowly print out the transmission.

"Oh, from Gunther," Andrew said as if someone was interested.

Need your help ID'ing this one . . . here's an attempt at drawing it. Please leave me voice mail at the Museum—I'll check it later. Thanks bud!

Andrew squinted at the poor detail of the fax, shaking his head. He referred back to the primitive drawing to help form the basic outline of the fossil. The loud clank of an outside hatch opening and then rapid footsteps broke his concentration.

"C'mon, what the hell is wrong?" Rebecca frantically followed the almost jogging Ian down the cramped hallway, passing but not noticing Andrew, fax in hand, at the communication station. He popped his head out inquisitively, smelling the lake water on the breeze their movement created. His eyes followed the moist footprint depressions in the carpeting of the hall to Ian, holding a heavy camera, and Rebecca. Admiring her figure in the tight wet suit, he wondered if she was interested in Ian and felt momentarily jealous. Andrew looked around the empty hall making sure his face did not betray his feelings to anyone. His head retreated slowly back into the cubbyhole.

Ian did not answer Rebecca's question. Trailing water-matted hair behind him, Ian continued towards one of the ships two darkrooms; a small red bulb perched over its door jam. He threw open the door and turned to Rebecca, inviting her to join him without speaking a word. The intense look on his face told her to ask nothing and follow him into the room. The door closed behind them and the red bulb illuminated.

Ian loosened the top of his still dripping wet suit and popped the seal on the watertight Plexiglas case of the camera he had brought back to the surface. He extended a small arm on the camera's metallic body and began to rewind the film.

"Need help, Ian?" Rebecca cautiously asked the livid looking Ian.

"I'm sorry, Rebecca," the color returned to his cheeks, "I did not mean to wander away from you down there."

"That's okay, Ian. You must have had a good reason."

"We will see in a moment. If I can get this bloody film out!" Rebecca gently took the camera from Ian's trembling hands and smiled. He dropped his weight into a padded chair, pushing the air out of its cushion with a hiss. Ian buried his face in his hands. A familiar click told him Rebecca had opened the camera and was removing the now rewound yellow film cartridge.

"I'll get this film started." Ian nodded to Rebecca in the reddish light and said, "I'll be right back, just going to get out of this wet suit. Won't be a moment."

"Okay. Take your time—you seem a bit, well . . . shaken up." Seeing the flame in his eyes, Rebecca expected Ian to scream at her when he said calmly, "Your right. Thanks. Three minutes for that speed film, Rebecca." He forced a smile and left. Rebecca carefully removed the film from its protective casing and wound it onto a plastic spool in preparation for development.

Once the door had closed behind Ian, Rebecca unzipped her wet suit exposing the bare skin of her chest to the cold air of the dark room. Carefully pouring a chemical developer into the canister that now held the spool of film, she set a small kitchen timer for three minutes and began to agitate the film and chemicals. Squeezing her still wet strands of hair with the fingers of her free hand, Rebecca shivered and goose bumps erupted on her skin making it feel one size too small. A muffled knock at the door startled her and, thinking Ian had returned, she quickly zipped her wet suit back up. When Rebecca heard Andrew's voice, she visibly relaxed. "Yeah, come in. Films in a tub." The door opened a crack and Andrew peaked in.

"I brought you a towel. Thought you might be cold after your dive."

"C'mon in." The pace at which she rocked the canister slowed as Andrew entered. "Thanks, Doc'," she smiled, happily taking the warm fluffy towel. His boyish grin made her full lips part ever so slightly, which neither noticed.

"Need a break?" He reached for the black canister that contained the developing film.

"Sure, it's only got a minute left before it needs fixer. Thanks." Rebecca passed Andrew the film after glancing at the timer and threw her head forward facing the floor. She slowly dried her long hair—starting at her neck and then wrapping it in the fresh towel until it stood upright in what looked to Andrew like a big marshmallow on her head—speaking all the while. "Ian got spooked by something down there, Andrew. He is a little freaked and, to tell you the truth, he scares me a little. I mean he is nice and all but —." She looked up and saw a look in Andrew's eyes that she recognized. "Why Dr. Wright, I do believe you are making eyes at me," she said with her best Southern Belle accent. She slowly leaned forward and, kissing him half on the cheek and half on his lips, whispered, "the attraction is mutual."

The clanging bell of the timer brought Andrew back. Rebecca stood and a knock at the door followed by Ian's voice made her move for it. She paused, winked and said, "See you later alligator." Ian then entered the dark room, smiling at Rebecca. "Film is ready for the fixer. My turn to get into some dry clothes," she smiled back.

"Hey there, big guy. How's it going?" Andrew unscrewed the canister and poured the developer into a recycling container. "Which one of these is the fixer?" Ian pointed silently at a bottle on a small shelf. "Wanna talk about it?" Andrew poured in the new chemical and resealed the canister.

"I saw something Andy," Andrew rolled his eyes but decided not to correct Ian's use of his name. "Something that kind of short circuited my brain, you know what I mean mate?" Andrew nodded and gestured for Ian to continue. "I pissed my pants down there." Ian plopped into the chair Rebecca had abandoned after shooing away several lingering water droplets.

"Did you get any pictures? What are we developing here?"

"That's from the main camera on buoy one. Most of it is what would have been shot automatically, but I did get a few manual shots off. They were almost blind, pointed at . . . shadows. That's long enough on the fixer. Rinse off the negative with water from the sink there." Ian pointed to what appeared to be a small pink basin in the unnatural red light.

"Oooh, I am all excited!" Andrew imitated the giggle of a teenage girl. Ian laughed and slouched a bit more in the chair. "Why don't you take over here Ian, I have a fax to answer. Anyway, you probably saw some giant, toxic waste deformed Sturgeon. Pictures of mutant caviar bores me." Andrew handed Ian the developed negative and pats him on the back. Ian stood, unrolled and hung the cellulose strip from a line that stretched between a cabinet and a screw on the opposite wall. After securing it with a wooden clothespin, he found a scissors-shaped plastic squeegee and ran the last of the water off the negative. He would let it dry properly before cutting the strip into smaller, easier to handle lengths and then examine them on the light table.

Ian reached for a switch and changed the rooms light from red to the blinding exposed main bulb on the ceiling. The blast of white light left purple spots dancing in his field of vision. He did not yet notice the strange, hazy image that had developed in one of the frames of the dripping negatives.

249-VONB

Chapter 4: Probing

1.

Captain Thomas methodically scanned the horizon from atop the starboard flying bridge of the Explorer. His lined and leathery face betrayed the punishment of wind, sun and rain it had endured. It was a crisp morning and the freshly fallen snow made everything glow a fiery orange in the rising sun. He smiled and drew a deep breath, holding the chilled air in his lungs a bit before exhaling.

"Ahhh." He squinted and tilted his good ear towards the west.

The birds alighting from the trees and the low rhythmic thumping that had first melded with the breeze but then became distinct and progressively louder told him to issue the order. He flipped a small toggle switch on the intercom.

"Prepare for arrival."

Those three words started an organized commotion on the large steel deck at the stern of the Explorer.

The giant Boeing Vertol CH-47B Chinook medium transport helicopter broke from behind the cover of nearby Colchester Point, startling some who waited for its arrival along the side of the Explorer. The Chinook's white paint job and large red *HeliCargo* lettering made it look more distinguished than the familiar military olive drab it often sported. It's Lycoming free-turbine turboshafts drove the two three bladed main rotors, shattering the stillness. Slung from its belly by two steel cables, a blue shipping container gently swayed in the wind. With direction by hand and radio from the Explorer's first officer, the pilot skillfully maneuvered the cargo over the rope net that was strewn across the stern deck. When the container was properly centered and steady but a few inches over the deck, the cable was released, delivering the heavy load with a muffled thud.

Captain Thomas smiled again when the intercom crackled, informing him the cargo was safely aboard. The Boeing rose to about one hundred feet hovered for a moment and then banked. Relieved of its burdensome cargo, the powerful transport burst towards Thomas, almost causing him to duck. Instead, he saluted the pilot's before the venerable Chinook sped off, it's task completed. The Captain surveyed the glorious morning one more time before turning for the doorway to the bridge and wheelhouse. He could feel the blood pool in his cheeks as he penetrated the warmth of the ship's interior.

2.

Josh Feeks ran crying into the snow, trailing two blue wool mittens from bright red shoelaces that hung from a small dee-shaped metal eye on his jacket sleeves. Rusty, the German shepherd that had watched him grow up, immediately followed. The door stayed ajar behind the black, brown and white blur of Rusty; allowing the screams of Josh's parents to momentarily drift out into the crisp silver evening before being absorbed and smothered by the freshly fallen powder. Rusty ran to his sulking friend who sat perched on the old black stump that pierced the white blanket of the back yard. He licked Josh's hand and watched a tear roll down his red, cold bitten cheek. Josh pulled a mitten onto each hand between sobs and wiped his moist, freezing face.

Rusty first got that attentive look he would get—with one ear straight up and the other one bending at a forty-five degree angle—when the sound first emerged from the deep woods. "Stay Rusty. Good boy."

Josh sniffled. Josh figured people were walking in the woods and he suddenly felt embarrassed by the, *YOU BASTARD, that* bellowed from the still open front door of his home. His embarrassment took over his sadness as he lifted his body, leaving a snowsuit butt print on the stump, and went to close the door. Laughter, now closer, echoed from the stark, bare branches of the nearby trees. This time Rusty could not resist. After a sneaky glance to confirm Josh was not looking, he bolted after the friendly sounds; his tongue flapping behind him amongst the warm breaths that floated in a trail. "Rusty!" He did not even look back.

"Hey fella. Look at the puppy-wuppy, Mike." Rusty approached the couple. Not only did his tail wag but the entire back half of his body. "Such a happy dog."

"Watch out Mare, you don't know him."

"Chill out, he's obviously friendly. Check your equipment or something." His austere glance told her to quickly smile or face a fight. Mental note, Mary thought, dump this jerk. "Kidding sweety." He may be a great spelunker but his 'caving' in bed left much to be desired. His total lack of a sense of humor and inability to take constructive criticism without flying into a defensive rampage was starting to wear thin as well. One last cave and he is history, she silently promised herself. Anyway, he claims to be the only one to know about the cave they would visit today. Mike stopped, Rusty still playfully circling and dragging his snout through the fresh snow with sporadic snorts. "What's up Mike?"

"We're here."

"Say what? This is a shrub Mike, a shrub."

"Check it out." Mike shook the large thicket of twisted snow covered branches. A cascade of crystals fell to the ground, chiming as the ice vibrated. After one last scan of the surroundings, Mike used his body weight to bend the bush, pushing it aside and revealing the natural fracture and a small carved opening. "I had to enlarge the crack slightly so you can slide in."

"Wild. How'd you find this?"

"I was uh, well . . . relieving myself." Mare laughed.

"Let's do it." Removing their winter coats, brightly colored coveralls were revealed, turning the almost black and white early New England winter scene Technicolor. "I ain't gonna miss that stupid dog. Let's get in there."

"He's just barking at that chopper. Haven't you ever had a pet? Jeez."

First Mike and then Mary entered the small fracture in the rock outcropping. Rusty jumped around the opening as they slid into a small grotto with a dark portal at the other end. Fast moving funneled air made ghost-like moans that echoed from the underworld. Mike pulled the jackets they had shed through the opening he had chiseled, Rusty growling and snapping at the fur lined collars, and put them on top of a small frame pack he had placed on the snow sprinkled corner of the cave floor. He began distributing equipment.

"Go home you mangy mutt," Mike snarled. Mary rolled her eyes in the darkness. "Okay babe, leave anything you don't need here." She turned on the battery powered halogen headlamp that jutted out from her high impact plastic helmet and scanned the small, smooth walled room. "This opening here leads down a wind tunnel I call the vortex." Mike pointed to the dark portal whence the sound came. "I put in a rope ladder last year and I have a safety rope slung. Once we're at the bottom your in for a treat also."

The shriek of the wind became deafening. Mary plugged her ears and glanced nervously at Mike who was securing and adjusting his harness. She felt as if she was being pulled towards the vertical shaft; imagining being caught in an invisible whirlpool of air, like you see as the last of a bath's water runs down the drain. Mary's shout was inaudible in the roaring air as she dug her nails into the rough texture of the cave wall. Mike's strong grasp reassured her as she began down the rope ladder, cautiously eyeing the purple and white rope upon which her life depended. Mike half smiled at the wild, dilated look of fear in her pale blue eyes and knew she absolutely loved it.

The banshee-like scream of the vortex subsided as they moved deeper into a lower chamber and rested against a multicolored column of stone.

“Damn, that was scary. Glad you had that safety rope. That first time I fell I woulda cracked my coconut for sure. Like that must be hurricane force winds I bet yah.”

“Good rush, huh?”

“Rad’.”

“Welcome to my kingdom. Check this out.” Noticing the way the sound of her footsteps changed from a loud rapid echo to a distant muffled reflection, Mare knew they had entered a large cavern. Mike reached for a gas lantern he had stowed behind a rock. As its white-hot flame grew brighter, it revealed a spectacle that stole her breath.

“Wow.” The stalactites, stalagmites, draperies, flowstones, oolites and even a few helictites that filled the ballroom-sized cavern were reflected in small pools of mineral laden water. The sculpted stone pallet of bright colors danced across the still surface. Mare scanned the gallery, mouth agape. The rainbow of color that adorned the rock is the result of impurities in the ground water, producing most of the yellows, browns and reds. “Beautiful.” She instinctively turned her headlamp off to conserve battery power. “What are those things that look like snakes coming out of the ground?”

“Well, I asked a friend of mine back at school and he said they were probably the, how did he put it, secretion-lined tubes of ancient tube worms that lived here when ocean covered the land and this cave was some sandbar.” Mike exaggerated an inhale after the run-on imitation of his friend. “He said he needed a sample to be sure so I was gonna bring one back this time.”

“Why do they stick up out of the ground like that?”

“I think the mud or rock eroded away around them, but for some reason they stayed.”

"Cool."

"Once I screamed just for the heck of it, you know, to hear the echo, and a bunch of 'em shattered; just from the sound."

"Weird." Mare ran her fingers along the varying texture of the rock walls.

"See those two entrances over there." Mike shone his headlamp at the two mouth-like portals across the main cavern and held the gas lantern higher aloft.

"Yep."

"Well, I have taken the right one as far as it went. I mapped about a mile of cave beyond it but haven't even gone through the other tunnel at all."

"Is that you engineer-like efficiency?"

"I'm not an engineer, yet." Mike did not see Mary stick her tongue out at him.

"Well, let's check it out."

"Okay!" Mike seemed giddier than he ever had. Mary paused, confused by her attraction to this jerk. They moved for the left cave opening. Mike dimmed and then snuffed the gas lanterns bright flame, making them once again rely on the thin bright ray of their headlamps to cut through the thick darkness.

3.

"Watch it, men. Get that rail seated nicely." Mark Guttier personally supervised the laying of the turnouts and tracks of the MTA's new subway system. The crew worked in a furious chaotic dance securing rail to concrete tie and continuously checking the gauge to ensure the proper spacing between the rails. "Get that frog in place." The foreman translated Chief Engineer Guttier's order into an action by getting a team together to install the piece where the track would divide and head down separate tunnels. Gunther looked uneasily at the surrounding concrete lined tunnel and swore it was closing in on him. Bag of Dunkin Donuts in hand, Gunther wandered down the spotlit passage and headed for his work area.

"Morning, Mark."

"Landers, how many times do I got to tell yah, put on a damn hard hat. We already got the lawyers all over us." A yellow hard hat flew from somewhere in the shadows and Gunther juggled his glazed Boston Creme and honey-dipped treasures in order to catch it. He placed the high impact plastic on his head and headed down the side tunnel, now the home of massive power mains and humming electrical substations. A hanging blue tarpaulin divided the concrete tunnel into his new workspace.

Even though the discovery of specimens had waned to a mere few per month, the Museum insisted on keeping a staff member on full time. He was relieving a volunteer student this morning. Gunther pulled back the tarpaulin to see an empty pizza box and the back of the young female paleontologist.

"Morning."

"Oh, Dr. Landers, morning. I am glad you're here. Check out this fax you got." She pushed her red hair back behind her ear, though too short to stay.

"Thanks. Let's see. Oh, from Andrew Wright. What does he have to say: *No idea what picture is you sent, scan the specimen into a bitmap file, E-mail it to me and I will check it out. Also, please forward any news, drawings, etc. of Richmond dig. Damn, I wish I were there.* "You and me both wish we were there my friend," Gunther said and laughed. *Check out these photographs Ian Chelsea took as well!* He squinted to examine the images.

"Check it out, Dr. Landers, you can see a flipper here, a long neck right here and what looks like a sponge covered horses head right there. Can you see it or what?" The young woman asked chewing her gum faster while she waited for a response.

"I, I guess so, yah. Strange. You are sure that is not just clutter from the fax transmission?"

"Nah, look closer." She rattled the page in front of him.

"Well, thank you for reading and analyzing my private correspondence. Have a jelly-filled powdered on me."

"Ah-haha, doooh-nuts," the student said in her best Homer

Simpson voice and reached for the offered pink, white and orange bag.

4.

Rebecca opened the watertight door and stepped carefully over the threshold and out into the freezing morning. She skillfully balanced a half-full cup of steaming coffee after taking a long sip. The freshly fallen snow had already hardened to a frozen coating on all the exposed metal of the Explorer making her footing precarious at best. Passing a deck hand who laboriously removed ice from the hand railing with a small pick and another who had the more daunting task of carefully clearing the teak planking, Rebecca shuffled down the starboard side of the ship heading for the stern.

"Morning, miss."

"Hey, guys," she smiled.

She rounded a corner and, seeing Ian and Andrew talking to an older fellow, approached the congregation. The short, stocky, mostly bald stranger who had surprisingly emerged from the container, rubbed his wire rimmed glasses while speaking with exaggerated articulation—looking old but emitting the energy of someone far younger. Rebecca feared she would receive a shock if she reached out and touched him. Andrew and Ian turned and offered a synchronous, "Good morning," while the man squinted, stopped his lens cleaning and put his glasses back on. He smiled at the now clear, focused scene.

"And who might this beauty be?"

"Dr. Attwater, this is Dr. McClintock." Andrew announced.

"Rebecca." She jutted out her hand out and almost curtsied.

"James."

"James has brought a new toy to help us out here at Lake Nowhere," Ian offered, growing bored with the formalities.

"This *toy* your colleague is referring to is the Deep Eagle. She's my baby. I like to call her an underwater flying vehicle. I think the term submarine is just too limited, conjuring up clunky images of steel cans and periscopes, don't you?" James' arms flashed about with the animation of a child.

"Where is she? And why is it that anything that goes in the water is automatically female?" Rebecca teased.

"*She* is right here." James pulled back a large blue tarpaulin revealing his creation.

"Deep Eagle II," Andrew read and asked, "What happened to number one?" He ran his fingers along the smooth white metal hull.

"Well, let's just say scattered over the bottom of the Puerto Rico trench. That's where I am going to test the Deep Eagle III, a two-man version I have just completed. I had the command module, this container that was just delivered, flown up from San Juan last night." Ian circled the vehicle, carefully studying its design. Basically this genius, Ian thought, has made an underwater airplane. It's cylindrical body, capable of holding a large prone man, had a bullet shaped clear Plexiglas nose and two fast looking propeller and rudder assembly jutting from the body at the other end. An almost delta shaped wing intersected the body. A triangular vertical tail provided stability while its modest maneuvering surfaces would surely provide excellent agility.

"She's beautiful sir," Ian said. "Real genius. Who is piloting her?"

"Well, I am." James exaggerated the offense taken for effect.

"Aren't you a little, uh, old sir?"

"Eee-an!" Rebecca shrieked.

"It's okay. I appreciate his bluntness. Not enough of that in this world. Maybe I am a little old Mr. Chelsea, but nobody is more qualified to pilot the Eagle. I designed and built her. She's mine. And let's just say I am a little familiar with this water hole as well." James' face grew momentarily foreboding as he scanned the lake.

"I just was hoping I could try her instead," Ian winked and James laughed.

"Once her batteries are topped off we are going swimming, so you all can watch on the closed circuit. See that?" James pointed at a teardrop shaped protuberance from the vehicles port winglet. "That there is a pretty good light-intensifying camera. You'll get nice pictures back here. They'll be black and white but real darn clear. You'll feel like you're down there with me."

"Cool. Oh, and you have to see Ian's photo's. They are really trippy," Rebecca smiled.

"Sweet." Andrew gave a thumb up.

"Raving mate," Ian spurted and posed.

"Be nice if someone would teach you kids English," James smiled, looked to the deck and shook his head.

5.

"Man, don't those stalactites make the cave look like a fang filled mouth."

"Shut up, dork, you're creeping me out." The tunnel had been slowly carved by the trickling water that ran along its rounded, slippery bottom over thousands of years. When the tunnel forked off into separate burrows, Mike took out a spool of nylon twine and secured it to a stalagmite.

"Mary, please." Mike handed Mary the spool and turned around. She secured it to a small roller on his belt that would dispense the twine evenly as they progressed deeper into the unexplored cave system. They headed towards the left.

"Do you think we're the first people, you know, ever down here?" Mary searched for her next footing on the uneven and moist floor.

"Maybe. I bet the Indians know about this place though. Once I was down here and I thought I saw a man, an Indian man, in the shadows of one of the caverns but it coulda been my imagination."

"My-eye-ike."

"No, serious. I'm not trying to scare yah, swear."

"The floor is slippery."

"Yeah. There are some good hand holds on the walls so use 'em, they help."

"I think I hear water."

"Me too." They reached a droop in the tunnel ceiling that forced them to remove all equipment, scurry through a crevasse with inches to spare, and then pass the gear through. The next obstacle, a sheer three hundred-foot drop down a shaft to what smelled like sulfur, required a bit more precaution. A small shelf allowed Mike to spike two clamps and establish a safety anchor for their crossing. Anyone watching would have thought two spiders had scampered across the sheer rock face, finding hand and foot holds where others would see only minuscule cracks.

"What the hell is that?"

"Wh-what?"

"See over there," Mike pointed into the blackness with his headlamp, "that weird formation."

"Yeah. Strange. Let's check it out." Both Mike and Mary shed the extra equipment they had donned in order to cross the deep shaft. They dropped the ropes, harnesses and clips into a neat pile for use on their egress from the network of tunnels.

"Let's do it."

"After you beautiful."

"Great, thanks. If there is a cave-in or something, I will be the first to get it. What a gentleman." They both stopped and scanned the large cavern they had now entered. Abstract formations of rock seemed to litter the otherwise smooth floor of the cave.

"You can tell this cave once held water, everything is eroded and smooth. Pretty wild." Mare reached down and ran her long fingers along the porcelain-like ground.

"What are these sculptures?"

"Don't know, but this one here almost looks like, like a-"

"A what?"

"Well, almost like a rib cage."

"Exsqueeze me?"

"You asked. And check this out, tell me that does not look like a long spinal column."

"Wow, your right. But they're glossy, feel like ceramic."

"Probably minerals from running water. Yah know, petrified."

"Cool. They look so nice, colorful. Where do yah think they came from?"

"Probably some animal crawled in here, got stuck and died." Mike removed from his pack a small pad of paper with a pen attached with some tape and string. He began to roughly sketch the route they had taken as well as details of the room they were now in. Mary slowly moved for a dark crack in the wall. Mike glanced up to see her frantically maneuvering to get a view through the tiny sliver before going back to drawing his primitive map.

"Shit. Freakin' Alien egg nursery."

"What do yah mean, Mare."

"Alien egg nursery. Yah know, when John Hurt gets that face hugger thing attached in that space ship—that one that had crashed."

"What the hell are you talking about?"

"Put that damn thing down and check this out."

"It's probably a reflection on a pool of water or something. The light can really play tricks on you down here." Mike moved over to where Mary had her head squeezed into the small crack in the wall that ran from the cave floor to its ceiling. Taunting her, he put his hand under his shirt and pretended an Alien was mercilessly tearing its way through his abdominal cavity.

"Laugh it up buddy. Here, look."

"What the-? Weird." Mike panned his headlamp in as wide an arc as possible through the small opening in the rock. "Giant chicken eggs. Omelet time."

"Would you be serious for once. I am no bio' major but I know enough to know that those are not giant chicken eggs."

"Look, there is a shallow pool of water in there. C'mon, let's try and find a way in."

6.

"Okay, batteries are juiced up. Green lights across the board, let's run the list." James' face went from the smile of a boy to the stern and concentrated look of someone about to take a risk, albeit a minimized and acceptable one.

"Need any help, chief?"

"Sure do, Andrew. Please get on that head set there and read off that checklist to me."

Andrew assisted James in checking the Eagle's systems: navigational surfaces, electrical, hydraulic, environmental and the submersibles propulsion. All were operational. "Okay, great, I'd say she is ready. Thanks for your help Andrew."

"Sure thing, I-"

"Hey, Andy!" Andrew cringed, removing the blue and black headset, and turned to see Ian approaching. "What's up, mate? Hello, Jim."

"It's James."

"Need a hand, Jim?" Both Andrew and James shared a glance of disgust that quickly dissolved into a smile.

"I think our rock star here is trying to get a rise out of us." Ian winked.

"Put me to work, Jimmy." James could only laugh.

"Okay, using that gizmo, I want you to loosen these ten bolts here around the Eagle's mid-section. Don't undo them fully. There are several o-ring gaskets that must be carefully manipulated before we open her up. Just loosen, understood." Ian picked up the large pneumatic wrench and held it as if it was a weapon. Andrew snickered.

"He drew first blood, not me." Half of Ian's mouth moved.

"How you going to live, Rambo," Andrew laughed.

"Day-by-day." James and Andrew crouched over in laughter that only grew more intense when Ian bellowed, "Adriaaaan."

"Wait, that's Rocky not Rambo?" Andrew wiped tears from his eyes.

"Okay, kids, lets get to it, we have to get this baby in the water in an hour." Ian gave a Benny Hill salute and pushed the green start button on the small, gas compressor next to the navy blue shipping container that held the command center for the Eagle. It burped a sooty cloud and noisily sprang to life. Ian revved the pneumatic tool and then carefully seated it on the first of the large stainless steel bolts that held together the two slender halves of the Deep Eagle II. James watched carefully and, once confident in Ian's ability, turned his attention to the small teardrop shaped housing of the Eagle's video camera.

7.

Miko Hakinen pulled up on the cliff road in his rented red sedan. He skidded to a halt in the gravel park road, digging shallow trenches in the surface. He threw open the door, initiating that dreaded ding, ding, ding of the car and said to his mercenary subordinate, "Hurry up, get out."

"Yes, Mr. Hak-, Hak-. Miko."

"Give me my scope you, moron."

"Yes, sir." The unnaturally broad shouldered bald man nick-named Ox complied; handing Miko the high powered black sighting scope. Miko snatched it from his henchman's paw and started up the small grassy knoll before the drop off to the lake.

"There she is," Miko aligned the red dot in the middle of the green image, "*there* is the Explorer." He panned the scope from the bow to stern, pausing on the large blue rectangular container. "Looks like they have had a delivery, and they are going to check out the Badlands. SCUBA flag is up. Come on, Mr. Moron, get in the car. It is time for us to get to work." Ox turned and waddled to the car and mumbled, "Yes sir."

8.

"Okay, be really careful, Mare. I've gotcha."

"Almost got it." Mary stretched to reach the rope that dangled over the large, dark crevasse that gaped below. Mike methodically placed his feet on the very small escarpment that jutted out before he reached for Mary. After systematically eliminating tunnel after tunnel and room after room, they had both realized that the only way to reach the room whose interior they had briefly glimpsed would be to accept the risk of traversing this seemingly bottomless rip in the Earth. Mary skillfully clung to the rock face and then, at just the right point swung on the creaking rope.

"Excellent. Man, you have more guts than most of the guys I do this with." Mary gave him a *don't make me have to lecture you again on the ways of male chauvinism* when Mike, realizing his fate, gave a quick peace-making wink. "Seriously, I am proud of you."

"Almost got—" The sound the rope made when it snapped seemed to echo through the intricate web of caves and tunnels, resonating in the ripples and folds of the rock walls.

"Miiiichael." Mike could only place the palms of his hands to his face as he watched her outline descend into the blackness below. He quickly realized that he had to tighten the brake on the safety line if he was to have any hope of slowing her fall. Just as his brain ordered his hands to reach for the aluminum braking mechanism, he heard the wathump of Mary hitting water. Mike began to breathe again.

"Mary!" Mike waited for the echo to degrade before cupping his ears to amplify the response, if any.

"I'm okay." Mare's voice came gurgling from below. "Get a line down here."

"I'm coming down."

"Don't be stupid. We'll both end up stuck down here."

"Okay—okay, your right. Is the safety line still attached to your harness?"

"Ya-ya-yes." Mike could hear the shivers in her voice and knew he had to get her out of the water as quickly as possible before hypothermia had a chance to settle in.

"Okay, Mary, I am going to start hauling you up. I want you to help me if you can by pushing off the wall when you can."

"Ka-kay."

"Here goes." Mike dug his heels as best he could into the smooth, slippery floor and began the task of getting his girlfriend back to safety. Sitting down on the cold rock, he leaned forward and prepared for the first heave of the rope.

"I sa-see la-light down here." Damn, Mike thought, I hope she does not have a concussion. It was hard enough to get across the two shafts when she was conscious but would be near impossible if otherwise.

"Honey, did you hit your head at all? Do you feel dizzy."

"Na-no. I'm okay. I did ba-bump it but my helmet did its job. It's getting brighter."

"Mare, we are at least a mile under ground. How can there be light?"

"It's greenish. I saw it under the water also." Mike was relieved to hear her voice warming up again as she gently swung over the icy water. Mike struggled against the weight of Mary; her water logged clothes and her equipment. The muscles in his arms, shoulders and lower back began to burn, as if his pulsing blood had become acid.

"Mare, I have to lock the rope a sec and rest." Mike slid a small roller forward on the metal brake loop of the safety line. Mike let out more slack, locking the rope in place and giving his aching arms and shoulders the break they needed. He sat down for a moment, resting his elbows on his spread legs, his eye never leaving the threshold of rock that the rope rested on. He noticed the rope jerk slightly and, between gasps for air he instructed Mary to keep still so the rope would not wear against the jagged stone. "Did you hear me? Mary? Mary! C'mon, this is no time for jokes." Frustrated, Mike rolled back onto his feet and peered down the cylindrical shaft.

He laughed when he first saw the expression of fear on Mary's face and the bulging of her eyes.

Mike stopped immediately when he noticed that her legs were gone and the last of her blood was slowly dripping out of the two tattered stumps that protruded from her waist. The echoes of his own laughter taunted him as the grotesque scene unfolded before him. "Ma-Mary, sweetheart?" Her lifeless gaze looked through him in response. "MARY!"

He realized he was slipping into shock and quickly tried to regain control of his nervous system. "Freak out down here and you are going to die Mike, stay cool buddy," he mumbled to himself. He felt faint when he saw Mare's body twitch as one last electrical command was sent from her dying brain: *RUN!* He fell backwards onto the cold, hard rock floor and began to sob. Mike slowly realized that she must have been attacked, and the acrid taste of fear began to slosh around in his otherwise arid mouth. But by what, he asked himself as his head began to clear. He looked at the shaft, with the black, slushy water at its bottom and thought, Oh my God, I have to cross that thing to get out of here. He tried to swallow but could not.

9.

"Oh my lord." Ian looked down so as not to break out in a torrent of laughter. Dr. James Attwater, dressed in an advanced, skin tight body warmth retention suit, looked the over weight, over the hill super hero with his red suit and white body length stripe. The Deep Eagle II sat in two five-foot sections on wooden, wheeled bogeys; it's white enamel-like skin gleaming in the clear air. James paused, attaching a rubber band to the arms of his glasses, in order to secure them to his head. "That's just going to cut off the blood to your brain Jimmy boy." James smiled momentarily and then returned to the robotic expression he held moments before.

Rebecca stepped forth and graciously said, resting her arm on James' back, "Best of luck James."

"Thanks dear. Worst part is I am a bit claustrophobic. This thing is looking like a high-tech coffin right now. Funny for a 'world renowned' sub designer, eh?" Rebecca giggled and shrugged. "See you all later." After plugging in a small beige earpiece, James slid into the bow section headfirst when his head appeared in the clear Plexiglas nose and he gave a thumbs up, two deck hands lifted his legs into the stern section. The deck hands then slowly rolled the stern section, with its horizontal and vertical planes and fast looking propellers, on its bogey until it was lined up with the bolt holes and rubber sealing gaskets of the bow.

James felt blindly for the foot peddle controls, sliding his shoes in. By moving his feet, he would control the roll of the Eagle.

"NEST? EAGLE. Radio check please."

"EAGLE, NEST. Check. Loud and clear."

"NEST, all systems spinning up nicely. Ready for lock in." The deck hands, reacting to a hand signal from their foreman, aligned the bolts with a red laser beam and began to lock James into the pressure hull of the Eagle. The whine of their tools barely penetrated the composite, HY100 steel and titanium vehicle. James felt sweat bead on his forehead as the feeling that the walls were shrinking and about to crush him intensified.

He concentrated on the scene before him. He lay on a padded mat and chest pad, his arms freely dangling at his sides. Two ergonomic control sticks protruded from the control panels at his fingertips. When he looked below where his rib cage rested, the small blue screen of the sonar and green laser ranging system were prominent. Looking straight down was a simple, icon driven readout of the status of the entire submarine's systems as well as battery gauges and artificial horizon equipment. A small yellow emergency oxygen mask and toxic gas filter were at the ready besides it. After all, he was locked in a cylinder with highly toxic and caustic nickel-metal-hydride batteries that, if breached, could kill him in minutes. James looked forward to the day when Teflon supported anode and cathode sandwiched polymer gel electrolyte, or, simply put, plastic batteries, would replace them. Until recently, an all-plastic battery had been an impossible dream, since most polymers that conduct electricity lack sufficient energy difference to act as electrodes. Engineers at John Hopkins University, James had heard, were close to overcoming this hurdle.

He knew the quick, reverberating knocks on the metal hull was a signal to tell him the seal was complete, inspected and approved. He felt a cool breeze from the environmental system duct hit his face and the noise of the air jets responsible for preventing the clear nose from fogging up, filled the chamber.

"EAGLE, prepare for hook-up and hoist."

James saw a helmeted crewman approach with a large steel locking hook that hung from above by a staunch cable. Once attached, it would be electronically controlled from the cab of the Explorer's deck crane and release the payload at the appropriate time.

10.

Mike tried to slow his breathing but could not. Realizing he was beginning to hyperventilate, he reached for his food bag and grabbed the largest Zip-lock bag he could find, and emptied it to the floor. Pushing it to his face, he exhaled into it.

"C'mon bud, get a grip. There was nothing you could have done. Not your fault." The added carbon dioxide of the sandwich bag slowed his breaths to normal. "Nothing you could have done. Oh my God, Mary." He began to sob again. *Get out of here first dude, then cry all you want,* an inner voice inspired Mike.

He rose, drew a knife from his pack and walked to where Mary's upper torso still dangled over the shaft. Mike put the knife to the multi-colored nylon rope, closed his eyes and whispered,

"Sorry, babe." The rope twanged as his sharp blade cut it cleanly, followed by a moment of silence as her remains fell the ten feet to the water and ending with an unnaturally light splash.

Mike re-established his lines and prepared to cross the shaft and exit the caves. His headlamp shone on the reflective rock, momentarily blinding him. When he first noticed the bubbling sound, he felt panic come over him again like a hot flash. He closed his eyes and took a long, deep breath. Despite better judgment, Mike looked behind him and down the moist, dark passageway and swore he heard a million monsters scurrying in the shadows towards him. He expected to see the long, slimy black head of the Alien, its metallic silver jaws poised to strike, when he turned to face the other pitch black tunnel.

"Why in Christ's name did she have to mention Alien's?" *I was responsible for her and now she is dead.*

Feeling the hairs on his neck stand straight up, he once again turned to look behind him. The levitating green orb at first made Mike laugh as if he had taken one step closer to insanity. He then gasped.

11.

The sudden jerk of the crane made James grunt. The initial rapid ascent made him feel momentarily queasy, exasperated by the bobbing and heaving horizon of the lake.

"Don't toss your cookies, old man. You'll short every circuit in the boat," James whispered to the control panel. James looked forward to hitting the water, like you look forward to the second an airplane's landing gear touches the ground after a rough, bumpy, nauseating flight. James knew Captain Thomas had brought the Explorer to a point over the lake floor where its powdery gray bottom became rocky and jagged. Both sonar and photo mapping had yet to reveal sufficient detail to warrant this part of Champlain to be considered 'clear.' The areas jagged and craggy outcroppings were known to all as the Badlands.

"EAGLE, we have you clear of the transom, feet are wet. Prepare for drop in three, two, one, drop," the earpiece whispered into James' ear canal.

The crane operator pushed a blue-lit button on his control panel, sending an electronic command through the wiring that coiled its way along the cranes main trussed arm and suspension cable until it reached the mechanism attached to the Eagle's spine. When the electric pulse arrived, a small motor slid a piston releasing the hook and then the weight of the Eagle to the lake below. A quick one-foot, slightly-nose-first dive and the Eagle pierced the oily surface of the black lake waters in an explosion of froth and foamy boils.

"EAGLE, away and free to dive."

James reached behind and above his left shoulder, just at the edge of his marginal vision, and increased the volume of his earpiece with the turn of a small silver knob. Taking a deep breath of conditioned air, he pushed forward on both control sticks. Immediately, the Eagle's dual processor main computer ordered the bow planes to adjust five degrees down. The stern planes followed suit but pointed up, and both General Electric motors spun their high-speed propellers in counter rotating fashion.

"Commencing dive." He nudged the control sticks forward a few more clicks and watched the read out that was projected on a portion of the Plexiglas nose. "Planes at seven degrees, 8, 9, 10."

"*Maximum recommended dive angle.*" A calm, soothing female voice filled the pilot cylinder. James knew the voice feedback points were very conservative. The Eagle could dive at ninety degrees straight down, hell, even inverted. James moved a small white switch on his right control stick and two bright wing mounted halogen lamps flooded the surrounding murky water with white light. Reaching for the central control panel, he engaged the proximity alarm and passive sonar; a small red bell and blue ear icon came up on the simplistic master display bar confirming the systems as active.

James had designed the cockpit like the people at McDonnell-Douglas had for the F/A-18 Hornet—maximum hands on throttle and stick or HOTAS, with a primary display near the pilot's center of field of vision. He looked forward to when he perfected his voice response system and could allow and trust the computer to take over more functions.

12.

Mike stood hypnotized by the bobbing, green-glowing orb before him. The sound that accompanied the light grew louder and louder: a hissing rush of air. He was barely aware, if not on the verge of unconsciousness, when a snarling snort echoed through the tunnel. Its echo was eventually drowned out by the pitter-patter of Mike's urine hitting the floor. The cave was black again, only its ceiling lit by his headlamp. Mike started breathing again in short, shallow gasps. Until he felt the warm breath on his face. Reaching to his head in a growing panic, he tried to widen the lamp's beam. A moment later, he felt the nudge. Mike tried to scream but could not. He turned to run when what felt like a truck hit his leg, followed by a hundred nails puncturing the meat of his limb. Mike blacked out when his face hit the hard stone floor, his nervous system having decided to shut down to prevent damage from another shock. He never reawakened.

Chapter 5: Flight of the Eagle

1.

"NEST, I have the thermocline at two hundred 'n' one feet, continuing dive. I will pause at around one hundred ninety five feet to get Rebecca's sample. Passing fifty feet." James watched the red digital numbers click off as the Eagle dove deeper into Lake Champlain. He looked at plankton-like particles that streaked by the nose, exaggerating the sensation of forward motion. The projected Heads-Up Display or HUD showed his speed as eight knots true. Always trust your instruments, he thought. The old brain can always deceive you. James plunged the Eagle into the chilly, eerie depths. He noticed the cabin temperature drop a few degrees and felt his weight slide down the mat upon which he lay, only to be held fast by the padded shoulder harness. Blood began to rush to his brain as he nudged the nose of the Eagle down farther still, gently increasing its speed. "Seventy five feet. Ten knots. I am reading a slight drop off in r.p.m. on the starboard motor, confirm."

"Roger, EAGLE, reading that as well. Wait a minute, it's coming back up holding steady in synch with port motor. I'm approaching one hundred feet, backing off the throttle." James eased the throttle towards him and the high pitched cavitation of the Eagle's twin propellers reduced to a hum which passed through the hull in pulses. Adjusting the pitch of the nose gently back to level, the submersible slowed to a near hover at one hundred and two feet below the surface of the lake.

James took a moment to look around through the now frosty

nose of the submersible. The water had a surprising abundance of suspended organic particulate matter, making it appear soupy in the bright cones of light that extended from the leading edge of the submersible's winglets. James looked upwards and into a small, contoured mirror. In it he saw the vertical stabilizer that protruded from the main hull. Below it and bolted to the either side of the hull were the motors. Sporadically the computer would detect the Eagle moving forward in the slight current which came from astern. Since James had ordered station keeping with a small toggle switch, it automatically reversed the propellers every three seconds for one second at half speed to maintain position. The Eagle's engineered neutral buoyancy aided in maintaining depth.

James looked out at the diamond shaped winglets and watched subtle corrections the computer made in the fore and aft dive planes. Engaging the sensor array, a small computer located under his thighs began a series of programmed tests of the water outside, storing its data for down load at a later time.

"NEST, this is EAGLE. Sample one collected, proceeding to two hundred feet."

"Roger, EAGLE, you are clear to two hundred."

James took one more look around, smiled at the blinking and glowing lights of his creation and turned off the floodlights before putting the Eagle into another dive. With the movement of the control sticks, the computer started a small impeller which pumped a half liter of liquid mercury from a compact, orb shaped stainless steel tank mounted on one of the stern bulkheads to one mounted under a forward ring strengthener. James snickered to the instrument panel and the darkness beyond before pushing the throttle to near full power and the control stick forward.

"*Descent rate warning. Maximum recommended dive angle. Acceleration rate warn—.*" James disengaged voice feedback, cutting off the synthetic female mid-word and pushed back with his right foot. A small flap mechanism extended downward from the trailing edge of the starboard winglet. The Eagle immediately began a crisp counter clockwise rotation. James let up on the pedal as the

Eagle settled into an inverted position. James held it for a moment and then, with an extension of his left foot this time, put the Eagle into a gentle, clockwise rotation until his vessel was again running straight and level. Giggling like a school boy, he glanced at the Heads-Up Display, noting the information on his machines performance that it displayed:

James pulled back on the throttle and control stick, leveling and slowing the Eagle as he approached one hundred ninety feet.

"NEST, EAGLE. I am taking sample two at one hundred ninety three feet." James pushed a red button, firing off a ping from the small, hockey puck shaped transducer mounted on the underside of the hull. "I am showing four hundred five feet to the bottom and nine feet to an approximately thirty two foot thick thermocline." The clicks and hisses told James the computer was being kept busy trying to hold position. He disengaged station keeping.

"Roger. Getting a bit of chop here. Must be some rough water sitting on top of the layer. Sample two complete. Descending." James had turned off the external lights to conserve battery power, but, nevertheless, could still see a few feet beyond the glass with his blue leaking cabin light. He heard the pressure hull pop and moan as it adjusted to the increasing burden of the lakes weight. Two billion cubic feet of water, all trying to get inside, he thought, twitching a little at a creak behind him. What he had always feared most was the Plexiglas nose cone giving way, letting water rush in and compacting him into a puddle of mush at the rear of the hull. Necessity had forced him to entrust the design, testing and manufacturing of the nose to others, others who would not risk their life in the contraption. So far so good. He would have knocked on wood if any were aboard.

"NEST, I am heading in."

2.

"What did I miss?" Andrew threw open the metal door to the Deep Eagle II control center.

"Shhh. He's about to do the thermocline." Rebecca put her hand up while the young man at the instrument panel held his finger to his headphone and squinted to listen harder.

"Say again, EAGLE." Andrew closed the door and absorbed his red-lit surroundings. Video panels lined one wall of the center with a single; track mounted padded chair running parallel. A three-dimensional wire frame video model of the Eagle gave real time feedback on the vessels exact position in space. The assistant had every instrument James had below with him, and more, before him on the panels.

"Encountering increased turbulence and buffeting. Gettin' thrown 'round a bit. Penetrating the layer in three, two, one." Static filled the audio speaker in the upper right corner of the center.

"Roger, EAGLE. Please boost signal, you broke up there a bit."

"Hi, I am Andrew Wright." Andrew offered his hand to James' buzz cut, polo-shirted, Filipino assistant. Andrew held it suspended momentarily while the assistant continued his keyboard input and, just as Andrew decided to retreat, the typing stopped and a firm hand met his.

"Pleasure. Name's Bobby." Andrew winked hello to Rebecca. The radio speaker crackled again, silencing the room.

"NEST, turbulence has dropped off a bit. Sonar is showing the layer as very well defined. Okay, let's see. Thermocline residing at two hundred four feet, it's almost thirty four feet thick and, according to returns, runs the entire length of the lake."

"Roger, EAGLE, data up link will record your findings." Rebecca studied the paper print out of the sonar returns and made a mark with a red felt tip pen every time she encountered an anomaly. She reached again for the microphone.

"Uh, EAGLE, Rebecca here. What is passive showing?"

"Passive is having trouble cutting through the layer. It is picking up a lot of commotion within the layer itself. I will let you know if it picks up anything once I am through. Okay?" James' voice had a lilt of affection. Heading below the thermocline." James again pushed the throttle forward, increasing the revolutions of the motors propelling the Eagle faster through the water.

"Okay, NEST, EAGLE approaching the lower boundary. A lot of chop here again." Andrew glided over to where Rebecca stood and gently came up behind her and whispered to the exposed ear: "How 'bout some lunch, Doc'?" Rebecca turned, slightly startled and smiled with her green eyes.

"Love to. How about in a half hour? Your cabin." Andrews heart raced slightly as he smiled and turned for the control room door.

"Later, Bobby."

"See you Andy." Rebecca looked at Andrew, frozen halfway through the open door, mouth open. Ready to correct the use of his name by his new acquaintance, they both laughed instead. Andrew gave a casual salute and abandoned the red light of the control room for the bright day beyond. He would first head for the galley to order their meal.

"NEST, I have passed below the layer. Water's a bit calmer. Man, that is one active thermal layer; Rebecca is going to have a field day with that data." Knowing the Eagle was collecting a treasure of valuable information; Rebecca smiled at the speaker and the red lit tan face of Bobby. Champlain's thermocline and general characteristics were some of the strangest she had ever encountered, both fascinating and challenging her.

3.

James looked out at the blackness, wishing he had sufficient battery power to run the floodlights the entire time he was down. A repeating chime filled the cabin, breaking his gloom-induced depression.

"NEST. EAGLE. Contact on passive sonar. Computer is chewing on it."

"Roger. Call it, EAGLE."

"I have a contact. Depth: five hundred sixty feet; range—two hundred yards; bearing: one eight seven. Sounds like . . . dolphins."

"Say again EAGLE?"

"Dolphins, sounds like dolphins. Yah know, clicking. Passing two hundred fifty feet. Contact is stationary. Creaking, sounds like a creaking door now. Three hundred feet. Going active to confirm depth under the keel." A SOund NAvigation and Ranging pulse again left the transducer and traveled the depths until striking lakebed; reflecting and returning to the Eagle. The computer read out confirmed the other instrumentation as accurate. Nearing the bottom as well as the dangerous Badlands, James became more focused and alert. As the submersible passed three hundred fifty feet, James quickly scanned all the familiar instruments in a sweeping head motion that lasted five seconds side to side.

"Looks like the contact is right where it starts to get rocky, the periphery of the Badlands. Anything on your charts Bobby?"

"Negative EAGLE."

"Four fifty. Going to intermittent passive." By pushing a small neon green button on the central panel, James instructed the computer to fire off an active sonar ping, called hammering the target, every ten seconds. In between, passive sonar would listen attentively. The sonar confirmed the target was ninety feet away, on the bottom and stationary. "Switching to terminal ranging, I'll bring the lights on at five feet and hold."

A small green laser beam fired from a protuberance on the otherwise streamlined underbelly of the submersible. The terminal ranging system could accurately measure the distance to an object far better than sound waves but was limited to a fifteen-foot range.

"Five feet, bringing the lights on. Wow, you guys see what I see?"

Ninety-four fathoms above, Rebecca and Bobby analyzed the foggy black and white images on the monitor before them.

"Looks like superstructure."

"Roger NEST, we have a pleasure boat on the bottom." James ran the spotlights over the white fiberglass hull and tangled rigging. Its long bulbous keel lay parallel to the now rocky bottom. "The sound is from the mast swinging in the current. Looks like she hasn't been here more than a month." James extinguished the floodlights and brought the Eagle to five hundred thirty feet. I'm killing the lights and coming up to five thirty; last thing I want to do is get snagged." The Eagle gently rose in the blackness to a depth of five hundred and thirty feet, putting several yards between her and the small American flag that seemed to still flutter in a breeze from the top of the wreck's mast. Her fouled boom hinge moaned, groaned and creaked eerily in the depths. "I'm going to approach the periphery of the Badlands. Once in, I am going to utilize the laser."

"Roger EAGLE, agree." Bobby shifted in his padded seat in the small stuffy but warm control center. He knew that the laser, on its gyro-stabilized articulated armature, was capable of twenty rapid-fire bursts in two forwards and one downward pattern. The downward pattern rotated the laser to point directly beneath the vessel, yielding incredibly detailed mapping resolution. The forward patterns were: first, cone shaped, meant for higher speed obstacle avoidance, and, second, rectangular, where the laser would sweep left to right for more detailed, forward imaging.

James had the option of projecting a computer generated, three-dimensional graphical representation of the forward outer environment. Bobby knew that, due to the complexity of the laser firing pattern, range was even shorter than terminal mode—down to a mere ten feet. Silty or very salty water, like near the Earth's poles, could further refract or otherwise interfere with the amplified light beam.

4.

Rebecca pushed Andrew to the bed, knocking over the fresh orange juice he had poured for her. Andrew smiled and watched her jump in next to him. Their lips met with a spark of static electricity but neither retreated. Andrew held her tightly to him, running his fingers through her silky and thick chestnut hair while the other rested on the small red Levi's tag of her jeans. They broke from their kiss and she immediately began to nibble on an ear, speaking intermittently.

"So, Doc', you really think there is something here?" He pulled her shirt out and ran his hand up her warm, smooth back. Their eyes met and they momentarily stopped, Rebecca now straddling Andrew who lay on his back. He smiled.

"I doubt it. Maybe some giant pike or sturgeon but a plesiosaur? Nah." Rebecca smiled back. "C'mere, lady." He pulled her to him.

5.

"All righty, NEST, proceeding into the Badlands; nice returns from the laser—should be a breeze." James expertly maneuvered the submersible as he studied the three dimensional outlines of the displayed laser returns. "Man, what a mess down here," he mumbled to himself, his breath fogging the Plexiglas nose cone.

"EAGLE, NEST. There is too much clutter with all the rock formations down there. Having trouble keeping a solid sonar lock on you. Would appreciate if you would check in every few minutes or so."

"Roger, NEST, will do. Call me if I forget; kind of busy down here." The Eagle glided around a pillar of rock carved millennia ago by dense ice and then gracefully passed beneath a bridge formation. "FYI, NEST, I will supplement laser with occasional active sonar."

"Understood." The Eagle climbed a small hill, hugging its surface; disturbing the fine layer of silt that had come to rest on the rocky bottom. James passed an escarpment that, unbeknownst to him, hid the corpse of a gunboat. It had belonged to a tiny American fleet led by Benedict Arnold—missing in action for two hundred twenty one years following an encounter with British forces during the Revolutionary War. Her slumber would not be disturbed on this particular voyage; a fresh water eel lazily wiggled from between two ribs of the fractured hull, disturbed by the high pitched whine of the passing Eagle's screws.

James scanned his instruments and then the dark abyss beyond. He gingerly adjusted the controls of the machine to avoid the dangerous obstacles that seemed to unexpectedly pop-up before him like targets on a firing range. Starboard, then port; up and down, the Eagle danced its way through the jagged outcroppings. James eased back on the throttle realizing he was perhaps approaching the environment too aggressively. The change in speed seemed to alter the reverberation through the titanium hull of the submersible, like choking up on a vibrating tuning fork. James spotted a small red light blinking when the familiar chime of the passive sonar warning system echoed through the cylindrical pressure hull.

"What's this then? NEST, EAGLE. Showing a contact. Very faint. Must be beyond the ridge I am approaching."

"Understood, EAGLE. Switch to active at your discretion. Sorry but I can't help you with the bottom the way it is." James clicked the microphone switch twice, telling Bobby that he had received his transmission but was too busy to respond verbally.

James activated the active sonar system and redefined the laser ranging to a combination of downward and forward patterns. The laser ranging system immediate told him he would reach the summit of this particular cliff momentarily. James pulled back slightly on the stick, raising the nose of the Eagle further, ensuring the vessel had ample room to clear the tortured rock cliff. "Contact is definitely over the ridge. Computer unable to identify," James said, watching the blinking green UNKNOWN in the Heads-Up Display. James prepared the Eagle to slow and loiter once over the summit, scanning the floor below for the unknown contact. "NEST, what do charts show for this area?"

"Uh, moment, EAGLE." Bobby jumped from his seat for the

chart rack, forgetting he was tethered to the control panel by the wire of his head set. He leaned back to slacken the taut wire, removed and threw the headset on his still spinning swivel chair, and reached for the rolled, laminated chart. Unrolling it on the floor, he glanced up at the display of the Eagle's position and ran a finger along the Y and X-axis of the chart until the respective numbers were located and his fingers met. Here the submersible hovered.

James and the Eagle passed a jagged formation called the *Bell Tower*. Deciding to sacrifice some battery juice, he energized the winglet-mounted floodlights

Relying on a slide rule to calculate approximate battery power that would be lost, James decided to keep the lamps on for twenty seconds only. James pushed the small, brass button on the side of his watch starting its small stopwatch hand. He looked out into the illuminated murky brown waters that surrounded him.

"These are about as effective as headlights in a blizzard, NEST. Looks like the bottom has been disturbed—very cloudy." Light danced about in shafts and sparkles, reflected off the soup of waterborne bottom muck.

James squinted and blinked to moisten the contact lenses that had become dry in the cold, arid artificial life support air. He rubbed his eyes, momentarily blacking out the world outside and filling his field of vision with purple dots. When he opened them again, he immediately detected motion. Blinking rapidly, he turned his head to port and again squinted, his breaths becoming more rapid and shallow.

James did not notice the dilated yellow eye looking through the other side of the Eagle's nose. He squinted harder to pierce the murk and was then startled by a series of events. First, the Eagle's proximity and passive sonar alarm sounded moments before the Eagle was knocked violently to port.

"Holy sh—." The computer immediately accessed its stabilization subroutine and within milliseconds was righting the bobbing Eagle with a series of whines, clicks and taps as it sent commands to the innards of the vessel.

"NEST. EAGLE. I have hit something. No damage except to my shorts." James confirmed as all systems reported in with either a green or red light. "Passive sonar has a solid contact. I'm gonna paint it." James reached for a button and fired off an active sonar ping. "Contact is dead ahead. Passive is locked on, beginning track."

6.

Rebecca rolled over, smiled and giggled, "Thanks, Doc', that will be all—you can go now." Andrew, still out of breath responded with a rolling of his glazed eyes.

The Explorer's address system interrupted their silent eye conversation. *Dr.'s McClintock and Wright, stern control room please.*

When the message repeated, they both began to move.

7.

"Call it, EAGLE."

"Roger, NEST, I have a contact dead ahead. Range: twenty-five feet; course: two nine three; speed: seven knots and accelerating. I'll have a bearing for you in a minute. Damn, contact just accelerated to eleven knots. It's tight in here." James pushed the throttle forward another two notches.

James eyed the laser and sonar display that painted an electronic picture of the world outside. On either side of the Eagle, steep cliffs, long ago carved by glaciation, formed a gauntlet of rock and crevasses. Pillars, buttes and boulders lined its upper edge as the Eagle sped in pursuit of the contact. James swore under his breath at his own poor eyes and the silty lake water beyond. He reactivated the computer voice feedback system with the flick of a small toggle switch so he could better concentrate on the forward view. The system immediately notified him that his proximity to the submerged fjord walls was too close.

Reducing the proximity alarm threshold to ten feet, James noted the corresponding reduced reaction times. At current speed, ten-foot warning would not leave much time for evasive maneuvering. Bobby scanned his duplicate readout of the Eagle's instruments as Rebecca and Andrew entered the control room, flooding it with light and cold air. James shifted his prone body, gripped the controls tighter, wiped a bead of sweat from his brow with his shoulder and concentrated dead ahead on the Heads-Up Display and the forward, outside view.

"Damn it," he cursed the scant visibility; barely exceeding five feet at times. He maneuvered again, dipping the starboard wing of the vessel, carefully following a small green arrow in the HUD that indicated the direction to the contact. "Man, you are all over the place aren't you?" He asked the pitch-black lake. He dipped the wing to starboard, then to port, brought the nose up and then down again as he frantically tried to follow the contact.

It took a moment to realize that the soft, female voice was alerting him to a hazard. His thought as he threw the Eagle into a tight left turn was he would change the voice feedback system to a more mechanical and forceful one. He felt the scraping of the starboard wing in his bones and closed his eyes for a moment when the hull creaked and popped as it flexed under the stress. He opened them again when the lake did not did not rush in to kill him.

"NEST, EAGLE," he paused to calm his voice. "I brushed against something. Luckily was sandy I think; definitely not solid cause the wing is not bent up and I am still here," he nervously laughed, peering out at the now bare metal of the wing. "Looks like I just lost a little paint."

"Roger, EAGLE, your call—abort or proceed?" James bit his lip, ordered the computer to run a full-system-diagnostic and, when it reported all was well, he drew a deep breath and responded.

"Proceeding, NEST. Passive sonar has contact as faint and intermittent but it still has a solid lock."

8.

"Whoa, the bottom just dropped out from under me!" James watched as the solid line representing the lake floor on the sonar display dipped away and off the screen. "Firing active sonar." When the pulse returned his instruments confirmed that the Eagle had emerged over a deep trough in the lake bottom, a feature not listed on the chart that Bobby studied at the surface. "NEST, I am now reading one hundred twenty feet below the keel." James tapped the battery level readout; noting battery power was down to a third but said nothing. "Uh, NEST. Computer claims the contact has descended into the chasm."

"Roger, EAGLE. Again, your call. You don't pay me enough to make these big decisions. We are definitely going to lose the comm link if you go in there." James' smile waned and then disappeared completely as he weighed the pros and con's of proceeding.

"NEST, estimate battery power for me please. Read out shows about twenty one minutes. Confirm this please and tell me how much I would need to get back up top."

"Roger, EAGLE, I'll get right back to you." The Eagle hovered a few feet above the ridge where the lakes bottom took a dive into what could only be called blacker blackness; above on the now choppy surface, James' request had set off a madness of calculations, guestimates and even an argument.

"EAGLE, I'd say you have maximum ten more minutes on the bottom."

"Okay, thanks, NEST. Proceeding then. James nosed the Eagle down, penetrating the tear in the bedrock.

"Talk to you in a few EAGLE." Bobby's transmission broke up at the last moment as the surrounding rock and the metals it contained interfered. James continued to speak aloud for the sake of the cockpit voice recorder.

"Passive has a lock on contact. It's continuing to dive. Computer still specifying contact as *UNKNOWN.*" James again started the timer on his wristwatch. "Ten minutes to surfacing. I'll follow the contact as long as I can." James noted the displayed information and formed a mental image of the terrain around him. The trough was really more of a chasm. It ran two hundred yards end to end and was sixty yards at its widest point; tapering off to twenty at its deepest. James eased the nose of his craft even lower, triggering the: *"Descent rate warning."*

This time he did not disengage the now annoying sounding voice feedback system but pulled back slightly on the stick.

"Six hundred feet. Contact is continuing to dive. Feedback from active shows the contact is large, but, there is so much clutter down here I would not take it as gospel." James' ears popped. "Atmospheres increasing; environmental struggling to correct. Better check on it once topside." As the Eagle passed six hundred thirty feet, the hull again squeaked and banged as adjusted to depth and the tightening grip of the lake.

"Firing active again to confirm surroundings. Have lost the contact in the clutter." The acoustic wave ricocheted among the twist and turns of the encompassing rock, returning an interesting display. "Looks like we have a cave entrance twenty feet below us and thirty eight feet to starboard. Moving for it; matches last known position of contact—assuming the fish has entered."

Fish? Fish! Is that what I am chasing down here? James wondered, freezing for a moment as the memory of the fear he had felt in these same waters so many years ago flooded forth from his subconscious. He cleared his dry throat, swallowed hard and continued to go about the business at hand.

"Note: next time bring something to drink. Approaching cave entrance, bringing the floods on for a quick peek." The floodlights once again lit the underworld, though dimmer this time due to the diminished electrical reserve. They revealed a scene never before looked upon by human eyes. The Eagle looked like a silvery fish in the now clear illuminated water, slowing and hovering before a jagged, pitch-black entrance in the sheer crevasse wall. Bubbles danced around the Eagle, tickling its exterior on the way to the surface as they exited the gaping shaft opening. "There is a vent down here. Bubbling like a son-of-a-bitch. Suggests we could have a magma pocket below." James noted the rock wall of the crevasse looked young—freshly fractured. Probably occurred in the last thousand years or so, he thought to himself. "Surrounding water temperature is rising but not dangerous. Now at one hundred and one degrees Fahrenheit." He noted the slight rise in the cabin temperature as he turned the volume up on his communications link. He wanted Bobby to talk him out of the idea he had in his head but heard only the static he expected. "Proceeding into the cave." James would have made the sign of the cross if he was religious but instead relied on his faith in engineering and his own piloting skills. He eased the throttle forward after leveling and centering the Eagle in front of the cave mouth and the curtain of bubbles.

The Eagle gently moved forward while the noise of the bubbles grew from a trickle to almost a roar. The water outside looked like Champagne, he thought. James selected forward scan on the laser range finder. The green beam refracted momentarily in the bubbles, but then successfully penetrated and offered a detailed computer generated view of the cave before him. "Cylindrical, about a fifteen foot diameter. Red dots on the display probably mean stalactites or something. The cave is probably an old lava tube but I am no geologist. It is sloping up now. No sign of original contact."

Peering out from the Eagle's nose James noted a blind cavefish lazily meandering along the relatively smooth walls of the cave. Occasionally a jagged outcropping dangled from its ceiling, causing him to slightly adjust the barely noticeable forward momentum of the submersible. James looked at his watch. "Two minutes left before surfacing. Commencing egress. I'm going to reverse her out." James' fingers danced in a blur of keyboard and control stick inputs. The Eagle began to reverse exactly over the course, with which she had entered, expertly keeping the Eagle level in the unnatural maneuver. "For another time." James and the Eagle exited the cave and began the routines for a surfacing.

He immediately felt the vessel lighten as two, twenty pound

conformal lead weights were released to the lake floor. He placed an ear against the cockpit wall, straining his already aching neck, to listen for a small hydraulic pump empty the two ballast tanks, further lightening the submersible. James confirmed ascent rates as safe. The chasm wall fell back and away as the Eagle began a vertical climb.

James slid back in his harness as the nose came up.

9.

"Thanks for coming. Dr. Attwater will be out of radio blackout any moment. Thought you might be—." Bobby adjusted his gold-framed glasses.

"Yeah, thanks." Andrew acknowledged while Rebecca simply smiled and moved for the display panel. Bobby turned toward the panel and again adorned the headset and microphone.

"EAGLE, come in please." Static. "EAGLE."

"Roger, NEST, have begun ascent. Got some cool video to show you when I get topside."

"EAGLE, start your beacon so we can get an accurate pick up." Bobby listened for the repeating homing beacon and then activated a switch. "Bridge. Stern Control Station. Eagle is two miles, course two nine zero degrees. Understood?"

"Roger, NEST, understood. Explorer BRIDGE out." Andrew, Bobby and Rebecca all nodded when they felt the deck vibrate as the Explorer's engines were prepared to make way towards the ascending submersible. Explorer Channel personnel scurried about outside the container, sounding like mice in the shadows of a crawl space. Eager to record every moment of the Eagle's surfacing and retrieval, they hastily assembled the film crew.

10.

James watched as the surrounding water went from pitch black to dark brown; to brown; to yellow, as surface light became more and more visible. James relaxed with a long exhale as the safety of the surface came ever closer. As much as he loved doing this, at heart he was an engineer and not an adventurer. He would much rather be sitting with a set of blueprints, a cup of cocoa and a pencil instead of piloting the contraptions he designed.

His love of the world beneath the waves had begun with books by Jules Verne, which had especially inspired his genius for building the machines to enter it.

"EAGLE, have you at sixty five and rising at thirty feet per minute. We are in position. Stern crane is clear."

"Roger, surface break in two minutes, NEST."

Chapter 6: Taking Care of Business

1.

Miko pushed the hook through the live pike's foot long snout while grasping its long slimy stunned body. He attached a three-ounce weight a foot up the wire from the hook. It would allow him to control the depth of the live baitfish more easily. Ox studied the color LCD fish finder, ready to tell the boss when it detected something. Miko hauled the bait over board after grasping his stout five-foot pole and Penn reel. He released the drag on the reel and the weight dragged the wriggling baitfish to depth. Only the friction of Miko's callused thumb on the reel slowed its descent.

When what he thought was three hundred feet of line let out, Miko engaged the reels lock with a sharp click. Smiling with childish excitement, he set the pole in the boats trolling mount. The sun would be setting soon and the lake was still and oily looking in the overcast sunset. A single bubble broke the surface.

2.

Ian Chelsea pushed the rubber membrane of the regulator, confirming a clear airflow, and put the mouthpiece between his teeth. The familiar taste of rubber, embedded sea salt and saliva was comforting, like a pacifier to a child. He took two deep breaths before giving a thumb up, grabbing his mask and rolling into the glassy water.

After grasping the video camera and its watertight housing, Jack Meder shuffled his weight and followed Ian off the Explorers wooden stern swimming deck and into the lake, surfacing momentarily to receive a yellow Canon video camera.

A third diver, Alfred, followed. Protecting two large lamps and a battery pack with his chubby body, he pierced the lake, surrounded by the bubbles of air exhaled by Ian and Jack some ten feet below him.

Their task today was to film the last moments of the Eagle's ascent. Ian was to capture footage of the submersible at the surface for use by editors when the documentary was on the cutting table back in Bethesda. The only special instructions he received were to avoid filming the slight damage to the Eagle's winglet. He signaled Alfred, an apprentice film maker, to follow closely with the two large lights. Having discussed and rehearsed the dive before hand in the comfort of the Explorers briefing room, Ian knew to dive to a depth of thirty feet and hold in the Eagle's general ascent area. He would wait until the last moment to illuminate the craft as it rose from the black void below their gently kicking legs.

3.

Miko adjusted the rubber cover-all that uncomfortably protected his clothes from the mess of fish guts, dried blood and spilt beer that seemed to coat the entire wooden boat he had rented for this outing. Despite a leaky bilge and being at least a winter late for a paint job, her aft deck and fighting chair suited him. A small cabin and modest flying bridge as well as a cramped bunk and head forward and below the front deck would serve him well. He eyed the taut monofilament line of the fishing pole he had set in the trolling rig; slowly following it as it traveled from the brass eye at the end of the black pole until it broke the surface of the pink lake water. Concentric circles radiated out from it in the otherwise still reflection of the setting sun.

Miko clasped his hands together and blew warm breath on them to try to temper the chill of the evening air.

When the toothless old man had rented him the old wooden cabin cruiser, he had said, "She's a fine girl, she is. Ain't pretty, no, but'll getcha where yah need to go."

The cabin cruiser rocked in the glow of the cold, early winter dusk. He looked forward into the small cabin to see Ox making a sandwich next to a small single burner stove and small icebox.

"Hey, one for me too," he snorted.

"Ya-yes sir, uh, Mr. Miko. Ma-mayonnaise or mustard?"

"Mustard. Bring me a beer awl-so." He watched as Ox carefully balanced the flimsy paper plate, bag of chips and beer and moved towards Miko.

"Here you a-." He did not see Miko's extended leg.

"Hah, nice, moron." Ox was sprawled out on the oily deck, surrounded by chips, beer and components that had added up to a nice looking sandwich but a minute past. Miko laughed heartily. Anger boiled up in Ox as he peered at the ice blue eyes of the boss he hated so much but refused to leave due to the generous pay he offered. "Clumsy as you are stupid, eh?"

"Sorry sir, I will clean this up right away and make you another." The line Miko had set jerked slightly behind them but went unnoticed.

Two hundred feet below, the live pike impaled on the hook was now but a head; its pectoral fins still trying to propel its non-existent body through the water.

The line jerked again, this time Miko caught the motion in the corner of his eye. Pushing Ox aside, who still pawed the broken, beer-soaked potato chips, Miko moved for the now bending pole, his rubber boots squeaking on the wooden planks with every step.

4.

Ian looked down between the neon green straps of his flippers and saw a faint white outline below. Ian signaled Alfred, who loitered but two feet behind and slightly above, to turn on the lights while he readied the video camera. When the hand held lights came on, drawing their power from a rather bulky battery pack slung across the wide back of Alfred, the submersible and the cascade of bubbles that surrounded it looked ethereal. Ian depressed the trigger of the camera and confirmed it had begun recording by the red light that came on in the oversized viewfinder. He placed its rubber eyepiece directly to his mask and centered the glowing outline of the Eagle in its frame. Intermittently, bursts of flash increased the lighting as Meder took the occasional still photo with the waterproof camera. Ian filmed the rising Eagle, careful to keep the camera as steady as possible in the gentle current. As it approached and then moved directly in front of Ian, James waved through the vessels clear nose cone. Ian laughed in a burst of bubbles at the smaller, distorted image of James through the thick Plexiglas. Ian maneuvered to get under the Eagle as it passed in front and then on top of Ian. The last rays of daylight penetrated the first few feet of the lake and then quickly succumbed to the darkness. Ian smiled to himself, confident the footage was both exactly what the Explorer Channel people wanted as well as artistically satisfying.

The composition and quality of Ian's photo and cinematography were very important to him. He had once ripped exposed film from a camera after a nauseating flight from Skagway, Alaska to Glacier Bay National Park. He knew the film was too shaky and refused to hand it over for processing. Despite the negative impact on the budget, he chose instead to wait out the rough weather and then once again took to the sky in the small single engine Piper and captured some of the most spectacular footage of the ice shelf and the glaciers it spawned. The glass, teardrop shaped award he had won confirmed and permanently set his perfectionist ways.

Ian watched as James brought the nose up on the Eagle in preparation for reaching topside.

"Surface break in twenty . . . ten, five, four, three, two, one." The tip of the clear nose cone pierced the surface first, and James saw the sky again.

A camera on the stern deck of the Explorer recorded the surfacing of the Eagle from above the water line while Ian filmed it from below. He captured on film the explosion of bubbles and foam as the white submersible, looking like a breaching whale, leapt from the water before settling back to the frothy, disturbed surface.

"NEST, EAGLE has surfaced."

"Roger EAGLE, we are on the way." Ian began to film again as several inflatable outboard-powered Zodiacs swarmed around the bobbing Eagle, her vertical tail looking like a shark. Once he was satisfied with the footage of the undersides and propeller wash of the busy vessels above and when they had begun to tow the now powered down Eagle towards the waiting stern crane of the Explorer, Ian signaled Jack and Alfred it was time to surface.

5.

Miko sat in the old, leather covered fighting chair and, once Ox had handed him the pole, braced his feet against a small plank and strapped himself in. He slid the butt of the pole into a small greened brass receptacle and pulled back on the bending pole to judge the resistance of the line. He grunted under the exertion and then loosened the reel drag somewhat to relieve the strain on the taut line slightly, lest it fail. The reel clicked three times as it succumbed to the pull and let a few feet of line out.

"Get a gaff hook ready. If it starts to run, be ready to reverse the boat into it." Ox did not answer but simply removed a large, shiny hook at the end of a stout wooden club from a small equipment locker. He then climbed up a small steel tube ladder to the flying bridge. Once there, he started the single diesel engine of the boat with a hesitant rumble but left it in neutral. He watched his boss below begin to reel in the line. He would first pump the rod back as far as it would go and then lower it again, taking up any resulting slack in the line. Ox gave Miko the finger while the opportunity presented itself and then sneered to himself, one paw gently resting on the cold, metal wheel of the boat. "More slack in the line. It must have moved underneath us." Miko brought the slack in as quickly as possible before whatever it was that was on the other end decided to take it again. The clicks of Miko cranking the large reel slowed as resistance again built; then, he could no longer turn it. He grunted again as the reel stopped and the pole bent dramatically.

"Ox, reverse her slowly. Make sure to follow the line in case we start to swing." After a slight pause due to the surprise of hearing the proper use of his name, Ox complied, pushing the throttle out of neutral and into reverse. The old wooden boat jumped slightly as her propeller engaged, biting the water. Water lapped the transom as she slowly began to move backwards through the now dark waters. "That's good, speed is just right." Miko's usually taunting tone became more and more respectful as the task at hand pushed his sarcasm aside. Miko looked skyward and complained, "Damn moon coming up. I can't see a damn thing on this lake."

Ox contained a laugh at Miko's accent. For once he was confident his command of the English language was better than some one else's.

Miko squinted to see the angle at which the line penetrated the depths among the shadows on the water surface.

"Looks like he is going to starboard." Miko braced the springing pole, circling the index finger of his free hand counter clockwise. Ox adjusted the wheel to port to swing the stern towards the right as the cruiser continued to back into the fighting . . . fish?

6.

"Okay, get that line secured to the eye." The deck foreman barked orders to the hands that were securing lines to the Eagle to steady her in the increasing chop and in preparation for hoisting aboard by the stern crane. James patiently waited, watching the activity from inside the bobbing Eagle. He looked forward to once again standing and stretching his stiff legs. The rumble in his stomach reminded him that he wanted a hot bowl of that wonderful chicken noodle soup from the Explorers galley. He would slowly slurp it to chase away the chill that had settled into his bones. His slightly running nose confirmed the Jewish Penicillin would not be a bad idea. A blunt clank of metal let him know the steel crane cable had been secured before the radio had a chance to announce, "EAGLE, we have you secured and are ready to begin getting you aboard. Won't be a moment." James sighed and rubbed his eyes, moving his dry contact lenses and irritating his red eyes further. The sudden jerk, the moment of suction as the lake hesitantly let go of the craft and then the dangling sensation let James know he was closer to that steaming, soul warming soup.

7.

"Satana, this is big whatever it is!" Miko gasped for air as he struggled against the bucking and bending pole. "Reverse her some more. Must be a big conger eel or a huge pike. Voy vittuu! Strong bastard." Ox sneered at the barrage of foreign swears that permeated the cold, evening breeze. The wooden planking of the boat vibrated as the square transom buffeted the small waves that had steadily formed over the last twenty minutes. A spray began to traverse the transom and hit Miko, stinging his skin.

"Looks like snow clouds, Mr. Miko." Ox peered up at the thin, wispy clouds that meandered past the rising full moon."

"Yeah, I am cold as a, how you say, witches breast." Ox laughed aloud for the first time they had worked together and started to wonder if all of the bosses prodding and insults were simply his way and meant nothing personal by it all.

"Hey, moron!" So much for that theory Ox thought, his smile fading rapidly. "Kill that engine and come down here and get your gloves on. I almost have it on the surface." Ox turned the engine off, which sputtered, trying to cling to life, and then died with a thump of its ancient pistons.

"Coming, Mr. Miko."

"It must to be about thirty feet below us. The wire leader is showing." Ox jumped off the ladder onto the soft, sagging plywood deck and moved for the transom, trying desperately to squeeze the cloth gloves over his plump, oversized hands.

Miko watched the translucent nylon line go totally limp, coiling back into the form it had taken on the reel. The wire leader, a length of piano wire about thirty feet long between the hook and a small swivel, floated on the now frothy surface.

"Damn, where have you gone now?"

Neither man saw the long dark green neck snaking its way across the bow. Moving with the grace and strength of an Anaconda, it terminated with the powerful bulbous head. The agape mouth revealed rows of needle-like teeth piercing its green gums at seemingly random angles, like those of a barracuda.

Both Miko and Ox gasped and turned when the cabin window shattered behind them. Miko caught a blur of motion in the shadows.

"What was that, then?"

"Da-don't know, Ma-mister Miko."

"Go, check it out. Go up to the bow with the torch." Ox's mouth dropped as he eyed the dark. He grabbed a large flashlight, moved for the bow along a thin walkway that lined either side of the boats small cabin and began scanning the pitch-black waters with the light beam. Shards of the shattered windscreen lay on the small forward deck, refracting the flashlight in a spectrum of colors.

Miko continued to play the pole, testing it for resistance and taking up as much of the wire leader as possible. A sudden jerk almost stole the pole for the lake but, bracing himself against the boat transom, Miko was able to hold onto it.

"Ox, get back here. I need your help holding this damn thing. Moron!" Miko strained to look behind him while still fighting the resistance of the pole. "MORON! Get back here now," he spit.

8.

"All I can say is, whatever it was, it was no pike. I didn't get a look at it but the returns from sonar, the way it maneuvered down there it was no pike." James took another long sip from the oversized mug of chicken-noodle soup and then scanned the semicircle of curious looks on the faces of Rebecca, Andrew, Bobby and Captain Thomas. Ian burst in, still in his dripping Body Glove wet suit and asked, "So mate, you see Jaws down there or what?" James sniffed, giggled and went back to the blank stare people often get when cooling their soup and peering through the wisps of escaping steam and heat.

"Bobby, what is the condition of the Eagle? How bad is the wing banged up?"

"Not bad at all, in fact I have already done preliminary repairs. Pneumatics must have a pinhole leak somewhere in the lines 'cause I keep getting a weird drop off in pressure, but really nothing to worry about. Batteries are a little lower than we like to take them. We have started recharging already so they don't remember being empty."

"Good, good." Another slurp of hot soup echoed through the quiet briefing room.

"Excuse me, I am going to change into something more comfortable," Ian winked and left the room, leaving a small puddle of lake water where his bare feet had stood.

"How's all the photography equipment and the samples I took?" James peered through the fogged glasses.

"Being removed now." The door again opened but all kept their eyes on James.

"Uh, 'scuse me," Brent, Rebecca's assistant, interrupted. "Dr. McClintock, they wanted me to tell you that you are scheduled for filming in an hour. Dr. Wright, then you an hour later. Ian's s'posed to be dere too. Can yah tell 'im? They want to get some of his interview stuff out of da way." A uniform "Uh huh" came in response but still, no one took their eyes from James. Brent sneaked back out, pushing his yellow personal stereo headphones back into the folds of his ears and his lollipop back between his grape colored lips.

"I want to plan a second dive as soon as possible. We have to get back in that cave." James tapped the bottom of the mug to let the noodles that clung for dear life fall into his mouth. "Ha, that is better." He shivered as the last of the chill left his body, replaced by the warmth radiating from his soup filled stomach.

"What was it like?" Andrew got down on one knee to come to the eye level of James who sat comfortably in a small padded chair.

"Tight and dark. I was scared to death but whatever went in there stayed in there. Bob, I figure if I do an un-powered dive to the cave, that should give me enough juice to get in, explore and have enough to get topside again. Right?"

"Yeah, true. It would take a while to get you to depth but the batteries would be almost full when you got there." Bobby played with his gold chain and cross as he thought, a thick lock of black hair hanging over his tanned forehead.

"Okay, start getting a preliminary dive plan together. I would like to be able to review it by breakfast if possible?" James shifted in the shadows and his chair.

"Sure, I'll get right on it after I post-dive the Eagle thoroughly."

"Thanks, Bob."

9.

"You, eeediot, where have you gotten to now?" Miko mumbled to himself, struggling to get the pole back into the trolling holder. He held it over the small tube in the gunwale of the boat, attempting to aim the butt of the pole over its center; a difficult task with the still struggling catch at the other end. He heard a splash of water alongside the vessel and again turned to look, this time forcing the pole into the holder with the last of the strength left in his burning arms. He was certain the bending fiberglass pole would soon shatter but it settled into a U-shape, wedged precariously inside the metal tube of the trolling mount.

Wisps of fog formed as the warmer water met the chill air of the night, drifting in and around the boat as Miko reached for a flashlight. The moonlight gave a blue glow to the cabin of the boat as he scanned the bow through its jagged shattered glass, looking for Ox on the fore deck. "Ox?" The light caught two forms through spider web cracks in the front window as he moved for the side walkway. A thick evening fog had settled upon the waters by now and his motions on the exposed stern deck caused the puffs of mist to twist and curl. Shuffling along the mist covered walkway, the flashlight cutting swaths through the darkness in random lines, Miko reached the bow and again scanned the deck with the light.

There, on the dark wood planking, was a single drop of now coagulating blood. Two feet from that, the green boots with the yellow stripe Ox had been wearing stood empty, sitting perfectly besides one another. It was as if a ghost had arrived with the cold fog and was standing on the front of the boat staring at the lake.

10.

Rebecca squirmed a little in her seat, excited with her role in today's filming but worried she looked haggard despite the thick layers of makeup. She was tired and wanted a hot shower desperately. Drawing a deep breath, Dr. Rebecca McClintock finished her lines.

" . . . London's Natural History Museum sent out H.M.S. Challenger to probe the globes oceans. It . . . *She*, returned with treasures from dredging at all depths, an incredible amount of data. It was also discovered that the deep oceans were about three degrees colder than thought at around two degrees Fahrenheit.

This massive collection of the rarest of specimens was brought back to Great Britain. Oceanography as a science was established to sort through and record the often never before seen specimens. That's why the science is only about one hundred years old." Rebecca exhaled and closed her eyes momentarily to rest them from the bright gaze of the spotlights. The director yelled, "Cut!"

When the spotlight came on, Andrew held up his hand to block it, reminding him of the harsh desert sun. Half his face contorted to shield his surprised eyes.

"All right. Sound, how-ya-looking?"

"Check. Sound is go. Cameras ready."

"Graphic up." A small line and white *Andrew Wright, Ph.D. Marine Paleontologist* underlined Andrews's nervous looking face in one of the camera video monitors. "Good. Okay. Dr. Wright, how's your view of the TelePrompTer?" The last of the scurrying grips, electricians, sound technicians and lighting people settled into their assigned position, readying the 'set' of the converted briefing room for action. The director rubbed the gray and black of his unkempt beard as he reviewed the respective storyboard for this shoot. "Okay, 'Doc'."

"Ready, Todd." Andrew cleared his throat.

"Okay, annnnd action!"

Andrew's dark suit and gelled hair made him appear to the camera a bit older than reality. With a chart of Lake Champlain in the background and one of those wooden models of a dinosaur's skeleton, this one a plesiosaur, at his side, Andrew focused on the TelePrompTer rendition of the material he and the director had written earlier. This scene was to be used in the first third of the documentary, where the viewer is familiarized with marine reptiles, and, specifically, plesiosaurs.

"Plesiosaurs are Mesozoic reptiles comprising one of the most successful and widely distributed groups of tetrapods. They developed a worldwide range early in their history and some representatives of the clade survived into the Maastrichtian, becoming extinct perhaps only at the terminal Cretaceous. However, the evolutionary and systematic relationships of the Plesiosauria are almost totally unknown. The group appears as isolated bones and associated partial skeletons in the Middle Triassic, Anisian, of Germany. The first unambiguous, fully articulated specimens occur only in the uppermost Triassic and Lower Jurassic, or Liassic, of England. By Liassic times, the plesiosaurs were particularly diverse, already fully marine or pelagic, and highly modified from the presumed terrestrial condition of their forebears." Andrew paused, blinked three times, and took a deep breath.

"Adoption of locomotion dominated by limbs, through two symmetrical sets of hyperphalangic appendages, or more simply put, flippers, was a unique functional response by the plesiosaur to a secondary invasion of the seas. In the Lias also, the group had already begun to exhibit specialization's that led to several distinct lineages in the later Mesozoic, although the origins of this lineage diversification are obscure. The lower Jurassic plesiosaurs, because of their often excellent state of preservation and well-constrained stratigraphic positions, currently provide the best potential for clearing up early plesiosaur diversification and testing of postulated lineage monophyly." Andrew swallowed hard and took another deep breath.

"Among the Lower Jurassic plesiosaurs, dozens of species of which have been describe, the archetypal genus is *Plesiosaurus*, created by De al Beche Conybeare in 1821 on the basis of isolated and disparate material from the Lyme Regis, Dorset, and the Bristol region of England. However, the first specific description of a plesiosaur, that of the type species *P. dolichodeirus*, was provided by Conybeare in 1824 for a complete skeleton found by Mary Anning in December 1823 in the Lower Lias near Lyme regis. This skeleton, ah, two-two-six-fifty-six I think," Andrew said with a glance towards Rebecca who leaned up against the far wall, one foot on its white painted metal, "is now universally recognized as the genoholotype. Thereafter, the lower Jurassic of Dorset continued to produce a number of fine fossils of this animal until the cessation of quarrying activities in the Lias Group, early in this century." Andrew swallowed and then smiled widely.

"Great! Cut. Print that. Doc', I think that was perfect, your a natural. I just can't believe your students can absorb that techno-speak. We can go on when you are ready." Andrew's face flushed as he sipped from a plastic cup of ice water, again clearing his throat with a raspy cough into a rolled hand. "But let's do one more, dumb it down a bit. New England getting to you desert boy? Angie, get Dr. Wright some lemon honey tea. That should help. I need to get some more out of yah before you lose that voice." Someone, presumably Angie, scurried in the shadows towards the coffee cart, complying with the director's order.

11.

The feeling that Miko was being watched became stronger and stronger. At first the sensation that someone's gaze was upon him was subtle, but, slowly, it began to grow until the hairs on the back of his neck stood on end. When his arms erupted into a field of goose bumps, he spun around, determined to catch Ox in the act. He must be hiding, he thought. Getting back at me for all the torment I have given him. Nothing, just the darkness of the night, the gentle rocking of the boat and the fog obscured waves.

The mist was now thicker as he whispered in a breath of vapor, "Ox. Where are you for heavens sake?" A trickle of water was all that responded. "Ox, come out now or look for a new job." For the first time in a long time, Miko felt the choke of fear rising in his throat until he could almost taste it. He spotted the pole in its holder, now relaxed and straight, the great weight lifted from its line that lay in what looked like a pile of nylon spaghetti on the deck. Did the line snap? He wondered. Or was his hooked quarry simply on the surface? "Must be on the surface. Nothing could snap that piano wire," he reassured himself aloud.

He moved for the pole, moving slowly as if it would again bend suddenly and violently. He reached out carefully, his fingers touching the smooth finish of the pole shaft. Reaching more confidently he grabbed it and again sat down in the fighting chair. This is all I need, he thought. Dealing with the American Police, filling out a missing person report, trying to explain how the moron had disappeared. "He must have fallen overboard," he thought aloud, beginning to rewind the slack line that sat in a tangled mass at his feet. The reel clicked with each turn, echoing off the banks of fog that now had settled into a dense, foot thick layer directly over the water, obscuring the depths below. Once the slack line had been taken in, wrapping itself unevenly around the reel cylinder, resistance began to build. "Satana, stupid moron." He cursed to the night when he decided to cut the trip short and start the hassle of dealing with Ox's accident. He would search for Ox in the immediate area with the boat and head back to the dock to file a report if he found nothing. He suspected that would be the case.

Miko noted that most of the wire leader was now around the reel. He could not see over the transom from the fighting chair but knew whatever he had hooked had to be close to the surface. He felt a weak but determined tug at the line.

"Whatever you are," he mumbled under the renewed strain, "you don't give up even though you must be as exhausted as me." Having brought as much leader in as possible, he placed the pole in its holder again and slowly began to gaze over the wooden transom of the boat. When he looked over, he saw the wire penetrating the thick fog layer and heard the motion of water beneath it.

He rested his lower body on the wood platform of the transom top and stretched his upper body and arms out over the lake. Fanning the white mist with his open hand, a feeble attempt to clear it, he thought he saw what he would best describe later as the back of a whale shark—dark, with small, round light markings.

"Hello there," Miko whispered, continuing to use both palms to fan the thick mist. Like digging a hole in sand, it quickly settled back into whatever clearing he managed to make. He noticed movement from his catch among the white curls of mist and the blackness of the water below. "Still have some fight left in you then, eh?" He reached back into the boat for the gaff hook Ox had left on the deck. The full moon, amplified by the reflective mist, reflected off the stainless steel barb.

As he began to turn around, Miko first heard the low snorting sound. He slowly turned his head meeting the creature eye-to-eye. Before him was a dark outline of what looked like a small head at the end of a snake-like neck. It cried again, splashing Miko with warm, moist breath. Miko's entire body spasm'd in response. He caught a glint of moon light in its reddish-black eye. Not the black, lifeless eye of a shark, he thought, but the expressive, 'thinking' eye of a whale.

"Hello there." He tightened his grip on the gaff hook handle. "Hold still and you will make me rich."

The creature's head swung from side-to-side in an effort to dislodge the hook that pierced the soft flesh of its lip, blood trickling down its skin to the cold water. It appeared on the verge of consciousness, drained from the hour-long struggle against Miko and his stout equipment.

"Hold still." Miko raised the gaff hook, silhouetting it against the full, round moon before bringing it down in a rapid arc. The muffled thump as it met the spongy head of the creature seemed unnatural. The high pitched screech of pain did not. "Just one more and we will get you aboard." The head and the exposed neck flopped to the water, obscuring it once again in the layer of mist.

As Miko wrapped the last of the wire leader around a rusty cleat to prevent his catch from sinking, he felt a warm moist blast of air on his neck, followed by a snort and then sharp stabbing pain in his head. The world went black.

12.

"Just do the next scene and then you can take a break and have that tea."

"I'm okay. Don't worry."

"Camera, are yah ready?"

"Yeah, we're up."

"Okay Chuck, get in there for the opening shot. Good. Camera tight in on him." The camera moved to within a foot of the narrator. The last pats of a make up artists' pad put a rose on his cheeks. "Aaaaction!"

"Dr. Wright, what role did the marine reptiles have in the early debates about evolution?"

"Cut. Good. Okay, camera on Andrew. Come on, quickly now."

"I'm ready Todd." Andrew shuffled in his chair and pulled the back of his blazer down to keep the shoulders from riding up.

"Okay then? Ready now people. Annnd action!" Andrew inhaled deeply.

"Chuck, the icthyosaur and plesiosaur were originally interpreted in a non-evolutionary manner. Their names were derived directly from the pre-evolutionary concept of the static Great Chain of Being; an explanation of ordered diversity within Divine Creation. *Icthyosaur* comes from the Greek for 'fish reptile' reflecting its position in the Chain between fish and reptiles and plesiosaur comes from the Greek for *nearer reptile* or *nearer to reptile*, depending on who you talk to, fitting between ichthyosaurs and reptiles such as lizards and crocodiles. The Great Chain of Being, however, as applied to the animal kingdom, was already an obsolescent concept because of internal inadequacies."

13.

Leaning against the railing, Rebecca watched the winch haul the net aboard. The nets geometric pattern was occasionally broken by a silvery fish or slimy eel, their gills holding fast like barbs. The Explorer, under Rebecca's direction and coordinates, would troll the lake for several hours at different depths. This would help her view the food chain of Lake Champlain. Rebecca snapped on a pair of powder coated rubber gloves and reached for one of the fish that flopped around in vain, drawing several desperate final gaps of air before suffocating.

"Give me a knife please, Brent."

"Here you go, Doc'." Brent turned his cap around, reached for a paper wrapped scalpel from his kit, and handed it to Rebecca.

"Thanks." Rebecca tore the sterile paper and carefully removed the sharp instrument. She positioned the small fish on its back, made an incision from the anus to the pectoral fins, and then scooped the small collection of organs from the cavity. Separating the oily mess, she located the stomach and also cut it open. The incision immediately released into her gloved palm a black hash with the consistency of paté. "You see Brent, we compare the stomach contents to known plankton levels in the lake. This in turn helps us estimate fish populations in the lake and whether or not it could support a top level predator."

"Cool."

"From the volume and the size," Rebecca stretched a small tape measure from the tip of the specimens head to its tail, "eight and half inches, I'd say we have healthy fish populations and a good chance that, yeah, the lake could support a predator at the top of the food chain." Most likely seal sized though. At least that's my guess. We'll see what the data has to say."

14.

"Okay, Ian, Chuck, you ready?" Ian's leather pants screeched a little as he squirmed in his seat patted his gel slicked hair and gave Todd an okay sign. Chuck just smiled and winked.

"All right then. Annnnd action." A red light on top of the camera illuminated.

"This is Ian Chelsea, chief expedition photographer. Mr. Chelsea, please describe your recent encounter here in the waters of Lake Champlain."

"Right. Well, the best way to describe it would be to show

you these photographs here." Ian raised one of the five photographs he held in his lap.

"Okay, cut it here. Make a note to film close ups of these photos for Ian's narration, okay."

"Got it, Todd." Acknowledgment came from somewhere behind the bright lights, tangle of power lines and people.

"Continue, Ian. Action."

"Well, as you can see here, I was able to capture what appears to be a flipper here." Ian traced the foggy trapezoidal outline. "The most fascinating of the shots is this one." Ian changed photographs as if holding up cue cards for a stage actor. "If you, well, look at it a little creatively, you can see what looks like a long neck and a strange head . . . looking like it's covered with sea weed. This one here is of the bottom of the Explorer, our expedition ship. I think I, uh, kind of took this one accidentally."

"Mr. Chelsea, do you think you have pictures of a Lake Champlain creature here?"

"That is a bloody tough question," Ian laughed and scanned the room full of film crew, squinting momentarily to shield his eyes from the spotlights.

"Well, I think, like when looking at a cloud, we each see something different. So, I would say what I have here *looks* a lot like what we all *think* a plesiosaur would look like," Ian looked to Andrew for confirmation which he received in the form of a nod, "But, it could be anything, from junk caught in the current to plant life from the bottom that was simply uprooted. This water is murky and plays tricks on you. If you are asking me if I believe there is something here? Well mate, I don't think I am daft enough to stick my neck out on television so, I would say no, I don't think we have enough evidence to say anything for certain."

"And cut. Ian, try to be a little less casual in your responses. Also, please don't look around. Just keep your eyes on or near Chuck."

"Right'o. Got it. Sorry mate."

15.

Miko first perceived a tunnel of light beyond the dark haze and then, blinking rapidly realized there was a bright light blaring on him. Finding his body would not move he tried to lift his head that responded with an agonizing stab of pain. Concussion, and I have been unconscious, Miko thought and again lay his head back down on the moisture of the dew covered punky deck planking. He heard muffled voices and the rumble of an idling engine.

Miko recognized the feedback of a megaphone being turned on.

"This is the Police, prepare for us to come along side and board. Stay where you are." Miko saw red and blue strobes in the darkness as the Burlington Police Departments Boston Whaler approached Miko. Her mast mounted floodlight still trained on Miko's prone body. Despite the pain, he struggled to open a single eye and, when he did, managed to see only the front end of what he recognized as a SIG Sauer P-226 semiautomatic nine millimeter pistol. All Americans think they are cowboys, Miko thought. Miko saw the broken wire, loosely wound around the old cleat. He slipped back into unconsciousness.

"Looks like we got ourselves a drunk heah, Chief."

16.

The moon was now low and big on the horizon. Among the fog, far out and in the middle of the vast lake, a mother gently pushed her near lifeless baby on the surface. Its dark, spotted limp body folded into a vee-shape around the nudging paternal head as life finally slipped away, a barbed hook and severed wire leader trailed from its small bloody mouth.

CHAPTER 7: UNDERWORLD

1.

"How did it happen, Andrew?" Andrew leaned back in his chair, throwing both hands up as if loosening his sleeves. He placed both hands on the back of his head and looked straight up. Rebecca instantly understood the weight he felt on his soul. "Sorry, I didn't realize —."

"It's okay." Andrew's gaze as his eyes again met hers was one of anger. She could almost see a little flame flicker in his dilated pupils. Rebecca looked away and around the sonar room, nervously donning her head set and intercom microphone that tangled for a moment in her long hair. She adjusted an instrument that did not require it. "What they call a random crime. I was a-way . . . away." Andrew's voice trailed off into the verge of being a sob when he stopped speaking and closed his eyes. Rebecca held her fingers to the head set earpiece.

"Andrew, James is on his way down again in the sub." She reached for a small button on the control panel and pushed it. She adjusted the headsets small-articulated arm that held the microphone directly in front of her mouth and spoke. "NEST and EAGLE, this is SHACK. I have sonobuoys one and two fired up and ready to assist. Thermocline is at two hundred nine feet and relatively quiet, over." Rebecca released the switch, smiling as both Bobby and James acknowledged through her earpiece. She looked back to Andrew who stared blankly at her and smiled. "Hey, Andrew. You okay?"

"Yeah. Sorry to have gotten all, choked up."

"Don't apologize. I appreciate you sharing this with me. Have you heard if the Police have found those two missing students?"

"Nope."

2.

Looking like a pudgy Jacques Cousteau, James wore a red wool pull down cap and his wire rimmed glasses. Despite their thick heavy lenses he had decided to wear them this dive instead of contact lenses for comfort in the dry cabin air. He carried two foil orange juice packs. The hull of the Eagle groaned as the submersible again entered the depths. The cold water reached around James and his vessel, waiting for the opportunity to occupy the unnatural air space that kept James alive. Dark shadows formed on James' face as the only cabin light was the red, back up lighting that fed off of two small independent batteries. James flicked a small analog depth gauge with his finger, usually relying on it only in the event of a main computer or electric system failure. He noted its red needle pointed to three hundred feet and then looked to the bubble in a green liquid filled tube to get the vessels attitude. The blank computer and digital displays were an attempt to preserve power.

The Eagle's propellers were still, her descent relying only on the mass of the submersible, her structure, the new lead weights and the water in her flooded ballast tanks. Her three-axis stabilization system was powered down, making the stick feel heavy in James' hand, hydraulic assistance no longer available.

James' eyes felt heavy. The absolute silence and darkness that engulfed the descending Eagle brought him to the verge of sleep. One of those pseudo dreams you see when falling asleep startled him back awake. He rubbed his eyes and focused on the brass ringed depth gauge. Its needle pointing to three hundred eighty.

3.

"It was a stray bullet. Yah know, wrong place wrong time, ha. She died on a cold sidewalk with groceries in her arm, just a little hole in her forehead." Tears began to stream down Andrew's cheeks.

"Enough." Rebecca moved for him. "I'm sorry I asked."

4.

"Okay NEST, EAGLE is in position over the crevasse." The submersible and James hovered over the great yawning rift in the rocky lake floor and, once again hesitated before entering the abyss. Having designed the pilots' cylinder for a six-foot, one hundred ninety-pound man, his larger two hundred twenty-pound frame made for a tight squeeze. He felt a bit like the cream filling of a Twinkie. However, his reduced stature, or, the politically correct vertically challenged, forced him to operate Eagle's pedal system on his tiptoes even though he lay prone. It was that or be unable to reach his Head-Down Panel—the dials, buttons, displays and switches that controlled the vessels near mile of wire, also pneumatic and hydraulic lines and various subsystems. James reached for the low frequency radio power switch flipped it and, when a small red light came on, pushed the microphone transmit hammer. "Powering systems up NEST."

"Roger EAGLE, welcome back." The ghostly silence was interrupted at first with the clicks of switches and then the building hum as machinery came alive, eventually combining to form the familiar droning background noise of the Eagle. James smiled. Fluorescent cabin lights first flicked and then ignited, circling his eyes in the reflection of his thick glasses. The now dimly lit cabin only served to make the outside world even darker. James switched back to red lighting.

"Okay NEST, all systems spun up. Got green across the boards."

"Roger EAGLE, I have you at four twenty three, diving for

cave entrance at six hundred twenty seven feet, steering for zero one fiver."

"Roger NEST. Six two seven at zero one five." James nudged the Eagle's control planes into dive position, dipping the Eagle's nose towards the agape rock, and slid the throttle forward one notch, starting the counter-rotating high blade pitch propellers spinning. James engaged the laser range finder and selected the appropriate forward scan pattern. The Heads-Up Display immediately changed to a projected wire frame topographical representation of the outside world. He watched as the Eagle was engulfed by the walls of the ravine on its way through its tapering jagged depths.

5.

"NEST, SHACK, come in please." Static responded. "NEST?" James switched on the cabin voice recorder. "Lost contact with the surface at five hundred and twelve feet. All systems functioning well."

6.

"I have the cave now." The Eagle's nose pointed towards the black opening in the sheer rock wall. Stalactites and mites in its opening made it appear like a tooth filled jaw, waiting to consume James and his machine. The small rock plume that had bubbled and shot hot water the last dive was eerily quiet. "Six two four. Water temperature normal. No hot smoker this time around I guess. Everything is quiet down here." James brought the submersible and her wing mounted still camera closer to the vent for a photograph. Rebecca had explained that hydrothermal vents, like those found along the Mid-Atlantic Ridge, spit forth hot mineral-laden water, composed mainly of toxic hydrogen sulfide and capable of exceeding four hundred degrees Fahrenheit. The superheated water deposited its abundance of minerals in what was called chimneys. Often the smoky water erupting from the earth was dark, earning them the name 'black smokers'.

He pulled back gently on the throttle and eased the nose up in front of the breach in the rock. When level with it, he let the throttles spring tension return them to neutral.

"Bringing the laser on. Good return. Looks like the cave varies from fourteen to seventeen feet in diameter. Firing a single sonar ping. Supplemental data returns show miscellaneous obstacles varying from one to two feet. The cave is cylindrical, tube like, and travels for about thirty feet before gently rising. No data yet beyond that point. Proceeding".

The Eagle's propellers spun faster, slowly pushing the Eagle forward into the cave. James shifted in the uncomfortable position he held, wiping his moist face and further opening his dilated eyes. He wormed his body forward a few inches so his head protruded further into the submersibles clear nose cone.

"Lights are on. Battery levels show as full or near full," James' voiced trembled slightly as he nervously eyed the now illuminated jagged and craggy rock that surrounded him. He fought back the claustrophobic feeling by sucking a juice, collapsing its fall package with a greedy vacuum. The bright lights in the crystal clear cave water made the cluster of stalactites and mites that clung to the otherwise smooth rock cast deep, disorienting shadows. James expertly maneuvered the Eagle, patiently edging forward at minimum speed: about one knot. He set the proximity alarm to one foot. If any part of the Eagle got within one foot of an obstacle, an alarm would sound. Looking around in fascination, James reduced the output of the forward pointing wing-mounted lamps slightly. This both reduce glare in his video screen display as well as further managed battery resources. "I'm riding the laser beam and have proximity alarm at one foot. She's steady as a rock. Forward speed: almost one knot."

As the cave began to pitch upwards, James pulled back gently on the stick, pre-empting the pull up order issued by the voice warning system. The proximity alarm sounded when the stern of the Eagle and her propellers got dangerously close to the sharp rock. Beads of sweat formed on James' forehead. A muffled rumble began to grow louder as the Eagle climbed the slanting cave before reaching its top.

"Almost at the peak of a fifteen foot angled section. There is some kind of noise outside, a rumbling. Water temp just came up a few degrees as well." James again leveled the Eagle as the cylindrical cave again became horizontal. "Water temp up again two more degrees to forty three."

7.

"Another cave fish just swam by. They're albino and look blind. Pretty bizarre. I'll see if I can't snap a photograph next time." James followed the meandering fish as it passed by the Plexiglas nose. "Okay, I am at the top. Wow, my God." James pulled the throttle back to the neutral position and placed the Eagle in a hover while he absorbed the scene before him. As far as the lights penetrated the otherwise pitch-black cavern, James could see the cave floor was littered with the same type of gas vent that he had encountered at the caves main entrance. "I have just entered a large chamber. Water temperature at fifty-two degrees and rising. Chamber approximately forty feet long by thirty feet high. It is full of gas vents on its floor. They look like two-foot tall volcanoes. They seem to be quiet like the one at the front door. Wait a moment, spoke too soon."

The smoker or gas vent closest to the Eagle began to spout bubbles and what James assumed was boiling water by the wavy, mirage like distortion of the otherwise smooth water. "The first one just became active. It's shooting water and bubbles pretty strong; uh, causing some turbulence." The Eagle shook slightly in the disturbed waters of the usually still cave. The computer immediately activated station keeping and did its best to counter-act the forces at work on the submersible's hull. "Second one is waking up now while the first is quieting down. I am going to try and time the pattern so I can sneak the Eagle by without too much trouble." James moved the Eagle back and forth slightly, directing the light to the far side of the cavern. "I have one more of these to deal with before getting to what looks like the exit, once I get past the first two." James watched as the first vent erupted hot water and gas, and then, subsided. The released bubbles rushed up to the cave ceiling, squirming their way through every nook and cranny as they sought to join the inaccessible atmosphere somewhere above. "The gas is collecting in a small pocket and then rushing up the exit tube at the other end." James watched as the two streams of bubbles merged before moving for the higher ceiling at the opposite end of the gallery. The third vent became active just as the second had ended its spirited spouting. "Okay, I am going to have to time this just right; don't want to brush against this rock." James scanned the columns and jagged pillars of green and yellow rock. He referred to his wristwatch, scribbled some calculations on a small note pad that could be slid open for use from under the padded board on which he lay. "Looks like the first one goes for three minutes. The second one kicks in twenty seconds before the first stops, going at it for one and a half minutes. The third then starts up ten seconds after number two quits and carries on for about one and a half to one and three quarter minutes. There is then a ten second lapse before number one starts the whole thing up again." James chewed on the already tooth marked pencil he held and eyed the far end of the cave. "My hope is to get across all three in that ten second lapse. I would then wait for the gases to rush up the tunnel before proceeding. The only thing I will have to deal with is the rush of gas and water that are certain to follow me up the tube when they start up again behind me."

James waited for the cycle to begin and finish again before moving the Eagle forward through the cave to the opposite side. Despite having only ten seconds to do so, he was hesitant to accelerate in the small surroundings and instead gently nursed the submersible forward. As he reached the opposite end of the vent gallery, his wrist watch alarm went off, warning him that the third vent was just about to start up again. The Eagle was directly over the third vent when James looked down into its dark mouth. "Damn."

A faint orange glow emanated from within, distorted by the violently boiling water. The submersible's tail caught some of the turbulence of the small eruption, forcing it to rise in the gaseous bubbles and the nose to point towards the rocky floor. Deciding not to wait for the computer to react, James pulled back on the control stick to bring the nose and the vessel back to level. Overhead, a rush of gasses moved for the cave exit and disappeared into the darkness. "Okay, I am at the opposite end. I caught a bit of number three's temper tantrum. The Eagle got pushed around a bit but no biggy."

8.

In the Eagle control center Bobby thumbed through the latest issue of a diving magazine. Listening carefully for any noise to come through the sonobuoy monitor speakers, Rebecca and Andrew did their best to maintain poker faces for this latest hand of seven-card stud. Brent, who had just joined them in the sonar shack, frantically defended his home base from the falling cubes and other shapes on his electronic game. Bobby eyed the radio speaker, as if looking at it might get James' voice to come through, and then went back to the article on the worldwide blanching of coral reefs due to human activity, waste and sedimentation. Rebecca yawned, stretched and, throwing her cards down, said, "Straight."

"Again?"

"Let's go see what's happening on the stern, 'kay?" Rebecca stood and said.

"All right, I could use some air anyway." Andrew moved his head side-to-side, cracking his neck. Rebecca asked Brent to takeover the monitoring of the two hydrophones.

9.

"Okay, ready to proceed." James cleared his throat. The Eagle hung motionless before the cave opening at the opposite end of the small cavern of smokers. In the small cracks and fractures that lined its ceiling, tiny gas bubbles clung to the uneven surface. James decided to wait and follow the next rush of hot water and gasses, maximizing the time he had another eruption would chase him and the submersible up the unknown tunnel. James gingerly adjusted the ballast tank inlet valve, allowing a little more water into it, slowly dropping the Eagle towards the cave floor. When the proximity alarm told him he was a foot off the cave floor, he again selected neutral buoyancy. "I have lowered the Eagle as close to the floor as possible. I want to give the stream of bubbles as much headroom as I can. Once it subsides, I will proceed into the tunnel. Once in the tunnel, I estimate I will have about fifteen to twenty seconds until the next eruption catches up with me." A growing rumble sent a shiver through the Eagle, telling James to prepare. "Okay, here we go." Overhead, a violent stream of the bubble laden hot water rushed passed the Eagle and into the cave tunnel. When the tail end of it had passed, he raised the Eagle and immediately steered her for the tunnel entrance.

Her long, sleek white hull, interrupted only by the shark fin-shaped tail, disappeared into the narrow opening.

"I'm in." James nudged the throttle forward another click, hoping to cover as much distance as possible. "Laser shows the tunnel is relatively straight and level for at least twenty feet. I have about three feet clearance to the tunnel ceiling. I think the tail is going to protrude into the next bubble stream slightly so I will have to prepare for shearing forces. A shame I don't have the room to invert her. Increasing speed again slightly. Now showing forward motion at two-point-two knots, about two and half miles an hour. Two-point-five knots now, I'll hold her steady here. About ten seconds before things get crazy again."

Five seconds later James brought the throttle back to zero,

slowing the forward momentum of the submersible until she was still. James again lowered her until almost touching the cave floor and then activated station keeping. James rubbed his gray and black beard stubble and scratched under the sweaty front of his red cap. He eyed the ceiling of the cave, noting the soft sponge-like carpet that coated the rock.

After checking the batteries, he again lowered the intensity of the floodlights. Battery one reported a full charge, the second, three-quarters. The now familiar rumble again emanated from behind the Eagle and, as it grew louder, James swallowed hard and gripped the control lever ready to assist the computer.

"Here it comes." A subtle shimmy through the metal hull of the submersible became apparent, slowly growing to more of a jerking and then finally settling into a hard vibration. Catching the top of the vertical stabilizer, the stream of bubbles and rapidly moving water tried to spin the Eagle around, but a quick reaction with James' feet pushed the rudder into the opposite direction, counter-acting the force at work. When this action became insufficient, James reversed the starboard propeller, keeping the Eagle pointed forward down the tunnel. The squeal of the proximity alarm told him to pump a little compressed air and thus expel some water from the ballast tanks, allowing the Eagle to rise slightly in the tunnel. As she rose six inches, the increased tail exposure to the overhead commotion started the Eagle rotating on its axis. "Damn it!" The proximity alarm sounded again, this time warning that the tail was now dangerously close to the tunnel wall. James increased power to the reversed starboard propeller and pushed the rudder fully to port. "I have the starboard screw at half reverse, rudder fully to port. She's coming back again."

The alarm stopped as the tail of the Eagle again settled into a position perpendicular to the wall. James exhaled for the first time in what felt like an hour. He removed his glasses to rub the stinging sweat from his eyes.

"Okay looks like we survived that." Wasting no time, James brought the Eagle higher into the tunnel as the last of the bubbles and hot water rushed by. "Water temp coming down again. I really don't want to go through that again so, getting on with it." He immediately brought the forward speed to two and a half knots and was tempted to go to three. "Laser shows the tunnel starts to rise in ten feet. Bringing the floodlights up to full power again. Looks like some strange reddish algae are thriving in this tunnel. Must be the combination of the hot water and what I assume is carbon dioxide and oxygen. It is almost luminescent in the floodlights. Weird that it is thriving here with no sunlight." James stared, transfixed by the sparkles of color that reflected off of the algae covered rock.

The proximity alarm reminded him to pay attention to the task at hand. He raised the nose of the Eagle as the tunnel began to angle gently upwards, turning her slightly to avoid a small escarpment of jagged rock that thrust up from the floor.

"Okay, the laser is indicating there is a chamber ahead, about fifteen feet. It could be just be the tunnel getting wider though. It wouldn't know the difference. Increasing speed." James looked down for a moment to verify the Eagle was now moving at three knots. "She's at three knots. Yeah, definitely have a chamber ahead. Should get a better look in a few feet." James looked at his watch, remembering the imminent blast from the vents in the last chamber and nudged the throttle again, nursing a little more speed from the machine.

10.

"Honestly, I can't believe we let Dr. Attwater do this. We should have tried to talk him out of it from the start." Bobby spoke after the control room had endured a long silence. Tension had grown as time passed.

"Nah, James was going no matter what. He is confident with his machine. He's an explorer at heart anyway, he just doesn't know it." Ian had joined Andrew, Rebecca and Bobby for an update; a giant turkey on rye sandwich in hand and bottle of Coca-Cola tucked under arm.

"He will be all right. James is a professional and has a superior vessel at his disposal." Rebecca offered, speaking more as Dr. McClintock. Andrew sat silent, hands behind his head staring at the clock. "What do you think Dr. Wright?" She smiled. Andrew blinked rapidly recognizing the focus was now on him.

"Well, uh, we can't consider him overdue for at least an hour, so why start the worrying?"

11.

The Eagle stopped as the tight tunnel gave wave to a larger chamber. The vented gases had formed a gigantic gas bubble in the upper area of the space, forcing the water to occupy only a small portion of the cave floor. The white light of the floods reflected in a spectrum of color off the shimmering, gelatinous looking wall between the water and gas.

"Unbelievable." James looked down to make sure the video systems were working properly. Green lights confirmed they were. He put the Eagle in a hover in the deep section before the trapped gas squeezed the water into what James estimated to be an eight-foot corridor. If there were obstructions, he thought, he was in trouble and would be forced to abort the dive. The Eagle moved for the shallow water, creaking under the pressure of both depth and the squeeze of the trapped gas. Expertly maneuvering to within a foot off the cave floor and several feet below the undulating perimeter of the gas, the Eagle headed for the channel. James momentarily saw through the gaseous distortion, like an iced over window, seeing small fissures in the dry cave above. "The gas must be forcing its way out through fractures. It's all backed up, but getting out a little at a time. Pressure must be tremendous. Eagle is making a little noise. Nothing extreme but it's making my heart beat a little faster." James slowed the Eagle as he noticed a small rise in the cave floor while the gas bubble stayed level, making the passage even smaller. The green outlines on the laser return display showed the floor to be rising at three degrees. "Floor is coming up slightly. I don't want my tails breaking the barrier between the gas and water. All that oxygen might be just waiting for a spark and I am sure there is a lot of static built up around me. Who knows what else is in there, methane possibly. I have lost a foot in depth, resetting proximity alarm to ten inches. The bottom in this chamber is flat and muddy. There are wavy ridges in the mud from the increased current in here. The mud that covers the rock is probably from ash or minerals carried within the vented gas, falling with gravity to the water layer, hydrating and settling on the bottom." James reduced speed slightly as he brought the Eagle two inches closer to the gray, silty cave floor.

Unseen, the tip of the starboard tail momentarily protruded through the water-gas border and then returned to the liquid environment. James lowered the lights slightly in a further effort to reduce the constant drain on the Eagle's two advanced primary batteries, the machines life force. What could only be described as wind grew louder as the Eagle progressed under the giant distended trapped gas bubble, the passage finally widening as the floor dipped away after the small peak.

"My God." James eyes widened and mouth grimaced as he unnaturally craned his neck to view the spectacle. Where a large fissure was present in the rock, a vortex had formed as the gas was allowed to escape rapidly. The vortex spout wound and danced across the cave floor, filling the Eagle with a roaring suction sound. James felt the Eagle slide a little. "There is a whirlpool. Got to move away." James pushed the throttle forward and pointed the Eagle's tail and propellers towards the vortex. Feeling resistance increase he nudged the throttle forward even farther, making the vessels two electric motors whine as they increased revolutions. Slowly, the Eagle traveled away from the whirling gases. James heard what sounded exactly like when the last of the water leaves a bathtub. As the Eagle moved away and the suction subsided, James backed off the throttles, watching revolutions per minute drop off on the respective gauges. "I have plenty of room now. Got away from that whirlpool. I sure hope there is another way out besides going by that thing again. Not looking forward to that." The Eagle continued into the darkness.

12.

After weaving through a web of tunnels and what at times felt like no more than cracks, James and the mechanical shell he wore arrived at another small chamber with what appeared to be a vertical shaft opening in the floor.

"Got a sinkhole here or something. Water temp is coming up again as I approach the opening. The low ceiling and smooth rock floor of the chamber made everything look like it's moving." Am I experiencing claustrophobia or something? James asked himself silently. James brought the Eagle over the pitch black water of the near perfectly round shaft opening. "I am over the hole. Active sonar spinning up. Single ping." The Eagle hovered momentarily before releasing the acoustic wave to the caves. The sonar ping echoed rapidly in the confined shaft. "Okay, it is definitely vertical, at least one hundred feet deep. Its wall diameter looks roughly consistent at eighteen feet. Proximity alarm to one and a half feet. Commencing descent."

The laser aperture rotated in its hull blister and pointed directly downward. Once locked on an imaginary point below, James could 'ride the beam,' knowing exactly and immediately any variance in the descent position of the submersible. Since the Eagles length, nose to tail, was ten feet, James could afford slight variations in course.

"Valves open. Taking on ballast. Slow descent selected." James reduced the candlepower of the floodlights, making the scene outside the glass go from looking like an overexposed photograph to one that had been developed properly. A pop outside the hull startled him momentarily. "Valves closed, tanks trimmed. Descent is looking good." James watched as the nondescript gray shaft wall passed by the clear nose, glancing to the graphical representation of the sub in its surroundings. "Water temp is coming up again. It's even getting a bit warm in the cabin." James tapped the small yellow digital numbers that said it was now eighty-two degrees Fahrenheit inside the conditioned atmosphere of the pilot pressure hull. "Hold on. Turning off the floodlights. Look at this."

A red glow, emanating from below, engulfed the Eagle.

"Eighty seven in here now. There is an orange/red glow from below. It's getting brighter as I descend. I have got to admit it, I'm tempted to abort right here." As if to make the choice for him, an incredible scene unfolded before James.

The Eagle breached the base of the shaft and entered a giant stalactite filled cavern. Its vast floor some ninety feet below was a lake of what could only be molten rock.

"Holy shit. Lava. I have just entered a large cavern. There is a lake of lava at the bottom." James watched as a bead of his own sweat dripped onto the cabin temperature display that now read ninety-one. So long as the temperature is bearable, I am going to try and take as many readings as possible. It's amazing, a crust forms on top of the lava as the caverns water cools it, then cracks apart and sinks; reabsorbed by the lava . . . and so on. Absolutely amazing." James turned off the floodlights, afraid they would overheat and burn out. The bright, fiery glow that filled the massive chamber made them unnecessary anyway. High on the far wall, James notices several openings. "At one time all these tunnels must have been lava tubes, when the area was more active. Water temperature is up to one hundred thirty seven degrees, I've got to make a move now or retreat." James looked at the battery level indicators. "Down to sixty percent on batts for the ol' girl. I am going to make a high speed dash across the chasm and shelter in an opening I can see at the other side." Large bubbles from the boiling water buffeted the Eagle while the snap, crackle and pop of the lava rapidly cooling and cracking filled the cabin. James looked around out of instinct. "James Attwater, you are a crazy old bastard." James' fingers moved on the small keyboard in a blur.

Five seconds later, he had programmed the computer to do a full power dash to the center of the chamber, reduce to half speed and fully stop approximately ten feet in front of where the laser thought the far wall was located. In this high temperature and mineral content water, its accuracy was fallible. James adjusted his position and tightened the stainless steel harness buckle that held his prone body fast. Holding a finger up, James hesitated for a moment and then brought it down onto the [Enter] button of the keyboard. Its click echoed through the submersible.

Despite having created the Eagle, the acceleration was stronger than James had expected, making him feel momentarily dizzy. The far stone wall now raced forward, the lava below just a blur of red, yellow, orange and black. James doubted whether the Eagle would stop in time, doubted his own calculations and data and, most of all, doubted having put his faith in the computer. He simply closed his eyes to try and dam the swelling panic. The Eagle came to an abrupt stop, her propellers reversing in a roar of bubbles past the now foggy nose cone. James slid forward in the harness, its black canvas strap digging painfully into his body, and shook his head while his glasses dangled from one ear.

"Wow." As soon as his head cleared and his glasses were again perched on his pointed nose, James scanned all instruments and then the view outside the nose cone. "I'll be a sonofabitch, it worked. Phew!" A dark tunnel was seven feet in front of the hovering Eagle, the computer keeping station in the cooler water of this vertical wall of the chamber. "Water is down to one hundred and three over here. Looks like a small ledge below shields this area from the intense heat of the boiling water. I wonder how deep I am in the Earth's crust. Who'da thought we'd need a damn geologist, sure could use a geologist. Moving on, battery power is-a-wasting. That sprint took its toll, down to fifty-five percent. I will definitely be using the five minute emergency reserve on this dive."

Normally, all dives would be planned based on ninety-five percent of battery power. For this dive, however, Bobby and James were forced to admit that, with the unknowns as they were, not considering the remaining five-percent was impossible. James began to feel the urgency of completing the penetration of the cave system and then an egress as quickly and safely as possible.

"Getting on with it." He again took control of the Eagle and guided her into this latest doorway of the underworld. James sighed, more out of stress than boredom.

13.

"Okay guys, by my calculations he is down to about sixty percent power, if not less," Bobby said and scanned the control room. Rebecca, Andrew and Ian looked up and then went back to what they had been doing: Rebecca reading Stephen King's latest nightmare, Andrew scribbling notes in a futile attempt to keep up with the pile of work he was certain was building up on his desk half a continent away, and, last but not least, Ian. Ian sipped from a small glass a potent mix of gin and tonic.

"Bloody suspense is killing me." Ian squeezed the last drops of a sliver of lime into the sweating glass. Andrew nodded concurrence but Rebecca only smiled without looking up from the bent pages of her paperback.

14.

This particular tunnel had been rather featureless until the Eagle arrived at the first of the holes. Farther ahead and on all sides, the cylindrical passageway was pitted with small, round black holes, about six inches in diameter. James slowed the boat, craning his neck from side-to-side, trying to peer into the holes as they passed by. He then looked forward. In the grayness ahead, just beyond the range of the dimmed spotlights, James saw a shape.

"I knew it. Tube worms. Hell." Slinking slowly from its tube, a segmented body and feeler encircled mouth poked blindly into the tunnel, hoping to feed on whatever had disturbed it. Several others protruded from their openings. "They look like the ones I saw near the Mid-Atlantic Ridge, but, they are albino, translucent—like a pupae. Guess cause they are freshwater. I'll have to ask Andrew and Rebecca if there *is* any such thing. Ha! They are too small to disturb the Eagle but they sure are creepy." James heard several bumps and what sounded like shoes on a waxed floor as the worms hit and dragged along the passing machine. The largest snagged for a moment on the tail, pulling from its protective tube and falling to the bottom of the tunnel. James did not see the crab-like appendage that scrambled the exposed worm to the nearest unoccupied hole. "Have passed them now and proceeding. I figure I can go another half-hour before having to turn back. All unnecessary systems are shut down. I am also switching from both batteries to just battery one. I will run it down and then have a relatively strong second battery to rely on and complete egress and surfacing. I can also kick in the strong battery two to help number one when needed." James smiled and whispered to himself, "I love this." With a sharp snap, James rotated an electrical switch from the position that read '1 & 2' to just '1'. The cabin and display lights flickered for a second and then returned to normal. James' dry, hard swallow made him reach for a stick of cinnamon gum from a small sandwich bag. It would help ease the ache in his ears as well. "Maybe I will be lucky enough to find another way outta here." He reached for the last of the orange juice as well.

15.

Andrew gently kissed Rebecca after cupping her chin in his hands. He then leaned on the stern railing, their hair flying wildly in the wind, and looked out upon the lake. Their warm breath rose in a mist and froze in a smoky cloud.

"Well, we did want air, didn't we?" he said smiling.

"Yeah, but this is ridiculous." Rebecca shivered.

Now that Bobby was alone in the control center, despite the futility, he tried to reach the Eagle on the extremely low frequency radio. He powered up the ELF and, when the yellow diode changed to green, pushed the button at the base of the microphone.

"EAGLE, this is NEST, come in, over." Static hissed back and he reached for the volume dial, lowering it. Bobby watched red lights dance back and forth as the radio hopped channels, scanning each for any possible response. "EAGLE, NEST here, come in please, over." Bobby pushed back from the panel, frustrated. He stood and posed as if about to yell, a twisted look on his face. He blinked, shook his head and took a deep breath. Sitting back down, he picked up the issue of Scuba Diver and thumbed through it for the eighth time that day.

16.

James' first thought as the chamber opened before him was, they must be icicles. From the ceiling and floor of this latest flooded cave were what appeared to be icicles, ranging in size from a few feet to at least ten. Behind and interwoven around the opaque shafts was what appeared to be a lacy material, like a giant brides veil tangled about the room. James, squinting to better see the icicles that jutted out at random yet harmonious angles, smiled and said, "Quartz." As the flood lights of the submersible arc towards the ceiling, its beam reflected back in explosions of pink, purple, white and red. "Beautiful quartz!" The fine, web-like lace formations seemed to reverberate in the disturbed water of the cave, filling the Eagle with a harmonic hum that was both soothing and painful to James' already sore ears.

James noticed some of the columns were hexagonal, others octagonal. Still other formations had so many facets that they appeared to be perfectly round.

"At some point these caves must not have been flooded. They definitely have had dripping and running water. This room and all the stalactites and stalagmites all over the place tell even this laymen that these caves have not always been entirely submerged." James reduced forward motion of the Eagle to a crawl and, smooshing his face against the glass, peered through the nose of the Eagle like the tourists on the submarine ride at Disney Land and World. "Incredible. I don't think I have ever seen this much color in one place in my life." James, tempted to turn the flood-light strength up further, more logically pulled his hand back from the respective dial to conserve power. As James reached the far end of the cave he found he would be forced to do some precision maneuvering if he was to utilize what appeared to be the exit from the camber. The quartz intersected in the lower portion of the cave in what looked like a rose bramble, thickets ready to scratch and sting. Hoping not to disturb the mineral formations that had taken millennia to form, James carefully angled the Eagle, so her port winglet dipped and her starboard rose. Gently raising the nose and then dipping it again brought James and the Eagle over and around the first of the beautiful but potentially dangerous quartz shafts. Carefully adjusting a small control on a panel to his left, James manually trimmed the Eagle by pumping small amounts of liquid metal from the aft to the fore reservoir.

"Oh, you are a beauty my love." James said, winking at the center control panel of the Eagle. He adjusted the contrast of the HUD that, at this particular moment was displaying the computer-generated, laser-fed topographical map of the surrounding area. James had also initiated a compiling program that would consolidate all of the readings he had collected this dive into a map of the underground cave system. This served both as a computer-generated trail of bread crumbs as well a means of recording the journey. James knew this task would take the computer some time so he wanted to have it ready when it came time to depart the caves. One of the main computers two central processing units was to be dedicated to the respective calculations and graphics generation.

Having left in his wake the last of the jagged quartz, James increased speed and selected forward scan on the laser.

"Relying on the laser. Active sonar would probably cause a cave-in and passive keeps picking up all the seismic anomalies down here. Just my laser and my eyes, how's that for sensors." James smiled at the two tiny slits in part of the plastic cabin liner, knowing they held the parabolic mike for the pilot voice recorder system. James peered down at the battery level. "Half power on battery one. Number two switched off-line and still holding at sixty percent. One battery alone is going to drop faster than they both did together. Got to watch that."

16.

"I am going to dim floodlights and fly on instruments so to speak for a moment, both to test the auto-nav and collision avoidance subsystems as well as to conserve juice. I know Bob is up there crapping a pickle: *Is he dimming the lights? Is he turning off unused systems? Is he, is he, is he?"* James imitated Bob's Filipino accent, and burst into a torrent of stress induced laughter. Knowing Bob would later analyze every foot of this recording, James said, "You know I love yah Bob." Squeaking off a big kiss and again laughing. James smiled, still feeling, somehow, despite his aging exterior, young at heart.

Fear built from some unknown quarter as he realized he did not want to die down here. The most serious look ever to occupy the flesh that was James' face settled in. At the moment he decided to turn back, a voice inside told him to press forward a little more. He looked forward into the darkness and realized he was tired and hungry. The adrenaline rushes had also given him a mild headache that threatened to grow.

"Twenty more feet or so and I will head back. This is just another old lava tube anyway. Feeling mortal again, James turned on the wing floodlights and set them at their lowest candlepower setting. Looking above him, caught in the periphery of the dim, forward pointing light, James saw his own reflection. There in the ceiling was his twisted face and neck peering up from the front of the Eagle. "Okay —." James stopped the Eagle. Slowly bringing

9-VONB

up the floodlights until they reached full power, illuminating the world in front of James and his machine. A grunt left James' throat.

17.

The great cavern was shaped like an amphitheater, with gently sloping walls and a natural, domed ceiling. The quartz embedded in its rock made the entire room sparkle as if a dance club waiting for the evening crowd to show. From its roof and floor, giant stalactites and stalagmites jutted into the clear, aqua colored water. The waterline, reaching about fifteen feet off the cave floor, was mirror-like, preventing James from viewing the world above its surface. Turbulent, bubbling water some ten feet in front of the still Eagle betrayed the presence of at least two waterfalls in the cavern, surrendering their mineral laden water to the cave lake.

Scurrying amongst the smooth stones and pebbles that littered the cave's bottom was a myriad of cave life. It ranged from tiny blind shrimp to an albino leech, waiting for its next victim to pass. The light from the Eagle's winglets danced about the room in divine looking beams that fired at the ceiling from the disturbed water's surface. Seemingly, the entire room was lighter than the others James had encountered and was certainly far less foreboding.

"I am going to pop the Eagle above the surface to see what we can't see. The surface is too reflective to see through from this side. "Ballasting up; trimming forward ballast tank." Triggered by a switch, the computer instructed the forward compressed air cylinder to evacuate two thirds of the water that now filled the ballast tank. Gently, the nose began to float while the tail of the Eagle remained steady in its original position. James watched as the clear nose of the Eagle broke the surface tension, the water sticking to its glass for a moment and then rushing down the sides.

The light landed in two giant circles on the cave ceiling, throwing long shadows. There off to his left and next to a large stone pillar that reached from floor to roof, two openings in the cave wall were the obvious end to an underground river. The waterfalls, one thin and veil-like, the other wider and more powerful looking, echoed a muffled roar throughout the cavern. James noticed water was dripping from the hundreds of stalactites that lined the arched ceiling, causing it to rain. After all, James thought, the word stalactite does come from the Greek for dripping, *stalaktos*. Now, where did I here that? James wondered and giggled.

"I wonder if we are directly below Champlain's lake bed right now. The pressure on this rock must be enormous." James turned the angled nose of the Eagle to starboard. "There is a small beach or what have you. Looks like a . . . yes, could be a skeleton. There is a large skeleton on the dry part, the beach. It looks like a rib cage, about the size of an elephant's. Amazing!" James suddenly forgot the pressing feeling it was time to leave, again high on the spirits of adventure. "Got good video. Dr. Wright, these will need your expert eye." James noted and confirmed two frames from the still camera had been taken. Strobes fired through the floodlights to properly illuminated the photographs. "Right, moving on. Trimming the forward tank." Water replaced the air in the forward ballast tank and the nose fell, dipping below the water again and coming level with the tail.

18.

Andrew and Ian shared a drink in the warmth of the library. Here, perhaps the most stately room on the otherwise utilitarian Explorer, countless books and antique navigation charts lined the walls. Andrew looked around during the silence that was interrupted only by Ian twirling his half-melted ice cubes against the walls of his glass. Turning his neck slightly to try and read the titles of the diversity of books, Andrew began to mumble.

"Moby Dick, The Haunting of Hill House, Jaws . . . even Tom Sawyer. Wow, nice selection. Even I could survive going to sea if I had a room like this at my disposal." James winked acknowledgment, tapping the bottom of his glass to get the last of the elixir that clung to it. "They even have books on dinosaurs."

"Yeah, any Playboy's?" Ian snorted at least five drinks ahead of Andrew.

"No Ian. In need of some shore leave are we?"

"You could always lend me that Doctor of yo-"

"Don't even go there, buddy." Andrew smiled harshly.

"Hah, I knew it! You two been doing the 'orizontal mambo 'ave we. C'mon geezer, tell us all."

"Ian, you are a character. Are all Britt's as colorful as you?"

"Only the upper crust my friend." Ian roared. "C'mon, let's have one more."

"Okay." Andrew followed Ian back to his stateroom. The bottle of Tanqueray Gin that had sat on the small oak table in the smaller lounge and reading room now resided there.

19.

James brought the Eagle through the sheet of fine bubbles that streamed up from the colorful porous rock below. As he penetrated the mist, what sounded like a glass of seltzer echoed through the cabin. Tiny bubbles raced each other up and around the Plexiglas nose cone. Noticing the control surfaces were sluggish, disturbed by the added buoyancy and air of the mass of bubbles, James passed through. On the cave floor, between two straw-like formations of minerals, James saw a break in the rock. He dipped the wing and reduced speed, pointing the nose of the now hovering sub at the opening.

"I have what may be a continuation of the tunnels and a way out. I have a feeling I am close to the bottom of the lake and may find an alternate egress route. Anything would be better than leaving the way I came. Laser is now saying that there is definitely space beyond the opening." James actually caught a momentary flicker of green light in his field of vision as part of the laser beam refracted off of minerals suspended in the cave water. "I will have to get the Eagle in a vertical position." James immediately selected the appropriate program from the computer display menu, starting the Eagle into a gentle rotation as the computer made the necessary adjustments to bring her over. These actions included everything from manipulating the wing planes to transferring ballast to one side. The hisses, pops, clicks and other sounds of a living machine surrounded James who waited for the computer to complete the maneuver. With the Eagle now standing on its port winglet tip, James made a final adjustment to align the new horizon with the cave opening. "Going to be tight. Proximity alarm to eight inches. Maneuvering r.p.m.'s only." The Eagle began to inch forward. James pressed unnaturally on his left side as his body hung in its harness. His pencil fell in front of him, rolling on the cylinder and then finally settling again. A bead of sweat rolled into James' right eye, scorching it with salt. Despite the burning, James' hands on the control stick and throttle did not flinch.

The submersibles nose entered the seven-foot by twelve foot opening. It was followed by the long, sleek body, then the thin, sharp winglets and, finally, the tail and electric motors. The propellers turned lazily, like a ceiling fan in a tropical bar. "Laser shows the tunnel to be straight for at least ten feet." Once through the opening and after resetting the proximity alarm range to two feet, James manually rolled the Eagle back to level in the now wide, roughly round tunnel. A faint glow emanated from the distance.

Daylight, James wondered? Impossible, he thought, remember the depth your at you fool. He increased speed when the Eagle was again on the natural horizon. Reaching a wye in the tunnels, he decided to take the high road, following the now brighter greenish glow. James lowered the lights in this smaller tunnel.

"I am proceeding up a smaller tunnel. The main shaft split five feet ago. I am following some strange green glow. Probably some luminescent minerals." As the glow grew brighter, James noticed that a brownish gray sludgy material coated this particular tunnel. "It's leveling. Not sure I can take her much deeper. The tunnel's also tapering." Just as James looked up after selecting reverse on the motors to begin an egress, his field of vision was flooded with bright green light. Momentarily blinding him he yelled, "Damn! Reversing!" Surrendering the Eagle to the computer, James looked through the prop wash out the nose. At first James saw a dark shadow among the bubbles and greenish water. As it grew closer and larger, James began to discern the shape.

"My God." He would later describe it as shaped like a horse's head, covered by sponges. It stared back at him through the Plexiglas. Its large yellow eyes locked on his own. As the submersible began to reverse out of the cave, James watched in horror as it lunged after him. "A snake or eel, some kind of eel!" James grabbed the throttle, automatically disengaging the autopilot, and increased reverse speed. Immediately, the right tail scraped the sludge-covered rock. A shower of debris and stone fell on the Eagle's back and a shudder traveled throughout the entire vessel.

"Damn it!" Two feet from the nose cone of the rapidly reversing Eagle and partially obscured by the torrent of bubbles and mud that the propellers kicked up was an agape, tooth filled mouth. "Shit." The Eagle suddenly emerged from the shaft and, immediately shifting to forward propulsion dove for the lower tunnel of the wye that James now wished he had taken instead. James slowed the vessel slightly, realizing his panic had nearly crashed the Eagle. *Down here*, he reminded himself, there is no one to save you. James calmly selected the aft view on the video system. A small aperture now directed the cameras peering eye down a fiber optic cable that terminated in open water at the stern. The view it transmitted sent a cold chill down James' spine. "The snake, it's, it's chasing me." James again pushed the throttle forward as he noticed a red light flashing in the center of the console. "Reactivating voice feedback system . . . I need help." The familiar and comforting female voice of the computer's voice feedback system announced, "*Collision warning. Obstacle ahead.*"

"Damn!" James put the motors into full reverse to try and stop the now flying Eagle. In the dimly illuminated darkness and approaching rapidly, he saw the dead end wall. "C'mon baby, you can do it. Stop for daddy." The Eagle decelerated, nearly stopping an inch from the solid rock. Its clear Plexiglas nose gently plinked against the wall. James waited to see the spider web cracks form, before the roar of the lake entering and death. The Eagle hovered and James kissed the cold metal. "Phew." James reversed her slowly, no longer seeing the frightening scene in the rear-looking video. Bringing the Eagle back over a vertical shaft he had flown over without noticing, James again spoke. "I found a hole to duck into for a moment. I think I lost it, the snake or eel or whatever the hell that was." James dropped the Eagle into the opening. After a few feet, the shaft yielded to another horizontal tunnel in the rock. "Found something. Looks like another passage. I am moving on." James switched the video display to forward view and watched its black & white, high-resolution image as he proceeded down the tunnel. In its center he first saw a shadow which grew to a shape which in turn became a form until, now wide-eyed, James realized he was again in trouble. For the first time on this frightening dive James screamed aloud, his nerves finally requiring a verbal explosion to keep from fraying all together. He instinctively leaned on the throttle and the Eagle jumped forward, speeding down the tunnel.

"Collision warning. Obstacle ahead."

"You bitch!" James yelled at the voice feedback speaker. Feeling as if finally defeated, as well as the realization that he had actually volunteered for this—no, correction, begged his old friend—James released the throttle after pushing it into reverse. As the reverse thrust of the propellers countered the momentum of the vessel, James realized he had one more chance.

Moving for an opening, nay, a crack, James threw the Eagle into a turn and rammed the submersible through it. The collision was relatively smooth, cushioned by the thick layer of muck that surrounded the crevasse. When what James thought could only be the sound of the tail impacting the rock, he blacked out. He awoke a few seconds later. A warm trickle of blood escaped a small gash on his forehead. He immediately looked for the main display but had trouble focusing.

"Looks like I am still here." James' voice had a resignation to it. "She is still intact." James rubbed his eyes and swiped the blood away with his sleeve. "I think I have snagged the tail, I'm lodged in here good." James pushed the throttle forward, hearing the motors whine against the resistance of the suctioning mud. With an evil sounding scrape and a damn-it-all push on the throttle, the Eagle popped through the opening and accelerated rapidly after being set free. James instantly backed off the throttle. "The rudder is sticking a bit, might be bent." He pushed with his right foot against a resistant pedal. "Right fair water plane also seems damaged." James looked out at the winglet and the slightly misaligned maneuvering surface.

20.

As the silt behind the Eagle settled the video display showed the creature poking its head through the widened opening.

"It looks like a sea horse head on the end of a long, snake-like body. The body, what I can see of it, is about three to four feet thick. It moves like a sidewinder snake. This sucker's got some set of teeth. Even with its mouth closed they protrude and are all crooked." James saw the creature focus on the submarine, which now hovered below the low ceiling of a small grotto. It then scanned the chamber, pausing on a smaller opening at the opposite end. The yellowish eyes locked on the sub and, like a cobra readying to strike, coiled its body. In a blur of both time and vision, James saw the head strike the rear of the submersible. Just as the video display went blank and the Eagle lunged forward, striking her right winglet tip against the exposed rock, James pushed full forward on the throttle. The Eagle bucked. My God, James thought, it has got its teeth sunk into me. James contorted his neck, peering back over the length of the boat. There, teeth scraping against the steel and titanium of the hull, was the creature. "Ugly bastard." Despite the thrust and noise from the nearest motor, it was not deterred from maintaining its grip. James applied full power. When he heard what could be best described as fingernails on a chalkboard, and the Eagle leapt forward, he was certain the creature had released its grip. The Eagle had won its high power tug of war with the animal.

James backed off the throttles. The rear video fiber optic cable now pointed downward from the violence of the attack. James selected the still operational forward view, noticing his shaking hands. Slowing and stopping the Eagle, he numbly stared ahead. James then looked at the battery gauge.

"Down to three percent." Blankly, James turned the electrical switch from the '1' to the '1 & 2' position. The sixty-percent full battery two and the three-percent left of number one would now take over powering the Eagle and its systems. James felt the breeze of life support cut out for a moment until the buffer dealt with the power spike of the battery change. The rejuvenated Eagle reminded James he was not yet dead. With a deep breath he pressed onwards. James weaves the Eagle in and out of a maze of formations, formations that blurred into a disorienting visual and spatial hallucination. If not for his instruments to confirm reality, James would have piloted the Eagle into the rock. He blinked rapidly to clear the latest mirage that fooled his tired eyes.

"Passing over an opening." James looked down nervously, certain the creature would strike from the black hole at any moment. He swallowed hard and then looked ahead. Squinting, he adjusted his glasses and leaned forward on the padded pilot couch. "Increasing floodlight candle power." James' stern, tortured expression went to a blank stare and then a smile cracked onto his face, spreading rapidly. He increased speed and headed for the opening that had presented itself when the Eagle rounded a corner. For a moment, James felt a panic building. An anxiety that, had there been a hatch in the boat, it would be in danger of being opened. When he relaxed again, saying aloud, "Get a hold of yourself old boy," he became certain that beyond the opening was Lake Champlain and that he had survived.

"EAGLE, come in please, this is NEST, over. EAGLE, come in, over." As the radio came to life, James began to weep. He hid his face behind his flattened hand as if someone might actually see him. "EAGLE, NEST here, come in please. Acknowledge. Over." James cleared his throat, rubbed his eyes and said to himself, embarrassed, "A grown man crying, look at you. You are lucky this is a one-man sub. Guess it's better than soiling your drawers, ha!" James cheered up. Switching the cabin microphone from the voice recorder to the radio system, James transmitted.

"NEST, EAGLE here. I am coming home." The cheers of at least ten people erupted through the Eagle's cabin speaker, distorting the sound for a moment.

Chapter 8: Snare

1.

The gears of the eighteen wheel truck whined as the driver used the engine to decelerate, guiding the rig down a steep hill and turn. Its twin chrome exhaust stacks belched black sooty smoke into the clear, crisp air of the early morning, filling Miko's nostrils with an acrid odor. Miko waved his hand in front of his face as if to fan the fumes and delivered a sharp stare at the pudgy driver.

Once the truck had squeaked to a halt between the bright white painted lines on the jet-black, freshly paved lot of the lakeside warehouse, Miko signaled the driver to come out of the cab. Clutched in his oversized fingers, the driver held a clipboard and, in a monotone voice created by miles and miles of stimulant induced driving, asked, "You Hakinen? Sign here for your cargo please."

"Open up first, lets have a look." In a hurry to get a plate of eggs, steak and hash browns in front of him, the driver rolled his eyes at this latest of delays.

"Okay, but everything on this inventory form has been accounted for. Checked it myself before leaving Boston." The driver swung one worn, leather boot onto the small foothold at the rear of the truck, lifted his weight with a grunt and unlatched the trailer door. "Knock yourself out," the driver said, waving a swollen hand, signaling Miko could get on board and inspect the shipment. The disinterested driver lit a cigarette, kicking at small oily puddles left by the snowmelt of this warmer day. Miko boarded the truck effortlessly and, clipboard in hand, began checking off item-by-item the contents of the trailer.

"Since this is several tons of equipment, we must to use the forklifts. When I am done please to pull up to the loading dock."

"Sure, no problem." The driver took a long drag on his cigarette in an attempt to camouflage the sarcasm he knew had slipped into his response. "Where'd yah learn English? You speak real good."

"*Well*, you ignoramus, *well*." The driver's glance betrayed the anger and insult he felt.

"Yeah, whatever. You want to get done up there? I'd like to get this stuff unloaded and get me some breakfast." Miko did not bother to respond.

"Miko Hakinen, you ugly bastard!" Miko turned, prepared to yell at the driver when he saw his friend Christian!

"Christian you product of inbreeding, it is about time you got here! How are you you son of a bitch?" Miko jumped from the trailer and embraced his friend. Both patted each other hard on the back as if trying to clear the windpipe of a choking victim.

"Good, good. The flight to Boston was long and the one to Burlington seemed longer, but I made it."

"And just in time. I am tired of these idiots I keep hiring. How are you with a welding torch?"

"Good enough. Why?"

"You will see. Let me get this stuff unloaded then we can go get something to eat and catch up."

2.

"I am telling you, there is something down there. I am not saying it is the damn Loch Ness monster, okay. But, whatever it is, it is big, fast and has a temper." James shivered and fell into a chair. Rebecca handed him a steaming mug of hot cocoa and wrapped a blanket around his shoulders. "Thanks love."

"I won't argue. After my little dive and those weird photos, I don't know what to think," Ian offered reinforcement.

"C'mon, are you telling me-" Andrew interposed.

"Look science boy, open your mind," Ian interrupted.

"Thank you Mr. Chelsea. I appreciate you coming to my rescue. I also understand Dr. Wright is trained to doubt. Damn it, get this blanket off of me!" James squirmed out from under the heavy blanket like a frustrated child stripping winter clothes after entering a warm room. The door to the boardroom swung open after a gentle knock. "Oh, Bobby. How is it going son?"

"Besides the fact that you have trashed that beautiful submarine of yours?" Bobby said, trying to sound funny but really to make the point that James takes too many risks.

"Don't worry, we'll get the Eagle back in shape in no time. Have you had a chance to look through much of the video?"

"Yes and it is amazing. I can't believe how tight it was in there. I am surprised you didn't turn right around. Some of the footage is cloudy and near the end it is a little under exposed since the batteries were drained and the floodlight dimmer. But I can always run it through some image enhancement software."

"Good, good to hear. Now, any of you kids have an appetite?" Without answering, Rebecca, Ian, Andrew and Bobby all turned for the door on their way to the galley and mess hall.

3.

Miko and Christian opened the large outer doors to the warehouse, allowing the chilly, moist air to enter the cavernous space. High above, hanging from exposed steel girders, trusses and I-beams, were bright lamps illuminating the concrete floor. Large heaters did their best to fight the infiltration of the winter through the relatively thin plate aluminum that made up the structures' walls. Miko pointed to a far wall that Christian noted with a nod. Two large floor-to-ceiling doors, like those found on an airplane hangar, took up much of it. Beyond them was a large wooden loading dock, and a ramp to the water's edge.

"The ramp can handle thirty tons. Obviously enough for our

purposes." Christian grunted in response, brushing his shoulder length matted blond hair back behind his ears.

"Looks like your crew has finished unloading everything and are ready to begin the work." At the opposite end of the warehouse men scurried about, some with blueprints in their hands and others with tools, but each concentrating on the large structure that was forming before them. A vertically sliding door to the truck loading dock slammed shut as the driver pulled his rig away. Several large wooden crates that had been unloaded earlier from the truck were now being attacked with crowbars and hammers. The squeak of reluctant nails being removed from the yellow pine crates echoed through the large area. Bundles of what looked like steel pipes were moved and stacked by a small yellow Hitachi forklift.

"Okay everyone! I want this assembled by six this evening. It is going to be a long day so everyone grab some breakfast now while the rest are unpacking the equipment. There are some breads, cakes and coffee in the small office near the bathrooms." Miko, realizing his lack of—what did the Americans call it: people skills—had immediately made his friend Christian overseer of this job. Having already experienced Miko's wrath several times for minor mistakes, the workers seemed instantly relieved to have the new manager.

4.

Andrew sat down in the small communication center of the Explorer, really more of a cubicle off the main hallway of the ship. He spoke into the small microphone next to a terminal on a small, stained hardwood shelf.

"Gunther? Hey pal, Andrew here." A frame-by-frame video image of Gunther Landers filled the small video conference display on the humming computer. "How's life in the tar pits?"

"Hello Andrew. Good, good. Still bringing up some interesting stuff from the subway tunnels. We are trying to re-organize here at the Page Museum to display the things we find. We will probably add on a small wing near the Dinosaur Theater entrance; make a small room and displays for the Red Line finds."

"Great, great. Hey, what is the word from Australia?"

"Well, if I tell you, you will probably pack up right now and book the next Quantas flight."

"Go ahead, I can take it." Andrew leaned closer, fascinated.

"Well, we have a fully intact plesiosaur. I have seen some preliminary drawings and photos of the site and they are spectacular. Right now a paleontologist from the University of Sydney has moved the find to proper facilities. I can fax you what I have if you want?"

"Yeah, please, go for it. Wow."

"Will do. By the way, Sue sends her best. She asks: When you will be back in LA again?" Andrew saw a brief image of Sue waving before it returned to just Gunther in the frame.

"Never, if I can help it." Andrew flashed an exaggerated smile. "Please fax me that stuff when you get a chance and, please, keep me posted if anything major happens."

"Okay Andrew. By the way, how is your little adventure going?"

"It's going. A lot to tell you when there is time."

"Okay. Take care buddy."

"You too. Talk to you soon. Bye to Sue." Andrew moved the mouse pointer to the small button that said disconnect and pressed it. Diving a hand into the inside pocket of his windbreaker, Andrew removed his small, worn leather covered phone and address book. Rubbing his sharp, two-day-old beard while taking the rubber band from around the small book, he began thumbing through the tattered tabs until he found the 'R'. "Ringoen." Andrew removed the telephone from its cradle and began dialing the long distance numbers. "Janet? Andrew. How is everything? Good, thanks. Listen, I wanted to get an update on my classes. How is everything going? Uh-huh. Okay, cool. Yeah, you can tell Molly she can have an extra week for her paper, just don't advertise it otherwise all of 'em will want more time." Andrew turned to see who was tapping him on the shoulder.

"Join me for some coffee?"

"Sure." Andrew mouthed in response to Rebecca, still listening to his assistant at the other end of the line. He held up a finger to tell her he would be a moment. She nodded, winked and turned for the hall.

5.

"Here, put this on." Christian tossed a pair of dark, tinted goggles to Miko before opening the door to the warehouse. The cascade of sparks that immediately enveloped them made him glad he had donned the protection.

"I knew I could count on you to get things moving my old friend. Impressive." Miko and Christian stood back to admire the work that had been done in but a few hours. A giant cage like structure had taken shape, made up of the shiny steel piping and other components that had been delivered that morning. The cage walls were at least twenty feet high and fifty feet long. The one end that was installed was thirty feet wide by Miko's eye. The floor or bottom of the cage, although seemingly made of smaller gauge piping, looked equally strong. One end of the cage was still being assembled on the floor at the opposite end of the warehouse, its stiles and rails positioned for welding. A system of tracks, weights and counter-weights was also being laid out on the floor before being installed on the open end of the cage. "Will that be the trap mechanism?"

"That is right Miko. Also, those thick rubber devices will keep the cage afloat with compressed air. Divers will be able to adjust its depth by flooding this small metal tank here with the lake water."

"Very nice." A sweaty worker approached the two gloating men.

"Mr. Christian, can I speak with you a moment."

"It is just Christian, that is my first name."

"Oh, Christian. Some of the men and I were wondering, well,

we heard that the reward for whatever it is you guys are up to is . . . huge. We were wondering, why it is you are . . . paying us so little?" The henchman immediately stepped back as if both men might take a swing at him. Miko's face turned bright red. Christian and Miko shared a few words in Norwegian and then simply told the man to get back to work. He did not argue. When he walked away, they reverted to their quite well spoken English.

"I think we just found our bait," Miko snarled and laughed. Christian only laughed, causing the still retreating henchman to turn nervously before continuing his meander back to the work area.

6.

The large warehouse doors slowly slid open, squeaking despite the thick layer of lithium grease that had been laid down in the metal guide tracks. When they were half-open, the brightly moonlit night poured in, carrying with it a few flakes of the snow flurries that had begun at sundown. Christian watched one land on Miko's face and instantly melt.

"If it starts to really snow, that could hinder our efforts."

"Yes Christian," Miko nodded, "but luckily the weather report says it is to be a very minor storm." The warehouse doors, now fully open, revealed the gaping interior and the giant cage the men had put together. Large wheeled dollies were placed under each of its corners in order to move it onto the lakeside dock, down the ramp and into the slushy waters of Lake Champlain. Miko stepped outside, turned and studied the creation. The largest of the steel piping had been used to make the basic cube frame of the cage, while smaller gauge pipe had been used to create a screen to keep whatever entered captive. High above and along the top frame member, several of the flotation bladders had been secured, as well as a planked platform for a small boat to tie alongside. A SCUBA tank had been welded to the pipe next to the platform so a diver or man on the surface could adjust the buoyancy of the contraption, allowing it to rise or submerge to the desired level. Christian proudly pointed out the steel wires of the trigger mechanism.

"You see those wires there?" Christian asked and Miko nodded acknowledgment. "By disturbing bait at the closed end of the cage, the spring mechanism at the open end will send that large, weighted gate crashing down, sealing the cage and preventing escape."

"Impressive." Miko patted his life-long friend on the back.

"Sir?" The senior henchman, draped in thick plaid flannel and wearing a white hard hat interrupted.

"Yes," both Christian and Miko answered in unison.

"Sirs, we are ready to get this puppy in the lake. I have instructed the men to set up a pulley system to prevent it from heading down the ramp too fast. It should do the job. Otherwise, I am putting five men on each side and one man in the small skiff to guide and secure it once in the water. Sound good?"

"Sounds good. Good job," Christian gave a thumb up while Miko only continued to survey the warehouse interior.

The resounding thump confirmed the cage had left the concrete slab of the warehouse. Its front edge and supporting wheeled dollies inched onto the wooden, piling suspended dock.

"Okay men, gently! One, two, three heave." The giant cage was carefully moved towards where the ramp began to drop off to the lake and, once there, the men paused, preparing for the task of keeping it from rolling too fast.

"Tighten up that pulley line! Okay, I want the five men on each side to move forward slightly. The lines should keep the cage from getting away from you so I want you to concentrate on keeping the damn thing in the middle of the ramp." After careful maneuvering, dug in heels and skillful manipulation of the safety lines, the team of men managed to get the cage to the water's edge. When satisfied that it had been secured properly to the dock and realigned correctly by the man in the skiff, Christian gave a thumb up and the cage was pushed into the silvery looking lake. Moonlight reflected off the disturbed water in small bursts, creating an ethereal scene in the bright night. In the distance, the forested mountains had a silky, gauze look, while the moon left a milky tail across the black lake. The cage bobbed gently in the still water as the last of its ropes were wrapped around dock cleats.

7.

"Run diagnostics on both sonobuoys please Brent. I want to make sure they are functioning properly, especially before I test the camera that Ian just reinstalled on number one." Rebecca moved about the shadows of the sonar room, checking equipment displays and making adjustments to the various instrumentation.

"Okay, Doc'." Brent sucked noisily on a tootsie roll-filled cherry Blow Pop. The headphones hung from his neck, despite not being listened to they continued to hiss and spit his music.

"Dr. McClintock . . ."

"Rebecca, for the hundredth time."

" . . . Buoy two is showing green lights. One of its batteries must be shorted 'cause power has dropped but the other two seem to be picking up the load. Buoy one has yet to respond to the diagnostic command. Are we sure Mr. Chelsea reinstalled the camera correctly?"

"We are sure," a voice came from behind. Startled, both Rebecca and Brent turned to see Ian entering the room.

"Hey Ian, how's it going?"

"Good Rebecca. How is everything here in the shack?"

"Okay. Sonobuoy one isn't responding to our computer commands. It may have been damaged by water intrusion when you *borrowed* the camera."

"So I heard your intrepid assistant saying." Ian sent a wink Brent's way. "Hey Rebecca, I wanted to show you these." Ian extended his arm that clutched a handful of black and white photos. "Bob ran these through his enhancement software for me. You have got to see some of the details it exposed." Rebecca spun her swivel chair after making a final adjustment to a small dial and reached for the photos. "Pulitzer here I come."

"Wow." Rebecca's mouth opened slightly and Brent stole a glance toward the two hovering over the photographs. "I, I can see an eye right here." Rebecca's long slender finger traced an outline.

"Yes. And look at this one. Tell me that is not a flipper."

"My God." Brent now stood, hesitated a moment and then took a step towards the now huddled Rebecca and Ian.

"You know that picture I took accidentally of the bottom of the Explorer?"

"Yeah. Yes."

"Well, take a bloody look at this." Brent now joined the huddle over Rebecca's lap where the pile of photographs sat. Ian threw one more down. "The artificial blue outline is computer added based on a dark patch." The grainy photograph clearly showed the black outline of the Explorer some hundred feet above. Between the camera and the boat, Bobby's image enhancement software had detected an area where the pixels were twenty percent darker than the surrounding outline of the ship hull. This had indicated that another object was between the boat and the camera, most likely at a range from the lens of sixty feet, putting it forty feet under the Explorer. A blue outline helped the human eye distinguish the dark patch from the surrounding area. A long, gently bent appendage seemed to jut from a wider body. From the end of this body stuck a smaller, stubbier appendage. Four trapezoidal flippers bent backwards, suggesting the object was moving at a clip. Brent made a loud slurping sound as he swallowed the melting lollipop.

"Brent. Has buoy one reported back yet?" She gave him a get back to work glance. "Ian, these are amazing. Have you shown them to the others yet?"

"Nope. Nothing from buoy one Doctor, Rebecca."

8.

From the small flying bridge of the rented cabin cruiser, Miko turned the wheel slightly and looked back to reconfirm the towed cage was directly astern. At the floating cage's sides, two runabouts were on hand should it go off course. Christian climbed the rusty ladder and informed his friend that they were approaching the sight they had chosen to set the trap Miko responded by slowing the vessel. Below, three divers on the small aft deck prepared to commence their dive. One of them removed his tank from the fighting chair and swung it around onto his back. Another cleared his regulator with a hiss and donned his mask. The other sat on a small empty metal beer keg next to two mushroom anchors, fighting to get his fins over the thick wet suit booties.

"What is it like, the lake?"

"Just ten feet down, pitch black. You can not see your hand in front of your face. Like being in a black hole. Very scary."

9.

"Sonobuoy one is reporting red lights on two circuit boards. We should still be able to get some useful information out of it still. Mr. Chelsea, you were right. The problem has nothing to do with the auto-camera. Wait a second." Brent held the headphone closer to his ear. "Sounds like several high pitch screws, probably a few outboard motors and there is a deeper one behind those. Sounds like a bigger diesel. We've got some activity on the lake tonight."

10.

One after the other, the divers rolled off the stern of the wooden boat. With a kerplunk and the sound of a bottle of soda being opened for the first time, they pierced the gentle rocking lake surface. Having released the cage from the towline, the runabouts had taken up position alongside in order to steady it. The cage's inflated rubber floatation bladders bobbed as the cage rocked and rolled. The driver of one of the runabouts watched the trail of bubbles from the submerged divers approach the cage. Miko and Christian rolled a one hundred fifty pound anchor off the stern platform and watched as hundreds of feet of inch thick anchor line unwound on its way to the bottom. When the anchor had settled and stopped taking line, Christian cut the rope and attached one of the small kegs to keep it afloat. They would deploy one more anchor line on the opposite side of the cage, and the divers would then string two guidelines from the cage to the adjacent anchors, keeping the cage in the desired position. Two trails of bubbles broke the surface, forming a line between the floating kegs and cage. Lashing one of the runabouts to the small, planked platform of the cage, its crew transferred a large cut of beef.

"You sure those anchors are heavy enough?" Miko and Christian stood on the stern platform of the cabin cruiser watching the operation.

"Yes Miko. The mushroom anchors are perfect for the muddy bottom and remember it would be very difficult to have a one fifty pound pull travel all the way down the line. The nylon anchor rope is very flexible. It is really more to keep a relatively good position."

"Good." Miko handed Christian a small Henri Winterman Cafe Creme cigar and a light from his brass replica World War One trench lighter. Christian tapped Miko to bring his attention to the now sinking cage.

"Divers have begun to submerge it. Good, right on schedule." Christian lit up his watch with a small button on its side. "What it is it you really expect to catch?" Miko quickly shifted his icy glance to Christian.

"I don't really know. But there is something in here my friend, something. And that money is too juicy to not try."

"And your police troubles?" Christian asked, looking out on the inky water.

"Well, they seem inclined to classify it as a boating accident.

They could not find, how did they say it, *evidence of foul play*. Anyway, they are still busy looking for those missing students."

11.

Rebecca leaned back in her chair, rested her hands on the back of her head and closed her eyes. Brent stared blankly at the screen of his pocket game, his fingers working frantically. It was four in the morning. The night watch, making its rounds around the ships exterior walkway, and the bridge crew, were the only ones still awake. Out of the corner of his eye, Brent saw a red light on the panel illuminate. He hit pause on the game, looked to the now asleep Dr. McClintock and saw that passive sonar of buoy one had detected something.

"Doctor . . . Rebecca." Rebecca stirred, opened one eye, and then the other.

"Yeah?"

"Passive on one has something. Recommend we go to active for a fix."

"Go for it." She stretched and yawned. "What time is it?"

"Four twelve. I'll call for some coffee. You hungry?"

"Nah. Some Java would be great though." Brent lifted the ship's intercom phone and pressed the number for the galley. After a long ring, a sleepy voice promised coffee within fifteen minutes.

"Going active. Contact is faint. Depth: one thirty. Wait, lost it."

12.

Gliding effortlessly through the cold waters and trailing a fine exhale of bubbles to adjust to the changing pressure; a dark green neck probed the darkness. At its front was a streamlined head, its long mouth and interlocked teeth pierced the water, swaying side-to-side like a snake. The creature's lighter underside helped camouflage it against the lighter upper waters when viewed from below. Its elongated body and balancing tail pulsed as the muscles of its giant flippers propelled it through the water with rhythmic thrusts. Chemicals in a small pocket above the nostrils combined and began to give off a green glow. Returns from clicks made with the air in the creature's mouth told the Elasmosaurus that something large was ahead. The light on its head grew brighter both to illuminate the immediate area as well as to alert others to danger had this particular male not been alone. When the green light began to reflect off the shiny metal of the cage, the Elasmosaur slowed and then hovered, its long neck and body becoming vertical and perpendicular to the bottom.

Slowly moving from one end to the other, the head inspected the cage, at times nibbling it for a taste or smelling the water by sucking water in and out of its mouth. Detecting the beef, it moved for the smaller side of the cage, brushing the line that secured it to the vertical anchor line and again paused. Carefully probing the opening in the screen of crisscrossing pipe with its head, its long neck entered the cage. Nibbling and shredding pieces of the tough beef, its head jerked and shook at the slab of flesh. The beef bait was attached to a small plate that, when moved, released the trigger, tasted unlike normal prey but was attractive nonetheless. Having tripped the traps pressure plate, a wire traversing the roof of the cage moved, releasing a brass pin at the opposite open end of the cage. When the pin had cleared its opening like a giant garage door, the trap door began to slide down small rails on its metal wheels. Lead weights ensured that its travel was swift and the cage closed as quickly as possible. When it crashed down and locked, the panicked Elasmosaur quickly retreated its head and neck from the cage interior and the meal it was enjoying. With a scream and a release of bubbles, the creature bolted for the depths.

13.

"Did you hear that Brent?"

"Yeah, weird."

"That first sound was metallic but that second one, it sounded like, like a child screaming underwater. Strange. Gave me the goose bumps." Rebecca looked at her arm and shivered. "Spooky."

Moving down the upper promenade, Andrew saw the floodlit stern deck and made for it. As he approached, Andrew saw James, Bobby and the Deep Eagle II on large wooden support chocks. An enveloping assortment of tools and equipment lay about on cloth sheets and in bright red chests.

"Hey Dr. Attwater, James. Hi Bob."

"Oh, Dr. Wright, how are you this morning? Up awfully early."

"Who can sleep. They have the heat on so high in my stateroom that it was giving me a headache. I think I must have a broken thermostat. What are you two doing up before sunrise."

"Bobby and I had a lot of work to do on the Eagle. I banged her up pretty good down there. It was perhaps the most incredible dive of my life. And being part of this expedition puts a spark in an old mans eye again," James winked. I owe a lot to my friend Dunham. He is hoping to solve a mystery we have pondered over many a drink and meal." Andrew came in closer and knelt down next to the cross-legged Bobby. "Pass me that three quarters socket please." Andrew looked at Bobby who pointed at the correct tool to pass to James.

"The sub has some battle wounds, huh?"

"We have the correct parts for at least temporary repairs. The Eagle should be available again for limited dives in two days should we need her." James unraveled several colored wires that protruded from the open area of the starboard winglet, exposing a small, stainless steel nut.

"Are you guys hungry. I was thinking of rustling up some breakfast." Andrews's puffy eyes and hunched stance betrayed the fact he was at least two hours shy of a good night's sleep.

"Yeah!" Bobby was enthusiastic.

"Mmm, sounds lovely." James put his wrench down and covered a small circuit board with plastic anti-static sheeting. He groaned and mumbled as he stood joints and bones creaking.

14.

At the thermocline this early morning, the water was calm and wavy. The thermal interaction zone distorted the scene below as a shape penetrated the oily surface of the layer. It was followed by two smaller shapes; all three moving at a descent speed. The female Elasmosaur and her two young paused to smell and taste the beef in the current. They immediately turned into it and followed the chum-like path; small shreds of flesh and particles suspended in the relatively still water. When the mother noticed the cage they were approaching, she grunted a stay command to her female and male calves. They immediately obeyed and floated still while their mother continued toward the strange object in the lake. She cautiously approached the bobbing, shining cage, her head carefully scanning as much detail as possible with slightly near-sided, binocular eyes. Despite the temptation of the beef morsel, she sensed danger and decided to return to her children. Her intuition was correct, as divers that had investigated the first false triggering had reset the trap. The large side of beef still held the marks of the sharp, serrated teeth of the earlier visitor. Rendezvousing with her calf's, the female Elasmosaurus signaled them to follow. She would give the cage a wide berth and return to the usual feeding ground, where many of the lake fish gathered in the dawn light.

Getting slightly ahead, the mother and male calf moved off into the darkness while the smaller female calf, overcome with the urge to eat, veered off toward the wonderful smelling meat. As with any child, the young calf swam swiftly but slightly awkward homing in on the object of its blind attention. Seeing with its sharp young eyes the tattered beef at the opposite end of the cage, she proceeded through the opening. Frantically realizing one of her children was missing, the adolescent mother immediately stopped and turned in panic. Nudging her older male calf she sped back towards the cage, her headlight beginning to glow. In response, her sons' headlight glowed yellowish and intermittent still learning control of the organ.

The young female Elasmosaur began to nibble at the white floating shreds and tugged at the flank of beef. Her eyes closed lazily as she chewed away at the tough meat. The thick, fibrous meat soothed her teething gums that bled slightly in the cold water. If it had not been for the loud crashing sound as the trap sealed in the creature, she might have actually fallen asleep. Her mother heard the crack as the trap mechanism activated. She sped to the cage, encumbered by the slower calf at her side. At first, the calf did not realize her predicament. Though startled by the noisy springs and pulleys, she continued to slowly chew the mouthful of fat and muscle. Beginning to sense a problem, she slowly swam along the bars of the cage wall, remembering an opening. After circling the entrapping structure several times, the young Elasmosaur began to panic. Though futile, she rammed herself against the openings between the pipes. Poking her neck through the openings, she lodged herself where her torso began.

The mother sped ahead of the male calf the last hundred feet and arrived again at the artificial object that held her now shrieking offspring. She pushed against the lodged baby and then gurgled sounds of reassurance. The youngster instantly calmed down. The mother cocked her head slightly, hearing something high above on the surface.

15.

"Okay, we have an indicator flag. The trap has been sprung. Divers, into the water!" Several seconds after the command was given five divers entered the water in a boil of froth and foam that dissipated into a hiss off finer bubbles. Far below, in a futile attempt to free her child, the female Elasmosaur bumped the steel cage—making the anchor line kegs bob violently at the surface. Her calf slowly swam around the small enclosure and then, tiring rapidly, floated to a rest on the cold steel bars of the cage bottom. The mother watched helplessly as the divers approached. Reluctantly, she dove into the darkness just as the divers would have seen her and her other calf in the cone of light their flashlights made. Forty feet from the cage, she paused again and considered attacking the divers. Her instinct to protect her other calf overrode the thought.

Chapter 9: Exposure

1.

The morning was especially gray and foggy, the worst Miko had yet encountered in Vermont. Though warmer, the sullen sky made for a depressing aura to the landscape, straining the otherwise good mood Miko was in after the successful capture of his quarry early that morning. Opening the door to the cargo bed of the rented black pickup, Miko reached for a pile of large, thick nylon net and began to unfurl it neatly on the ground. He watched as several cars of his men pulled up in unison on the cliff above the small gravel beach on which he was working. The sheer rock formed a gauntlet around the small, eroded shore, enclosing a small, deep-water inlet in the protective outstretched arms of the land. Miko had decided to create a holding pen for the creature. It would have to offer more room than the metal cage for his captive as well as have an area where he could have the press or guests observe from above. His idea was to string a taught steel cable one-foot above the water from cliff to cliff as well as another line across the inlet bottom. Between these two lines, the gill net he had purchased would prevent escape from the pen.

Christian practically skipped down the small twisted road that lead from the overlook to the pebbled beach below, carefully balancing a plastic Dunkin' Donuts mug in his hand.

"Miko!"

"Eh, Christian, over here. Just in time. I need help unwinding and keeping this net from tangling."

"Great. Put me to work right away. Don't even let a man enjoy a glorious morning and a strong cup of lousy American coffee?" Miko and Christian laughed, smiling from ear-to-ear. Christian took another sip from his cup and looked out over the small inlet. "Looks like a fjord back home. Should do perfectly. How are we going to secure the wires in the cliff?"

"Here, I have some deep set spikes that should do the job. Once we are set up here, let's tow the cage over and figure out how to get the bloody thing into the pen." Miko took a long deep breath of the moist air and stretched in the warm light of the now higher sun. "As soon as the animal is in the pen, we will alert the press. In the meantime, we might want to let our usual good customers know what we have for sale."

"We are going to be riiiich!" Christian practically leapt, spilling half the steaming oily black coffee from the mug he still carried.

2.

"Chip Johnson, please. Chris Dunham here. Sir Christopher Dunham looked out over Hong Kong's Victoria Harbor and the Kowloon peninsula, waiting to be connected. A new twin towered suspension spanned the water to the man-made island of the new Chek Lap Kok airport. A large container ship carefully navigated the tight deep harbor on its way to a berth. Once there, giant cranes would unload her cargo and then again fill her hold for the trans-Pacific voyage to Oakland, California. He hovered over the speakerphone that sat perched in the middle of a large, dark hardwood table. Broken only by a finely carved wooden screen depicting a forest and gentle swan covered lake, the red satin wall coverings glistened in the sun beams that angled through the window. Two large woodcarvings of Chinese lion-dragons with paws rested on a globe flanked the sliding door to the office. Half sitting on the table, Sir Dunham dangled one leg, brushing it gently against the thick, Bordeaux colored carpet. Chris drew closer to the star shaped speakerphone.

"Chris, how are you?" The muffled voice came through, hearing the delay and echo of the international call.

"Good, and you, Chip?" Half a world away in Bethesda, Maryland, Chip Johnson paged through the latest proposal for an Explorer Channel *Signature Series* documentary. He had already decided to kill the idea of a documentary that would follow an AIDS patient, from contraction of HIV, to the slow agonizing death of AIDS. He felt it too graphic and depressing for the popular Sunday night slot.

"I'm okay. In desperate need of a decent writer. The last good documentary we put together was for last years *Shark Month*."

"I personally enjoyed that one last week on life aboard an American aircraft carrier. Also, that two hour series on that Chicago firehouse and the arson investigation was fascinating."

"Okay buddy, I am sure you did not call to discuss our lineup."

"No, I did not. I have gotten word that a creature has been caught on Lake Champlain and that it will be put on the market at the highest bid."

"What?" Chip Johnson sat upright in his chair, dropping the thick, heavy teleplay he had been perusing. The ash of a cigarette that jutted from his pursed lips fell to the green leather center cover of his desk.

"That's right. I don't think it is public knowledge yet but it is obviously not your team that has got it."

"No, certainly not. I would hope I would be the first to know. Who got it? Are they circulating a price yet?"

"A Norwegian and some other mercenaries. There is a price and it's astronomical. The only nibble I know of so far is from a Tokyo aquarium."

"Well, I would at least pay to get Ian Chelsea in close with a camera, maybe even from underwater. Is it . . . what we expected? You know, what we thought might-"

"Yes it is. I just wanted to tell you that, under my proposal, I am forced to give this character the reward. Now, it is my intention to pay him the full bonus only for the live capture and the main reward to your organization. After all, it was your people that got the first evidence and photographs of this bloody thing."

"Chris, you crazy bastard, you were right! I can't believe it."

"See, I am not senile yet."

"It goes to show, throw money at something and even history can be made."

"So true. Talk to you soon, old friend."

Sir Christopher Dunham strolled to the window and looked out through the droplets of water that had formed on the tinted glass. Far below, the new convention center was bustling with its latest gathering. A junk maneuvered in and out of the morass of other boats on its way to sell goods at one of the many dockside markets. Sir Dunham's secretary knocked, entered and announced, "Dr. Mobius to see you sir." Chris sighed, again confronted by a routine life. The excitement and vindication of the find had buoyed his soul. He sighed and wished he could join the team on the lake and, most of all, that he was young again.

3.

"Okay, Christian, take the cattle prod and get ready to move it along." Miko's mercenaries had brought the cage and its captive to the shallow waters near the inlet. After hours spent enclosing the inlet with the net, they felt it was now ready to contain the animal. The Zodiac's, their outboard motors idling and spitting cooling water back into the lake, were lashed alongside to steady the cage. At the middle of the enclosing net and between two large blue flotation buoys, Christian had rigged a sag in the net. This would allow access to the inlet from the lake beyond and could be closed to again restrict it.

When divers had secured the area between the cage and the netting, the order was given to raise the cage trap door. Christian jumped from the rented wooden cabin cruiser that was now also alongside. He landed with a clang onto a steel bar that formed part of the trap's roof. Being slippery and unsteady, one foot slipped between the metal tubing and into the freezing lake water. He recovered to see the brown and yellow spots of the bulbous back that floated motionless but a foot away. Despite the commotion of the raising of the trap door and the lowering of the net on the opposite side, the creature was absolutely still. Christian stared at the textured body to confirm life and finally recognized the shallow breaths of the mammal.

Activating the shiny prod he clutched in his large, weathered hand, Christian waited for a small green light to tell him it was fully charged. When it did, he drove the sharp prod tip into the soft flesh of the creature's back. It released its charge with a blinding flash and an arc of electricity.

4.

"Ladies and gentlemen, one at a time, please." Miko held up a palm to the enveloping army of press camera operators and journalists. Each stretched unnaturally to get their microphones an inch closer to the mouths of Miko and, at his side, Christian. For the first time in a long time, Miko smiled.

Squinting in the glare of blinding video lights and reflector panels, Miko looked down to the small, makeshift table and then to the dew on the grass at his feet. Finally the babble of tongues quieted and one question emerged. He found it hard to understand Americans but, for some reason, women's English was clearer to him. Her voice seemed the calmest, as if she had waited for the others to finish their nonsensical chorus before uttering a word.

"Madame?" Miko acknowledged, still not seeing her. She pushed to the outer periphery of the seemingly single creature—made up of individual human components in mob mentality.

"Have you found a Plesiosaur?" His eyes met her cold blue stare and Miko smiled before responding.

"Yes." The crowd of reporters mumbled in unison.

"And what do you plan to do with it?"

"Well, the Japanese have offered a deal to acquire it for one of their aquariums—." With that, the crowd erupted into a roar.

5.

Rebecca and Andrew did not have a chance to respond to the hurried knock at the door before it flew open. Ian looked surprised to find them locked in an embrace, their lips but inches from the others.

"Wow. Sorry. Lovebird's, huh? Who would have known." Ian looked to the thin commercial grade carpet that covered the steel floor and turned slightly red.

"No need to blush Mr. Chelsea," Rebecca smiled, putting him at ease.

"Yeah Ian, what's up?"

"You have got to see this. Johnson and Dunham are holding a press conference. It will be on CNN in two minutes. Come to the board room to watch." Ian did not wait for an answer but spun and made for the wardroom and its television, practically running down the echoing hallway.

"Shall we?" Rebecca teased.

"I guess so, as long as you promise to meet me right here again afterwards."

"We'll see." She smiled, shot a glance at Andrew and stood.

Andrew and Rebecca entered the wardroom and were met by the stares of most of the ship crew and the Explorer Channel personnel. Even Captain Thomas was watching on the bridge. Refusing to leave it, he had instead ordered a portable black & white television be brought up to him. One of the deck hands stood, allowing Andrew to sit in the last of the chairs while another rose to accommodate Rebecca. He saw Ian leaning against the far wall.

The familiar theme of CNN Breaking News silenced the many conversations that had melded into a single murmur.

"Good afternoon, this is Natalie McAllen in Atlanta with this breaking news. On the heels of the announcement that a Plesiosaur had been captured in Lake Champlain, we now have announcements being made by the British tycoon who's challenge and reward gave impetus to this quest—Sir Christopher Dunham. We will also hear from Chip Johnson of the Explorer Channel. He has organized the largest expedition to the lake and will soon announce the airdate for the upcoming special documentary being produced by that network. Gentleman, thank you for joining us." The television screen was now split into three windows—one with Natalie McAllen in Atlanta, the next with Chip Johnson in Bethesda, Maryland, and the third with Sir Christopher Dunham in Hong Kong. A small brown and beige graphic of a Plesiosaur adorned the background screen.

"Thanks Natalie," Chip Johnson answered.

"Good evening Natalie." Chris held his earpiece, waiting for the slight delay in the satellite signal to come through. He brushed aside his gray hair and adjusted the wire tucked behind his ear.

"Let's start with you Mr. Johnson. Can you please tell us the progress your team has made in Vermont?"

"Sure. Well, as you know we put together a team of the top minds in the fields of paleontology and oceanography. We also have the finest videographer in the world. We were also lucky enough to have one of the worlds foremost nautical engineers join us. So far, this team has conducted extensive sonar surveys of the lake, completed several investigative dives and has some interesting photographic evidence of what lurks below the lake's surface. We are currently negotiating with this, Mr. Hakinen to allow our scientists to get the chance for a first hand examination of the creature."

"To remind our viewers, Miko Hakinen is a Norwegian that has actually captured the Plesiosaur," the news anchorwoman interjected.

"That's right Natalie," Chris Dunham endorsed, "and we are

trying to prevent him from selling this creature. I would like to announce that it is my intention to out bid those that are currently interested in acquiring the beastie, specifically the Japanese. I will facilitate its release once the scientists are satisfied they have sufficient information. I am also arranging to get counsel from the British Natural History Museum. As you know they have the worlds finest collection of marine specimens in the world. Their knowledge of ancient biology will be a great asset."

"Natalie," Bethesda broke in, "I am also working with the government here in the Wash to get some kind of protection for this discovery. We are afraid that this find will cause others to hunt the creature and we want to make sure there is no way such a resource could be exported from the States of New York or Vermont, or, worse, from the country." The screen flashed from close-ups of each man, full shots of the Atlanta news studio back to the three participants together.

"Where you going headed?" Andrew asked Rebecca as she stood, his eyes still glued to the television screen.

"Someone's got to tell James and Bob to come watch. They are on the stern aren't they?"

"Yeah, I think so. They're working on the Eagle."

"I'll be back." Remembering neither had shown up for lunch, Rebecca grabbed several finger sandwiches from a small serving tray on the table. She pushed aside a bottle of Diet Cola and lemonade to get a napkin to wrap them in.

"M'Kay."

6.

"Okay Bob, next one." Bobby moved the circuit-testing probe from one transistor on the circuit board to the next.

"Amps look good. The short must be in the passive sonar control circuit's."

"Yeah, I think you're right. Remove that access panel and let's check those as well."

"Will do."

"Hey grease monkeys!" Rebecca carefully maneuvered under a blue tarpaulin, around a red toolbox surrounded by a pile of its former contents as well as over the power cord of a small, portable Zenith television that was precariously perched on an upside down blue plastic milk carton. She placed the sandwiches that were wrapped in the cloth next to the television and top of the white stenciled words on the carton: *Property of Burlington Dairy. Removal Punishable by Law.* "Hoodlums." She smiled widely and looked at the television. "Look, I am a big fan of M*A*S*H also, but don't you guys ever watch the news?" She reached down and, with three clicks of a silver dial, changed the channel to thirteen. James reached for one of the salmon salad finger sandwiches.

"Mmm, thanks love." James smiled widely. Bobby continued the task at hand, barley acknowledging Rebecca's presence.

"Excuse my assistants manners Rebecca. He tends to get overly absorbed in his work."

"Oh, I am sorry. Hello, Dr. McClintock." Bobby wiped his hands on his jeans but decided not to offer his dirty hand for a shake.

"Hey Bob. How's the Eagle?" Bobby shot a criticizing glance at James.

"Fine, fine. Some minor electrical system problems but nothing we can't fix. Oh, sandwiches. Thank you." Bobby reached for one, tuna salad on wheat.

"Your welcome. Hey, wait . . . shhh." Rebecca pointed at the minuscule black and white screen. The three huddled around the glow of the crooked television.

"We are now joined by the Governor of Vermont, the Honorable Howard Dean. Governor, can you hear me."

"Yes Natalie, go ahead." The governor sat in a large chair on the porch of his log home in the Austrian Alp-like Green Mountains of Vermont. Dressed casually in a thick flannel shirt and jeans, he sat back in his rocking chair and crossed his legs.

"Sir, as you know, there have been announcements that an attempt is being made to remove the Plesiosaur from the lake and, more importantly from the state and country. Can you comment on that please."

"Well, I can confidently say that is not going to happen anytime soon. A court order has been issued temporarily denying an export permit. Until a permanent decision can be reached, both the Vermont Department of Fish and Wildlife as well as the Humane Society of the United States will conduct examinations of the penned creature. As a MD myself, I think it foolish for us to think we know how to care for such a unique specimen. We are also attempting to get the EPA to list the creature as endangered under the Endangered Species Act. This would give us much more legal leverage. But, as you know, any of our great American bureaucracies takes time to react so we are making sure temporary provisions are sufficient to offer the creature the protection and care it deserves. I have ordered the Burlington and State Police to guard the pen area twenty-four hours a day. As I have said before, if it was up to me, this thing would be free right now. But, since the laws don't address dinosaurs, this Norwegian might as well have a giant lake trout right now. And there is nothing that says we can take a fisherman's trout away." The governor smiled both to add humor to his last sentence as well as to signal Natalie McAllen in Atlanta that he was done for now.

"This is unbelievable." Rebecca looked to Bob and James who huddled closer to a small orange glowing kerosene heater to take the chill from their limbs. The changing lights of the television strobed shadows against their faces and the cluttered aft deck and wounded submarine.

7.

A ring of at least ten various sized shiny, brass keys jingled and jangled at the side of the running, slightly overweight police officer. From his black belt hung a baton, flashlight and holstered nine-millimeter. A large sheriff's star adorned his lapel under various sharpshooter awards.

"Where Johnny?"

"Ovah heah, sheriff." The two officers slowed to a stroll as they passed beneath the last leafless oak and maple trees, sliding on the moist peat-like ground cover. "Ovah heah, by this bush next to the big flagstone." They paused and stood over the browning and thinning bush. "See the footprints heah?" The Vermont trooper pulled the bush to the side, breaking a few outer branches with a crackling sound. "And look heah. You can see someone's been a chippin' away heah at the rock around this fractcha." The sheriff removed his hat and sunglasses, placed them on the gray, craggy rock and reached an arm in. "Sir, looks like a dog has been coming round as well a couple times; lotsa prints yah know."

When the arm retreated from the enlarged entrance to the earth, the trooper released the bush from his leaning body. The sheriff's hand held a small black fanny pack. Removing his cowhide gloves to regain dexterity, he unzipped the small front brass zipper and found a Velcro closed fabric billfold. Opening it with the rasp of the tearing Velcro, he flipped through the collection of credit cards and identification that were held in a clear plastic fan.

"Drivers license for Mary Gerardy. Get some caver's in here and tape off the area."

8.

Ian watched as the overloaded Boston Whaler attempted to come alongside the Explorer. A man stood, rocking the usually steady craft and reached down for equipment at his feet. He swung a camera onto his shoulder and a bright lamp came on and shone in the misty air in a cone-shaped beam. A second man stood in the small outboard powered boat, holding a microphone and wearing a fine suit. His carefully jelled hair was incredibly still despite the wispy breeze. The seventeen-foot boat was low in the water and pitched and yawed as the two foolish men tried in vain to maintain their footing. When the reporter, yelling, "Can you comment on your expedition! We want to come aboard," began to stumble, Ian straightened from the leaning position on the second level's railing. The cameraman removed his right eye from the soft foamy rubber eyepiece and looked at his flailing colleague. When the reporter finally fell overboard into the frigid, black lake water and knocked the cameraman to the teak plank seat, Ian began to laugh heartily. His usually pale complexion reddened as his face clenched and contorted in laughter. The reporter floated, still holding his microphone, to the surface.

"Just like those bloody stooges, ha. Ah, what the hell . . . MAN OVERBOARD!" Ian yelled. A passing Explorer deckhand froze, grabbed a floatation ring from a nearby freshly painted bulkhead and made for the cry in the night.

9.

The giant hunter green sport utility vehicle plowed through the hoards of reporters, camera operators and light and sound technicians that had massed along the compound's perimeter fence and entrance gate. Andrew looked out the tinted window at the squeaking hands that tried in vain to slow the vehicle or get a window lowered for a hurried question or photograph. One enterprising young person, tape recorder in hand, jumped up on the large passenger step that ran underneath and along the two side doors. He tapped on the one way glass with the corner of the small plastic recorder. Ian sat in the front of the trucks cavernous interior, listening to the driver honk the horn and swears at those that blocked his way. The crowd reluctantly moved after nudging with the large front bumper of the truck, which inched towards the chain link fence.

"People, kindly allow the vehicle to pass! There will be no statements so give it up," a man from beyond the now opening gate yelled. He had climbed several feet up the fence to help him get the attention of the mob, a tactic that readily failed.

"CTN, man, all the networks are here." Rebecca counted off the satellite dishes and trucks as the SUV moved slowly past them. "Anyone see Peter Jennings anywhere?" Rebecca winked and smiled. The wavy, distorted reflection of the diamond shaped links of the open gate passed along the door window. Despite the now louder yelps from the reporters and the wide-open gate, none dared cross the line onto the property. When the truck had entered, the gate was closed again on the small track imbedded in the brown clay road. It latched shut with a click before a worker replaced a stout looking brass padlock on its mechanism.

Rebecca looked back to see a beat up school bus arriving at the small field outside the fence. Its doors opened and disgorged a sign toting mass of people that made for the fence and confluence of media. Soon lights and cameras were instead aimed at the new arrivals, abandoning the chained perimeter and the truck that had now driven towards the shore of the lake.

10.

Andrew immediately recognized the tall, shoulder length blonde hair and stout build of Miko Hakinen from the recent interviews on television. Miko stood, arms crossed his smaller, stoic friend at his side slowly sipping beer from a brown glass bottle. The vehicle slowed on the gravel road as the lakeshore drew closer.

Rebecca saw a small pebble beach that occupied the convergence of the two sheer cliffs. They radiated from the shore before opening and falling to the vast lake.

Ian examined the string of orange buoys that stretched from one end of the cove to the other. The lake was still. A wisp of vapor hung over it where the cold waters met the warmer air. Except for the occasional disturbance of the silvery surface, the lake might as well have been a mirror. It reflected the deep blue sky of the clear day and the intermittent passing of long, willowy stratocumulus clouds. The gravel road crunched and popped beneath the oversized tires of the truck as they finally came to a stop before the two fidgeting Scandinavians. All four doors of the vehicle opened, disgorging the gang into the sunny morning. Ian made for and opened the back gate of the vehicle, unloading his SCUBA and film equipment.

Rebecca stretched her arms to the sky and let out a groan.

Andrew immediately made for Miko and Christian, arms extended for a hand shake, eager to see breathing what he studied in bone.

"Hi there. Last time I saw you were in town. The bar wasn't it? Dr. Wright. I'm Dr. Andrew Wright." Andrew offered his hand to Miko first.

"Yes, I remember. Good to see you. Welcome." Miko's voice was monotone. Despite hating the over used American custom, Christian also shook Andrew's hand. He said nothing.

"Well, looks like you beat us to the prize. So, where is this beauty of yours?" Andrew already started for where the water lapped the shore and a small, temporary floating dock had been installed. "Thanks for having us." Miko smiled to Christian, knowing they had been paid handsomely to allow the Explorer Channel's people to examine and film the creature.

11.

After a short wade from the stony shore, Ian entered the dark green water wearing only a wet suit, fins, snorkel and mask. He clutched his watertight video camera that he used for filming dives down to a depth of thirty feet. Beyond that depth, more specialized equipment with a better water seal would be called upon. A temporary aluminum structure had been erected on the shore to provide shelter to the personnel responsible for monitoring the creature. A narrow, Styrofoam filled dock floated in segments for about thirty feet from the shoreline. Flanking the encampment and the shiny, moist black stones and pebbles of the beach, the two cliffs stabbed into the lake. Between them, small white floats set every three feet supported an orange nylon line.

A rifle-armed guard patrolled the outer perimeter of the enclosure in a small red Avon inflatable runabout. The boats 7.5 horsepower Mariner outboard vibrated on its transom mount, slowly pushing it through the calm-as-a-mill-pond lake. High above the make shift pen, on a grassy knoll at the top of the cliff, were several state troopers and reporters.

Penetrating the icy water, Ian immediately felt pain from the parts of his flesh that were exposed to the outer environment. They would soon numb in the cold and the pain would turn to a dull throb, easily ignored in the greater excitement of the moment. Despite the almost complete darkness of the water, Ian immediately felt a presence near him. He could not yet see anything and heard even less. Only the gently lapping water at the lake's shore echoed in the distance.

Ian began to feel as though he were not alone. He felt a wash of water brush up against the exposed skin of his cheeks and turned to see a blurred passing of brown, green and yellow. As the form passed, it left a wake of cold, rippling water. Ian disengaged the safety on the video cameras trigger and confirmed that the batteries were properly charged. When the green light at the side of the camera verified that he was ready to shoot, he pressed pause and then the record button before lifting the camera to his eye. Floating motionless on the surface, gently pulling breaths through the narrow snorkel air pipe, Ian waited for the creature to reappear. He lifted the lens of his mask above the surface for a moment and, several feet away, saw the small humped back of the baby Plesiosaur as it meandered towards Ian. Peering through the reticule of the camera, he waited for the shadows to clear and reveal the form in the darkness. When it finally became clear, Ian could barely hold the camera, wanting instead to peer upon the creature with his own God given eyes. He pressed the trigger of the camera, disengaging pause and starting the recording to the magnetic tape that was held inside its watertight compartment.

For a moment, Ian forgot to breathe. When the shock of the spectacle subsided and his body resumed its autonomic duties, he inhaled a mouthful of cold lake water. Choking for a moment, Ian then cleared the snorkel tube with a mighty exhale, appearing to those on the pebble beach some fifteen feet away that a whale had breached and was clearing its lungs. There, but three feet in front of Ian, was the head and long neck of the juvenile Plesiosaur. After placing the rubber reticule of the camera against the glass of his mask, Ian zoomed in gently on the detail of the face before him. The large, black glossy eye reminded Ian of the moist, sad eyes of a cow and was far from the lifeless, doll-like black eye of a shark. A lacy material lined the head and jaw of the creature, looking like seaweed swaying gently in the current. Ian thought it looked similar to the lobes of a Tasseled Wobbegong he had filmed in the western Pacific. The dark green almost scaly looking skin would camouflage the creature when viewed from the surface and the lighter underside, when viewed from below.

The Great White shark, *Carcharadon carcharias*, had evolved a similar disguise for predation on pinniped's, that tend to mass near dark, kelp covered seashores. The long neck snaked gracefully back and forth, seeming to help the creature hold its hovering position in front of Ian. He thought the child looked tired and lonely before again concentrating on the task at hand. Slowly, beginning to swim around the side of the creature, Ian hoped to completely circle it with the camera running. This would give an uninterrupted panorama of the marvel. He moved slowly and carefully, trying not to spook his subject into leaving its hover. Moving along the side and down the neck, Ian reached out to feel the extremely soft hide of the animal, feeling as if he were stroking velvet. The creature reacted by craning its neck and head back towards Ian and followed him with a cautious eye. Ian reached the bulky torso of the Plesiosaur, zooming out to allow the larger form to fit in the camera's viewfinder.

Ian brushed against the left, forward flipper, scraping him with what felt like sandpaper. The calf reacted by pointing the flipper downwards. Ian panned the camera, pausing on the small bones of the large flipper that were outlined in the tight hide that covered them.

"Fingers." Ian mumbled, releasing a barrage of bubbles and causing the creature to twitch. It quieted immediately, seemingly calmed by Ian's presence or perhaps just thankful to have another living creature within sight. Ian continued his orbit, zooming the camera in for details he wanted to emphasize, and then out again to give the viewer the complete picture. Swimming over the creature's rump, Ian was gently nudged by the restrained strength of a stub tail. He noticed that it tapered at its end, most likely to act as a paddle, assisting in great bursts of speed. Perhaps it instead acted as a rudder, allowing rapid changes in direction or depth as it pursued its quarry or both. Leave the theorizing to the scientists, Ian reminded himself and again concentrated on his job. What started as a humming sound soon became a raspy, breathing. My God, it's, it is purring, Ian realized. The long neck slowly swung around to the side he now swam along. When the head again turned to Ian, its piercing gaze transfixed him. Ian was certain he could see both intelligence and emotion behind that black eye but decided to keep that sentiment to himself. He turned off the camera and allowed it to float free at his side on its tether.

Gently, almost tickling, he stroked the creatures hide. Ian felt goose bumps erupt and a loud series of clicks exited the bulbous protrusion of the creature's skull. It gently snaked its neck along Ian's wet suit, like a cat might rub its owner's leg after a long day of anticipating their arrival.

Chapter 10: Action and Politics

1.

Andrew watched as the golden Jack Daniel's sour mash whiskey clung to the side of the glass, leaving an oily looking residue that slowly cascaded down the sides.

"Tell me when mate." Ian tapped the bottle against the edge of the glass.

"Keep it coming Ian." Andrew watched as the glass was filled to the top. Just as the liquid reached the rim and was about to overflow, Andrew said, "That'll do it." Ian poured himself a large glass as well and, clinking his ring against the crystal, took a large gulp.

"I'm going to do it mate, it has to be done."

"Look my friend, they have the cops and their own security. Anyway, PETA are probably planning a raid as we speak. You know them they don't mess around. You know how passionate us yanks can be." Ian smiled for a moment and then returned to the earnest look that covered his face.

"By the time the bloody politicians work all this out, the poor thing will be dead. I'm telling you Andy, this thing thinks and feels. Don't ask me how I know that but I sensed it—felt it." Andrew leaned back in the reclining chair and scanned the wardroom. A knock at the already open door brought them both from the depths of their thoughts. One of the Explorers deckhand's, Robert from Wisconsin as he came to be known, stuck his head in and simply muttered, "CNN," before again disappearing into the hallway. Andrew and Ian looked at each other.

"Did you hear something?" Both laughed as Andrew rose from his chair with an exaggerated groan and turned on the twenty seven-inch television that had sat dormant on a stained wood stand.

"—again, the latest development in the Lake Champlain discovery comes today from Quebec. As a party with territorial waters in Lake Champlain, Quebec believes that the fisherman should have the right to do with his catch as he pleases. Ottawa, the Canadian capital, immediately released a counter statement saying that Quebec does not speak for Canada and, any official stance that Canada will take with regards to the welfare and disposition of the Plesiosaur will come from Ottawa and not Quebec."

"God damn politics. Bloody hell!" Ian pounded the table, now more animated by the alcohol in his blood.

"Look Ian, I agree with your motivation for trying to do this, but, I'm afraid of the consequences, both to you and the animal."

"Yeah, yeah. Blah, blah, blah." Andrew thought Ian was now well on his way to being drunk and decided to quit while he was ahead.

"All right. If I cannot talk you out of it, maybe I can help?"

"Just keep this between us, I will take care of the rest."

"You got it." Andrew conceded, too tired to argue.

"Cheers geezer."

2.

Chuck McClure, narrator for the documentary that continued to be filmed around the goings on of the scientific expedition, leaned against the railing of the promenade deck of the Explorer. In the background were the densely wooded rolling hills of Vermont, the city lights of Burlington and the calm black lake.

"Get a light reading." Todd said as the last fill light came on, directing his crew and camera team into position for the scene. "Okay, everyone ready? Chuck?"

"Yeah—." Chuck made one final adjustment to the position of his foot on the steel rail and the forced casual stance he held. "Yeah, ready. All set." The last of the tripod mounted lights came on, illuminating the scene.

"Okay, quiet folks. Take it Chuck. Annnd action."

"It's July 1883, Sheriff Nathan H. Mooney looked out at Lake Champlain and saw a gigantic water serpent about fifty yards away. The creature, which rose about five feet out of the water, was twenty-five feet in length and had what eyewitnesses called: round white spots inside it's mouth. The dozens of sightings that comprised the monster flap that followed Mooney's sighting would predate the public Loch Ness controversy by fifty years. Lake Champlain has been called America's Loch Ness. Her monster is nicknamed, Champ, and has been sighted over two hundred forty times. The one hundred and nine-mile-long Lake Champlain is also similar to Loch Ness in that both are deep, freshwater lakes that were created some ten thousand years ago. Both bodies of water also support enough fish to feed a small group of predators."

Ian Chelsea exited a hatch onto the teak planks of the promenade. Despite the nudges of several of the film crew, he walked between the camera lens and the narrator that was reading his lines from a black TelePrompTer.

"Cut! Damn it! Cut! C'mon buddy." Ian continued to stroll towards the stern of the Explorer and his cabin.

3.

Ian shook the last of the alcohol effects from his brain and splashed the frigid lake water on his face. Sitting on the small floating platform at the Explorers side, he dangled his wet suit and booty clad feet into the lake. Stowing a small paddle, a divers knife, his fins, snorkel and mask into a small, six foot black Boston Whaler inflatable, he removed a small two horsepower Johnson outboard motor from the small teak transom. Gently resting it on the wood planks of the platform, he would not be needing it tonight. He looked to the wispy cloud filled sky and confirmed the moon would not illuminate his deeds this dark night. Even the usually abundant stars that twinkled in the crisp and clear New England air seemed to have taken a respite this evening.

"Perfect," Ian mumbled to the water that lapped against the wooden dock. He carefully lay the silver SCUBA tank on the planks of the floating platform. When he left the Explorer's small compressor room, Ian did not realize he had grabbed a partially empty tank from the shallow tub of water. He removed a small tin from a yellow mesh bag, opened it and began to smear his face with the oily black muck that would blend him into the night. When done, he carefully rolled the air tank into the small inflatable and, using the oars to balance himself like a flying Walenda, boarded the dinghy. Ian looked at the compass on the small dive computer at the end of his regulators' air hose. He needed to head south for about one mile and then east towards the faint lights in the distance. Recognizing them as the floodlights the Vermont State Police had erected on the lake side cliff over the holding pen, Ian dipped the first and then the second of the oars into the black, frigid lake water. The sound of his polypropylene suit rubbing against the reinforced rubber dinghy made a comical sound that normally would have demanded a laugh from him. But, tonight, Ian did not feel like laughing.

4.

"About one-third of the sightings are of a creature with a *long sinuous neck* and a body with one or more humps. Some describe this long sinuous neck as giraffe-like; others, snake-like," Chuck held his arm in an S-shape. "They tend to be fifteen to thirty feet long, and dark in color. The rest of the eyewitness sightings are of a creature with multiple humps, but with no visible head. The theories as to what type of animal Champ may be are identical to those suggested for the Loch Ness Monster. Opinions have ranged from schools of sturgeon or walleye, to zoogledon's, a snake-like primitive whale. As with Loch Ness, some photographs and motion picture footage of Champ exists, but, most of it, though tantalizing, is inconclusive. A Sandra Mansi of Connecticut took the most significant photograph on July 5, 1977. Mansi took a photo of what she thought was a *dinosaur*, whose neck and head were some six feet out of the water. Scientists, who concluded that it was original and not manipulated in any way, have examined the Mansi photograph. The photograph appeared in the New York Times and Time magazine in June and July, 1981."

"Okay, cut! Beautiful. Chuck you're a one-take-wonder. Pleasure workin' with yah.."

"Thanks Todd. Anyone got a smoke?"

"Okay! Get McClintock. Where is she? Can somebody please get me a grinder—roast beef—I am starved? Oh, with American cheese and some potato chips . . . and an ice tea."

Rebecca was surrounded by reporters that had met her on the Explorers floating dock when she returned by launch from a stroll in town. Despite the cold air, bright floodlights attracted every tiny insect within two miles. A whirlpool of bugs swarmed around the bulbs, occasionally colliding with them, only to fall to the lake after being singed by the hot glass. She finished answering the young journalists' query before succumbing to the tugs and pulls from the film crew staff that had run down the long plank way from the ship's deck.

"Even though Champlain is one fifteenth the size of Lake Ontario, it was in fact created in the same ice age—some ten thousand years ago—that created the other North American Great Lakes. So, I guess the proposal to have it join its sisters and earn the right to be counted among the Great Lakes isn't ridiculous. If you ask me, the proposition put forward by the senator from Vermont is motivated more by the prospect of federal marine research funds that the designation, if signed by the President, would make available." Rebecca turned and ascended the ramp, ignoring the frantic follow up questions that chased her. She looked up to see Andrew skipping down the plank toward her.

"Hey Reb', seen Ian?"

"No, haven't. Don't go down there. They're in a frenzy." Andrew heard his name called in an attention getting manner and mistakenly looked up to make eye contact with the shouting reporter. It was too late.

"DR. WRIGHT ANY COMMENT ON THE CREATURE?" The man screamed above the crowd of his competing colleagues. "DO YOU FIND IT HARD TO BELIEVE?" Andrew looked at Rebecca, rolled his eyes as she patted him on his back before resuming her climb. With shoulders bent and hands in pocket, Andrew stumbled forward, as if a condemned man making his way to the gallows. Rebecca laughed and paused a few feet up in order to hear Andrews's response. By the posture he had taken, one foot on the walkways railing, another on his hip, she knew it would be one of his now familiar mini-speeches.

"In New Zealand," Andrew paused to make sure he had their attention, "over two dozen different kinds of shellfish fossils and fifteen previously unknown species of algae have been found under the seabed off Antarctica."

"This discovery indicates the Ross Sea off Antarctica was six to seven degrees warmer about 1.2 million to 1.8 million years ago." Rebecca interjected, shifting the lights and microphone booms to her momentarily.

"My point is that we really know very little and are discovering new species daily. I think this find, a live plesiosaur, takes us by surprise because it is not an ancient algae, seaweed or mollusks, but a large air breather. A legend come true if you will." Andrew's tone had fallen back into its familiar teaching voice.

5.

This will be just like the time you freed all the sharks from that Chinese long line, Ian thought. Rowing quietly, he lifted the oars from the water, carried them through their arc with the pitter-patter of water droplets on the still surface, and turned them to present the thin side of the blade to the lake before they slipped back in. Ian pumped another strong stroke on the oars. He looked over his shoulder to insure the small inflatable dinghy was still on course and hunched his back even further to present a minimal silhouette.

The night had come cold and quiet. He could almost hear the mumbled, far off conversations of the patrolling officers over the pen. Ian gave a quick check of the SCUBA tank by opening the valve and pushing the regulator membrane. The hiss of air confirmed it was clear and ready for use. Drawing stealthily closer to the pen, Ian confirmed with a compass that he was indeed approaching the correct cluster of shore lights. When he could see the orange marker buoys of the pens entrance and the gold stars on the cowboy hats of the Vermont Troopers high on the cliff, he placed the clear rubber snorkel in his mouth, lowered his mask to his face from his forehead and rolled silently into the lake. He pulled his knife from its ankle sheath and swam alongside the dinghy. Occasionally he would pop his mask above the water, always getting closer to the marker buoys. An outline on the cliff pointed at him. Another wielded what appeared to be a rifle. When a light came on and was trained in his general direction, Ian reached into the raft for the air cylinder. He quietly lowered it into the water, donned it and exchanged his snorkel for the mouthpiece of his regulator hose. An amplified voice broke the silence warning that use of deadly force against trespassers had been authorized. Just as he prepared to dive, he heard the first bullet spinning through the air, whiz by his ear and then splash into the lake some twenty feet away.

"Shit." Before diving below the surface to save his life, Ian caught a glimpse of a scene that seemed to play in slow motion, like someone had pressed the frame-by-frame button on the VCR of life. Amongst the shadows, thirty feet from the marker buoys, he saw a long stout neck and powerful head jutting out of the water. It peered across the pens net barrier to where its caged progeny meandered at the surface. Ian watched as the creature turned to him, and then again returned to watching its weakened child. After what sounded like a horse snorting in the canter, its long neck gracefully slid below the water without a sound or disturbance of the surface. When the next bullet penetrated the dinghy Ian towed along, collapsing one of its compartments with a whoosh of air, Ian jackknifed his body and submerged.

6.

James ran his finger along the backbones of the Explorers video collection:

"Back to the Future Part II, Jaws, African Queen, Raiders of the Lost Ark. What do you feel like seeing, Rebecca?" James' voice was raspy.

"What else is there?" Rebecca shifted in her chair, tucking one leg under the other.

"Halloween, Bladerunner, Lawrence of Arabia . . . hey, how about this one: The Longest Day? It's even the colored version." James grew giddy like a child trying to convince a parent that this was the tape to take home from the local Blockbuster. He slid out the two tape boxed set.

"M'kay. I doubt I can stay up for two tapes though."

"Feel free to dose kiddo, so long as you keep me company. How 'bout some popcorn from the galley?"

"Sounds great." Rebecca again shuffled her weight in the soft chair, settling in like a cat before a nap. Andrew appeared in the doorway.

"Whatcha two up to? Anything good on?"

"About to watch a movie. Come on in."

"And I was getting us some popcorn."

"Have either of you seen Ian?" Rebecca grunted no and James headed for the intercom phone to the galley, his attention on the image of warm, buttery popcorn. Andrew shrugged his shoulders and eyed a very large, deep, comfortable looking lazy chair and Ottoman stool.

"I'm warning you Andrew," Rebecca raised her eyebrows with concern, "that chair can put you to sleep in five minutes flat. I was wide awake one minute, sat down, and next thing I knew it was the middle of the night and I had drool running down my cheek." Andrew laughed.

"Don't sweat it, I'll be okay." Andrew fell into the lush chair, instantly feeling at ease.

"Don't say I didn't warn yah."

"What's on?"

"James wants to watch the Longest Day."

"Oh, a great one."

"Yeah. He'll be back with that popcorn from the galley; shouldn't be a moment." Andrew felt his eyes grow heavy but widened them and looked to Rebecca to confirm she did not see him getting drowsy. Andrew reached for the remote to keep his mind busy. "Hell, this chair is more comfortable than the bed in my cabin." Andrew surfed through the channels provided by the marine satellite dish mounted high above other instrumentation on the Explorers flying bridge mast. He paused on CNN when the red and yellow Breaking News graphic filled the screen.

"Here we go again. Doesn't the press ever sleep?"

"Ladies and gentlemen, we interrupt Moneyline to bring you this press conference live. Edward Banes, Director of Greenpeace's Clean Lakes campaign is speaking at Logan airport in Boston. Let's join them now." The image changed from the studio in Atlanta to a hectic surrounding of a passenger attempting to disembark a United Airlines flight from Dulles in Virginia.

"Look people, one question at a time. Judy."

"Thanks Ed. What does a creature have to do with your Clean Lakes campaign?"

"I believe this discovery proves we have neglected the awesome responsibility we have to all life on earth. To think this thing has been living down there for thousands of years and could easily have been killed by some boater dumping waste oil or bilge mess over board, or, worse, dragging a net. What it has to do with our *Clean Lakes Campaign* is that we intend to propose the designation of Lake Champlain as a National Park, and that all boat traffic upon it be limited in order to protect this wonderful find. We also support immediate listing of the Plesiosaur as endangered and application of all rights, privileges and funding that this designation under the Endangered Species Act allows. Good evening to you all, I need a shower." They cut back to the studio.

"That was Edward Banes, Director of the *Clean Lakes* campaign for Greenpeace. We will now replay the governors conference held earlier today before returning to our regularly scheduled program."

The governor stood behind a wood podium with the Seal of the State of Vermont in polished bronze. Behind him as he scanned the crowd, waiting for the last person to stop talking before speaking, was the lake. It glistened in the clear, sunny day. For the first time, its waters looked a deep, dark blue, instead of the usual dark green or yellowish brown. He had chosen the site high above the cliff for its superior vantagepoint. The wind was stiff and cold, pooling blood in everyone's cheeks. When governor Dean heard only the sniffles and coughs of the crowd, he began to speak, slowly at first.

Andrew was now deeply asleep in the chair; shadows fell on his face from the glowing television screen. Rebecca propped her tired head up with one hand while James sent a piece of popped corn airborne, arcing it into his waiting mouth.

"Good afternoon," the governor shuffled his stance, "and it is a glorious afternoon here on the shores of Lake Champlain—one of Americas Great Lakes—and I mean that in both senses. We all know why we're here so I will get right to it. "I stand before you with irrevocable proof that a piece of the Lost World still breathes air today. Citizens of Vermont, these glorious United States of

America, and to the entire world, I give you a creature thought extinct for millions of years. I give you a baby plesiosaur." The governor stretched an arm out and pointed down towards the pen and the trapped creature below. The press and distinguished guests did not see the two divers, Miko and Christian, that held the weakened baby at the surface for the gawking crowd. Rebecca noticed as the news camera zoomed in on the plesiosaur that its skin had grayed since she had last seen it.

7.

Ian secured the still floating dinghy to the marker buoy anchor line. He did his best to breathe shallow and release his bubbles as slowly as possible, minimizing the white foamy bubble trail all divers leave behind. Wish I had one of those yank SEAL team rebreathers; zero bubbles those, Ian thought, surveying the mesh net that extended from the silvery surface to the smooth gray pebble bottom. He positioned himself between the two large orange marker buoys and found where the net could be lowered on a series of rings threaded on a steel wire. He scanned the black water for other divers. He was certain they would have been alerted and deployed by now.

When he looked back across the mesh he saw a slowly moving form. It rose and fell and at times rolled slightly on its side as if disoriented. Adrenaline surged as Ian remembered why he had come here this night. Swimming for the opening in the net, he untied the small ropes that secured it.

When the net-flap began to lower, he saw the large round eye of the small plesiosaur. The frills of its head gently floated alongside. The neck and the creature looked gaunt to Ian, thinner than last time they had met.

Jesus H. Christ. Another bloody day and it might have died, Ian thought, quickening his attempt to fully lower the ten-foot wide flap. He swam side-to-side in order to evenly lower the guide rings, but continued to keep a wary eye on the surrounding waters. *Maybe they didn't see me after all, maybe they were just shooting at shadows?* Ian decided he had to assume he had been spotted.

When the flap had finally been fished down its guide wires, Ian crossed from the lake, over the net and into the pen. He made for the now hovering animal. It looked at him with its dark eye and blinked, almost signaling that it understood what Ian was doing. Swimming alongside the creature, Ian gently wrapped his arms around its solid neck. With a ginger tug, he started it swimming for the opening in the encircling net.

Ian felt it muster strength and start to move through the water. Its neck snaked back and forth as it gained speed while side flippers flapped at the water in long, slow gliding motions. Ian watched as, like an oar, the front flippers pushed down and back to propel the animal forward, retreating with minimal profile to reduce drag until they again pushed downwards. At times the rear flippers would trail along horizontally, acting as fair water planes to aid in diving.

They passed through the opening and the net and shooters finally began to fall behind. The slight increase in speed of the creature seemed to confirm the freedom of the deep lake waters had been reached. As the animal accelerated, Ian slid down the neck slightly until reaching its base at the wider beginning of the torso. He felt the creature begin to surface for a breath, probably before a deep dive, he felt a burning in his leg.

When Ian looked back in horror at the sudden pain, he saw the glint of a blade and the mad eyes of his attacker. Ian responded with a kick that at first missed and then met the divers jaw with the crunch of breaking teeth, knocking the regulator from his mouth and mask from his face. The diver dropped his knife and bolted for the surface, the usual panicked response that only training and experience can overcome. Ian grabbed where the blade had sunk deep into the flesh of his leg and, watching a trail of his blood enter water through the tear in his wet suit. The cold should slow the bleeding, he hoped. I pray the knife did not hit the artery.

When the creature breached the surface for its breath, Ian stayed below and therefore did not here the deafening report of the high power rifle. He did notice the creature wince and begin a sluggish dive. When Ian realized it was not only his own blood that filled the surrounding water, he searched for its source. The wound was on the upper right side, midway down the neck. It squirted blood in the rhythm of the creatures beating heart.

"Daaamn!" Ian screamed underwater, loosing a torrent of bubbles and spitting his regulator from his mouth. Replacing it, he made his way up the neck towards the wound as the creature dove. Upon reaching it he applied pressure to slow the bleeding. The creature's neck twitched and it let out its own cry. For a moment, the plesiosaur's neck slowly came around—looked at Ian with pain, fear and blind trust—then again resumed its attempted dive, as if all salvation lay somewhere below.

Ian felt the need to surface. As the pressure of depth increased, his own air seemed to thin and he worried that a violent attack from an adult animal could kill him. He decided to maintain pressure on the wound for a few minutes more and not look at his air and depth gauges; one hand on its neck, the other on the wound. Ian's legs floated freely behind him, naturally angled at the degree they were descending into the blackness.

8.

"Is that gunfire?"

"Dr. McClintock, you are watching a war movie." James laughed. Andrew stirred from his slumber in the Easy Chair.

"No, really, in the distance, coming form outside." James paused the tape when he saw the concern on Rebecca's face.

"You're right." James and Rebecca looked at each other, agreeing silently to investigate. It took James longer to get up from his seat these days. By the time he had, Andrew was fully awake.

"What's going on?"

"I hear gunfire. It's too late to be hunters isn't it?"

"Did Ian ever come in while I was sleeping?"

"No, why?" Andrew rose and rubbed the sleep from his eyes.

"How long was I out of it?"

"About twenty minutes. Why, what's up?" Both Rebecca and James paused in the doorway and turned to look at the groggy Andrew.

"Well, I am worried he might have done something . . . stupid."

3

Chapter 11: Consequences

1.

James, Rebecca and Andrew all exited the starboard entryway and entered the cold, star filled night. There was another clap that echoed between the hills until absorbed by the dense woods.

"That's definitely gunfire," James edged through the others to get to the railing that lined the promenade of the Explorer.

"Why didn't you tell us sooner Andrew? We could have done something." Rebecca looked disappointed.

"I didn't think he was serious. Anyway, I thought he was too drunk and barely would have made it to his bunk, let alone try to free the damn plesiosaur."

"Look kids, first things first. Let's determine whether or not Ian is aboard before we go assuming he is being shot at. He could be curled up drunk as a skunk somewhere—the engine room, a gear locker—after all, it could just be hunters." James felt very tired.

"James, I looked everywhere before I passed out in that cursed chair." Andrew crossed his arm. Rebecca and James looked at each other and nodded.

"Okay. Andrew, keep searching the Explorer. Rebecca, get to the sonar shack with that strange assistant of yours . . ."

"Brent."

"Brent. I'm going to wake Bobby and get the Eagle in the water. If Ian is out on the lake, I can get to him faster and quieter than any of the Zodiac's." Andrew and Rebecca immediately began their respective tasks. As they turned and left in opposite directions, James mumbled, "I am getting too old for this," before heading for the stern of the Explorer and the Eagle. He wished he was in his bunk watching Baywatch on the small cabin television and smoking one of the cigars he had brought on board. "Darn kids."

2.

Ian increased pressure on the neck wound. He noticed the blood flow slow and the interval between beats of the animal's heart lengthens. His own wound continued to bleed, although luckily not at the volume one would expect had an artery been severed. He looked up and saw the wake of two high-speed boats, probably belonging to the Police, cutting the surface in a continuos vee-shaped wake.

The high pitched whine of their propellers seemed to disturb the creature who's back Ian clung to. Estimating, he thought there was some eighty feet before he would be forced to let go and begin a slow ascent with the appropriate decompression stops. Ian still did not check his tank gauge.

The creature continued its dive, occasionally releasing a fine stream of bubbles as it adjusted to the increasing depth and pressure of its own mass.

3.

"How long by the checklist Bob?" James leaned against the long white cylindrical hull of the Eagle.

"Thirty-five minutes, maybe forty. But we haven't even completed repairs and batteries aren't fully charged."

"You have ten minutes."

"You're crazy, boss." Bobby immediately got to work, summoning three of the Explorers deckhand's, that had stood around watching, to assist. James knew Bobby could not refuse a challenge.

4.

Ian felt the animal slow its descent, eventually coming to a stop. The creature floated for a moment and then began to heave, seeming to choke or cough. Ian saw a trail of blood exit the small mouth, with its young, fresh white teeth breaking the thick gums. Internal bleeding, perhaps pneumonia, he thought. The creature floated still and suddenly Ian realized how dark, silent and heavy the surrounding lake was.

He moved underneath the animal, running his fingers along the lighter shaded underbelly and its softer hide. Gently urging the plesiosaur towards the surface, Ian knew it's only hope for survival lay there, in the very hands that had harmed it in the first place. Human hands. At first it grunted under water and refused to move but then began to slowly ascend. Since Ian saw no movement of the fins, he concluded it must have a type of swim bladder, an oil filled organ that adjusted the buoyancy of many fish. He then concluded he was not qualified to make that conclusion. He was just glad it had stopped diving and was now making for the surface, albeit at a snail's pace.

Ian noticed it was becoming harder to inhale and that the bubbles he exhaled were far smaller. Running out of air, he thought. Years and years of carefully planned dives. He knew the only time diving became dangerous was when rules were broken and he had broken every one on this dive.

5.

From the stern of the Explorer, Bobby watched a helicopter in the distance. The large searchlight it carried began to sweep the water side-to-side as it approached the area where the creature had been held. The rhythmic pulse of its blades echoed erratically between the broken shoreline, sending sound waves in every direction. He shook his head and entered the trailer that sheltered the computers, electrical boards and sensors that made up the Eagle control center.

"This is going to get bad before it gets a whole lot worse." Bobby sat in his swivel chair, donned his headset and microphone and turned on the master power feeds that drew electricity from the Explorers generators and batteries through a heavy gauge yellow wire. Underneath the floorboards of the trailer were also batteries for a few minutes of emergency power should the mother ships' systems fail. "EAGLE, this is NEST, radio check. Come in please."

"Loud and clear NEST, let's get to it."

"Roger, commence that shortened checklist I gave you, I will have the computer do the rest from here." A small serial cable ran from a junction box on the trailer to a small connector on the Eagles underside.

The submersible sat on its chocks while deckhand's continued to make her ready for hoisting and launching. James had been secured in the Eagle in record time and Bobby confirmed its seals as good. James could be seen through the clear nose furiously running the checklist and still in his civilian clothes. "No time for those," he had barked. "Anyway, temperatures should be okay; don't plan to dive too deep yah know." When James took that tone, Bobby had learned not to argue and instead threw the special body suit into a ruffled pile on a toolbox.

"I have run the checklist. Ready for launch. Good job Bobby, twelve minutes."

"Roger EAGLE. CRANE, NEST here, commence hoisting and prepare for launch."

"Uh, EAGLE, SHACK here. Good luck."

"CRANE 'ere. Okay." The Eagle was lifted from its chocks, swung over expertly and released to the black hole.

"EAGLE away."

6.

Ian struggled to breathe. The weight of the animal had grown geometrically as oxygen to his own muscles diminished. The creature was no longer helping him get to the surface but, instead, was floating immobilized. Ian continued his slow ascent, knowing he should have paused ten feet below for three minutes to properly decompress. As he rose towards the surface, he took slow shallow breaths, holding them longer than was safe.

7.

"Okay, I have a contact on passive sonar. Port engine is acting up. Revolutions keep spiking and then dropping off. Strange, hope the motor isn't burning out. They're damn expensive."

"Roger EAGLE. Recommend you reduce rpm's on port engine or cut completely."

"Negative NEST, I need the additional thrust. I need to get to contact as quickly as possible. If it's not Ian, I will need to search for him immediately." Despite James' decision, he watched as revolutions per minute peaked again and then dropped rapidly to zero on the small illuminated dial. "NEST, looks like I have lost port engine anyway. Counter acting with right rudder. Contact now may be two individual contacts, one larger. Computer is chewing on the data. About three hundred yards now."

"EAGLE, I have you at eighty feet, fifteen knots heading zero nine five degrees."

"Concur, NEST."

"EAGLE and NEST, SHACK here," Rebecca took a moment to giggle, feeling instead like saying *Apollo. Houston here.* "I am going to go active on sonobuoy one to get a fix."

"Go ahead, SHACK." Rebecca nodded to Brent who pushed a green illuminated switch on the wall panel. Immediately a series of acoustic waves left the bulbous transducer of the hydrophone that floated some one hundred feet below the surface. She planned to retrieve this one in three days with Ian and was glad to get the extra work out of it. The one on the bottom, number two, would release from its anchor automatically. A bladder would then inflate, slowly bringing it to the surface. This equipment had been removed on buoy one to make room for the photographic pallet.

"Okay. EAGLE, I have you at eighty-three feet, sixteen knots heading zero eight five. Your contact is at seventy-nine feet and rising, bearing zero eight zero. Range approximately one hundred ninety yards. I'd say we have two contacts. One larger, one much smaller. Could be Ian and the beast. Thermocline solid at one hundred ninety two feet."

"Roger SHACK, thanks. Making my way towards contact. Batteries at around forty percent. I'll save the lamps for approach. Speed steady at fifteen knots, starboard engine only."

8.

Ian heard the deafening sonar wave. The creature twitched, disturbed by the high frequency pulse. Its neck drooped, unable to keep level with the body.

Thank God. They are looking for us, Ian thought and closed his eyes for a moment. The glimmer of hope pushed away the dark feeling that had settled in. He realized the euphoria he was beginning to feel was due to oxygen starvation. He drew another stale, shallow breath from the nearly empty tank on his back. His throat was raw from the dry air.

9.

"My God. I see them." The winglet-mounted floodlights came to full power, illuminating the area where his instruments said the sonar contact was. James shuffled forward on the body board that held him prone in the Eagles tight interior, looking through the Plexiglas nose window at Ian and the creature floating nearly lifeless and beginning to descend.

James tightened his grip on the two control sticks of the Eagle and cursed at how much maneuverability was lost when the port engine had failed. He brought the Eagle in close to Ian and the creature that floated above him. A pool of blood had collected around the two, orbiting in small droplets. "I am moving in now." James steered the Eagle underneath the two and slowly began to ascend. He craned his neck to see the two floating above him.

Voice feedback announced: "*Passive sonar contact. Designate contact three.*"

James looked down for a moment at the screen and mumbled, "Another contact. I think we are being watched." Ian began to move his legs slowly. "Come on kiddo, you can make it. Uncle James is hear to save your ass."

The Eagle slowly leveled and ascended, her dive planes and trim tanks expertly controlled by the computer and software that interpreted James' inputs. Doing his best to bring the Eagle directly under the abdomen of the Plesiosaur, James allowed its large, slender flippers to hang behind and in front of the submersibles winglets. He hoped this would present minimal disturbance to the machines navigational surfaces. The Eagle contacted the creature and shuddered.

Once underneath, the added weight immediately stopped the Eagles ascent. James increased buoyancy in the fore and aft tanks by adding pressurized air to each, returning the appropriate amount of water to the lake. He realized he would be unable to use the remaining propeller to maneuver, as the risk to the animal was too grave.

Ian watched as the Eagle rose beneath him and the animal. The halo around the submarines' floodlights confirmed he was suffering the ill effects of breathing too much carbon dioxide. What little air that remained in his air cylinder was bad, laden with chemicals that, in the right concentrations, were toxic to the body. Despite knowing this, Ian continued to draw what little oxygen he could from the mix.

Once the creature had settled onto the submarine, Ian made

his way along the Eagles spine. Wrapping his arms around her cylindrical shape, he shimmied his way towards the clear nose cone and the cabin light that filtered through the gloom. He looked over his shoulder to see the still bleeding wound on the creature's neck. A look back and along the Eagle and Ian saw his own leg continued to spurt blood into the lake, coagulating immediately into a spongy substance in the icy waters of Champlain.

Ian reached where the steel gave way to the clear Plexiglas. He felt as if he were dreaming, reaching his gloved hand over the nose cone.

James startled when the hand appeared. The Eagle groaned and thumped as the creature's body rose slightly and then bumped again with the rising vessel. James kept the ascent slow and constant to avoid additional risk to Ian and the Plesiosaur. Ian's face now appeared in the nose cone.

"NEST, SHACK. EAGLE here. I have them." James smiled to Ian and gave a thumb up. Ian lay his head on the glass while the creature's neck now floated by, bumping him. The animal's glassy eye opened slightly and James stared at it, transfixed until it again closed.

Ian, now on the verge of unconsciousness, mustered the last of his strength to reach for his air gauge. He pulled it up towards him and opened his eyes confirming what he already knew. Ian tapped the gauge against the nose cone, capturing James' attention from the various lights and switches he fiddled with on the control panel inside. When James saw the needle in the red zone and almost on zero his eyes grew wide.

"Jesus." James looked to Ian who winked before closing his eyes. "JESUS!"

Ian heard James' scream through the steel hull and felt its vibrations, drawing him momentarily back to the moment. James immediately commenced emergency ascent procedures, making sure to prevent the computer software subroutine that utilized the propellers to aid the ascent from running.

"Depth: seventy-two feet. Ian is out of time. Beginning emergency ascent procedure."

"Understood EAGLE." James initiated the sequence, freeing the computer to carry out the one hundred twelve tasks that made it up. The hisses of air, clicks of machinery and trickle of fluids confirmed they had started. The Eagle assumed a nose up position of several degrees before several small compartments blew open alongside the submarine's body. James adjusted the up angle of the nose slightly, bringing it down a few degrees so as not to risk loosing the precious cargo in a steep, rapid climb.

James watched the computer display confirm that the several large yellow air bladders along the Eagle had deployed and were inflating. These bladders would nearly double the buoyancy of the vessel. Ian decided to worry less about the threat of the Bends to himself, than that of asphyxiation.

He remembered to disengage the strobe on the submersible spine that would automatically come on, fearing it might startle the animal. The bright light, had it not been shut off, would aid rescuers in locating the Eagle on the surface in an emergency.

"Damn, the added weight is slowing us." James grumbled to the controls. He watched as Ian's face turned a sickly blue color and the creatures' limp neck dangled alongside, pushed down by the momentum. A single tear rolled down James' cheek as he watched the depth click off.

10.

Rebecca reached the teak door. She was out of breath, having run the Explorers stairs and corridors to get here from the sonar shack. She grabbed the handle and burst in. Turning on the lights of the warm berth, Rebecca made for the bed and its sleeping occupant.

"Captain! Captain Thomas!" She shook the comfortably sleeping Captain. "We need to move the Explorer right now!"

"What? What are you doing in here?" The Captain was quick to wake.

"Sir, the Eagle is surfacing with Ian and the creature—they are both hurt—and it's surfacing about a mile from here!"

"Dr. Attwater's boat? What's it even doing in the water?" The Captain threw back his blanket and, wearing only his red striped pajamas, made for the rack next to his reading chair that held his pressed uniform.

"Sir, pleeeease."

"All right, all right." Before getting in uniform, he reached for the intercom on his stateroom wall. "Yeah. Raise anchor and prepare to get under way. I know, I know," he looked at Rebecca and then at the small speaker, "Just do it. Tell the watch I am coming to the bridge." Rebecca smiled and thanked him before moving for the hallway. "Don't go anywhere missy. You come to the bridge with me. You do have exact coordinates don't you? It is night last time I checked, or maybe this is all a dream and I am still asleep in my bed." The Captain gave a sarcastic smirk and then motioned his head towards the open doorway. Rebecca made for the door. The Captain yawned and followed.

11.

Andrew stood on the promenade railing, raising his body some two more feet. Peering down on the aft deck, he heard the rumble of the Explorer's two Cummins diesel engines starting and taking over from a Fairbanks-Morse diesel generator that powered the ship when at rest. He felt the vibration in the deck plates increase in frequency.

Scanning left to right he saw the trailer that contained the Eagles control center, the large cradle and chocks that supported the submarine when it was aboard, the yellow crane that hoisted it overboard and the large open work area with now frantically scrambling crew men. Bobby leaned against the trailer. Andrew then noticed a boil of foam astern and then another as the propellers were engaged and began to churn the water.

The increasing breeze and the moving shore lights confirmed to Andrew the Explorer was now under way, making way.

"Finally," he mumbled to himself and considered making for

the bridge. Andrew felt like a third wheel, out of place on the voyage. He did not have the technical skills pertinent to the situation. After all, he belonged in the desert, removing layers of ancient worlds, not afloat on some lake.

Andrew sighed and decided to stay for a moment, wondering where Rebecca could be. He felt like having her near. Dressed only in a cardigan, he shivered in the cold night. His two day beard betrayed gray that had settled in the last year or so, confirming the passing of his youth. Andrew hugged himself and sighed a cloud of fog.

Rebecca stood back in the shadows, away from the green light that emanated from the main instruments of the Explorer bridge. A radarscope, sonar, global positioning system, compass and multitude of other equipment lined an angled panel underneath the large main windows of the bridge.

Captain Thomas stood behind the left shoulder of the crewman that worked the large, spoked steering wheel. A jungle of curly radio wires hung from their ceiling mounted units.

"Sir, we have reached the position entered in the GPS."

"Okay. Full stop on engines. Do we have a fix on the submersible?" Captain Thomas peered through the angled bridge windows and the misty night.

"Aye sir. Surfacing at two eight five—fifty yards—two points off the starboard bow. Depth currently eighteen feet and rising."

"Thank you mister. All right, I want all deck lights on. Get men on the spotlights and crane. I want divers and the support boats to assemble at the fantail in three minutes. Let's do it!" The bridge crew broke down the Captain's broad order into the many details and individual orders that had to be given. The bridge erupted in a hash of tongues.

"Eagle at ten feet and rising, sir." Rebecca stepped forward to better see the hooded sonar display. "Five, four, three, two, one."

12.

Captain Thomas sighed and, looking tired, made for a door. He grabbed a pair of binoculars from the thin neck of a freckle-faced yeoman.

"Captain off the bridge." A deeper voice than seemed appropriate for the young red head informed.

Thomas exited the port doorway, flooding the warm bridge with the cold air of the still dark early morning. With his own steel blue eyes and before raising the large binoculars to his face, he scanned the blackness.

"See them?" Rebecca had joined him on the flying bridge. He lowered the binoculars slightly to express his annoyance at the interruption and then continued to reconnoiter. Rebecca watched as a crewman on the bow removed a canvas cover from one of the large deck spotlights and turned it on, training it on the lake water. Two Zodiac inflatable runabouts came alongside the port bow of the Explorer and idled, awaiting surfacing of the Eagle and its occupants. Their outboards vibrated in neutral and billowed small puffs of blue smoke into the clear night.

13.

James watched as the gloomy liquid world outside lightened slightly. Despite the dark night above, he could still see the dark brownish-black lake was becoming a lighter soupy-brown. Knowing the surface was near and, wanting to avoid a violent breach, he slowed the ascent further by beginning deflation of the floatation bladders. An eruption of foam and bubbles above and around him told James the creature was now on the surface. He selected station keeping on the master control panel. As the Eagle neared the surface, and in order to maintains neutral buoyancy, the computer immediately ejected the floatation bladders. The Eagle, and the animal that floated on it, was some five feet below the lake surface.

Chapter 12: Passing

1.

"No, I don't see 'em yet. Wait. Got 'em." The captain bent down to speak into a small pipe that tapered wide like the speaker from an old phonograph.

"Breach! Breach! Surface contact at three ten degrees. Range approximately twenty yards," a voice called from the bridge.

"Get the Zodiacs in there." Captain Thomas' voice was raspy with sleep but calm nonetheless. With that order, Rebecca turned her gaze to one of the men in an inflatable. He stood in its bow, a taught line stretched from a metal ring at its tip. When it reached his arm, it was wrapped several times around the wrist. The constriction turned his blood starved hand a ghostly white.

Raising a portable radio to his ear, static filled orders from the bridge pointed the runabout in the correct direction. Immediately the outboard went from a rhythmic rumble to a higher pitched whine as its propeller engaged and cut the water. The second inflatable was close behind.

Rebecca stepped up on a small, heavily painted support spar and leaned half her body over the open flying bridges' barrier to better see the surfacing animal.

"Here, use these." The Captain handed Rebecca the binoculars and then made for the bridge interior to continue directing the operation.

2.

Alfred choked up on the line as his Zodiac jumped a small wave and left the water slightly. Jack Meder and a cinematographer occupied the other boat running parallel at speed. Ahead in the mist he could see a form. The form then became a shape and then the shape began to take on color as the Zodiac sped forward through the night. Al squinted to pierce the darkness and then signaled the driver to slow down with the shaking of his hand. He saw a brown and green spotted hump protruding from the water and a white froth that formed around it. A few feet away he saw the long, snake-like neck and then the stub head.

"Whoa." He raised the radio that hung from a lanyard. "Zodiac Two, time to get wet." Alfred turned to see the two divers roll off the side of the other Zodiac that had taken up position besides the floating animal. Looking down through the murk, he knew the large Eagle floated unseen some seven feet below.

3.

James heard and saw two divers enter the lake. He powered the submersible's one good engine and engaged its propellers by manipulating a transmission lever. Wanting to be ready to assist if the creature began to sink, James looked at the drooping head and concluded the creature was unconscious. The divers made for Ian first. Swimming rapidly, they got to him and maneuvering him into a lifeguard carry, returned him to their boat. Once they had Ian's limp body aboard, it immediately sped off for the Explorer.

James sighed, relieved to know Ian was finally getting medical attention. He shifted his focus to the divers that trailed a small net between them. They made for the creature. James rubbed the Plexiglas nose with the heel of his hand, clearing the fog his breath created as he pressed his face closer for a better view. He saw one diver hold position while the other began to swim around the motionless animal.

James eased the throttle forward, bringing the Eagle in closer and increased candlepower on the winglet mounted floodlights. The appreciative diver gave a thumb up as he encircled the body and flippers with the net. James settled the Eagle into a hover some ten feet behind and below the creature, divers and two inflatables above. The submersibles tail pitched down and then hovered. He lowered the pilot cabin lighting twenty percent to increase the effectiveness of the winglet floodlights by minimizing reflection in the Plexiglas nose cone.

4.

Rebecca saw the glowing patch of water and the beams of light that shot from the agitated lake surface like a disco light. The two brilliant lamps of the Eagle looked like swimming pool lights, except for the brown, matter-filled water. She could see the crisp silhouette of the animal sprawled at the surface. First, a stubby, flattened tail, then, widening at the haunches, two large diamond-shaped flippers flapping in the surface current. The torso, wide with the fat of youth, slowly tapered to the shoulders. The smaller forward flippers folded back at forty-five degree angles and the neck looked like a black Anaconda. It ended in a powerful looking head and jaw, like the oversized square head of a pit bull.

The divers surfaced one after the other and made for the Zodiacs that lay in wait, their outboards idling in neutral. Rebecca now distinguished the shape that had surfaced behind them from the rest of the surface shadows. The heavier head pulled the end of the neck under the water. The creature rolled slightly, revealing the taught net that now towed the animal slowly behind the Zodiac's.

The Eagle finally surfaced. Her tail pierced the surface first, followed by the nose, then the cylindrical body with the two electric motors mounted at the stern, and, finally, the winglets. Rebecca saw her afloat some thirty feet behind the three wakes of the creature in tow. For a moment, as a small wave lapped the Eagle's clear nose—or beak as James once said—she saw James' pale face. The propellers, half above the surface, came to life in a violent froth, slowly pushing the Eagle towards the mother ship.

The Zodiacs will soon be free and able to assist, James reasoned. In the meantime, while they aren't, I'll close the distance a bit.

From where Rebecca perched, the submersible looked like a large white manta ray plodding along at the surface.

Ian was brought aboard carefully. His flippered legs and arms dangled limply. Rebecca turned away for a moment, covering her mouth involuntarily, as she saw what looked like blood streaming from his ears and nose. She looked into the bridge through the icy window to make sure no one had seen her cringe. As all attention focused on the creature that was nearing the stern platform, none had. She decided to leave the flying bridge for a better vantagepoint.

' Strolling slowly down the promenade towards the stern, she walked with her head down and was looking sullen. She looked up, blinded momentarily by the bright spotlights that lit every outside deck of the Explorer. When the purple orbs they burned in her retina cleared from sight, she saw Andrew leaning against the promenade railing, carefully observing the turmoil below.

"Hi."

"Hey, Reb'. Ian didn't look too good. They brought him inside to the infirmary and I heard the supervisor radioing for a paramedic team from Burlington. This is not good." Andrew looked to the four-pointed star anti-skid pattern on the metal decking and shook his head from side-to-side.

"It's not your fault you know. Ian is a big boy and can make his own mind up. I'm sorry if I made you feel otherwise."

"Yeah, but I knew what he was going to do and I knew it was dangerous."

"Look, Ian from day one has been the Sturm und Drang type. You can't control his actions. He's a risk taker. I was sure of that after just one dive with the guy."

Andrew simply smiled at Rebecca's attempt to make him feel

better. Though futile, he appreciated the effort. They again turned their attention to the chaotic ballet of motion on the deck below.

5.

When the Zodiac's and creature in tow approached the rear platform of the Explorer, James slowed and then stopped the Eagle. He loitered some twenty feet away in the light chop that was developing as the night breezes grew stronger. He watched as the divers again entered the cold lake and gingerly maneuvered the animal and net that wrapped around it into the correct position for retrieval.

The yellow stern crane erupted in a cloud of diesel as its engine revved and its arm swung into a position directly over the floating mass. A deckhand reached for the hook at the end of the cranes dangling cable. He precariously perched himself on the lip of metal at the edge of the platform and grabbed the heavy hook.

He signaled the crane operator to allow some slack in the cable so he could bring the hook inboard. Once accomplished, the deckhand placed one side of a heavy canvas sling over the hook while allowing the other to droop freely. Normally, the sling was used to get a large, solid hulled launch aboard. The foreman estimated that it should be capable of lifting the weight of the young Plesiosaur. He signaled the crane operator with a twirling hand to begin lowering the sling into the water. The lifting cable slowly unwound from its spool and the sling slapped the water.

The divers, having removed the net that enshrouded the creature, began to guide the sling into position. They carefully aligned it perpendicular to the towering transom of the ship. When roughly in position, one diver grabbed the side of the sling that was not secured to the hook and dove underneath the surfaced animal. Coming up on the other side, he lifted the two steel eyes that adorned either end of the sling and strained to slip them over the lifting hook. When secured, he gave a gloved thumb up. The two

Zodiacs backed off slightly and prepared to come alongside and assist the patiently waiting James and his Eagle.

Andrew was the first to spot the red strobe approaching from the horizon in the distance. Rebecca then discerned the engine sound rising above the general background noise. It seemed to emanate from all directions, bouncing off the surrounding shores and hills.

"Must be a boat bringing out the EMT's." Rebecca responded with a sigh. "This sucks."

The immense weight of the animal settled in the sling. Its torso was supported while its four flippers, the rear ones being slightly larger, and its neck hung freely. The engine of the crane strained and its cables whined as the individual steel strands that comprised it stretched. Happy with the position of the animal, the deck foreman signaled the crane operator to begin slowly hoisting the load.

The operator manipulated a lever, taking the crane engine out of neutral, and slowly pushed another to begin the lifting. The crane exhaust pipe belched a cloud of thick, soot-laden diesel smoke into the clear night air. It struggled against the five thousand pound animal and the suction of the water.

Andrew and Rebecca shimmied along the railing to better view the fireboat that had come alongside the Explorer. A firefighter lassoed the cleat of the side boat platform and three paramedics, dressed in red uniforms with reflector strips that glowed silver, carefully disembarked. They carried triage supplies in tackle boxes and, once on the dock, began the steep climb up the ramp without a word. A crewmember met them at its top, handing them radios and pointing them on their way.

"It took them about ten minutes." Rebecca pulled back her sweater sleeve, looked at her small wristwatch and mumbled. She and Andrew moved back to the position that gave them the best view of the stern activities. Guidelines radiated from the slung animal to deck hands that braced against the weight. They would utilize the lines and the strength of their backs to prevent the slings tendency to swing outboard.

"Watch out, that sling is moving." The foreman pointed at where the creatures weight had shifted and more of his torso was now unsupported. "Let's get him on the deck as quickly as possible. Okay, easy gentlemen, easy." The creature swung gently in the canvas cradle over the fantail of the Explorer, its neck and flippers dangling in the cold night air. "Easy now. Okay, I want a few men to support that neck when we swing it over."

Bobby had now joined the foreman and was carefully eyeing the Eagle, the two Zodiacs alongside as well as a diver in the water securing her to a towline. He stepped to the side when bumped by the foreman and given a Get Out of My Way look. Bobby again leaned against the cargo container that held the Eagle control center. The foreman turned his way and gave a quick wink, silently apologizing for his rudeness. Bobby nodded acceptance.

"My God, look," Andrew stretched and pointed at the animal.

"What? Where are you looking?"

"Look at its neck," Andrew stepped down from the railing he had perched on and made for the stairs to the lower level. Rebecca watched as he then emerged from below the promenade deck onto the stern deck, moving towards the foreman and the deck hands that had assembled to receive and guide the injured Plesiosaur aboard. He pointed towards the creature's neck where Rebecca now recognized a small stream of blood. The foreman immediately got on his radio.

6.

Rachel had just become a paramedic but displayed the calm, cool approach to the situation that one might expect from a veteran.

Though more senior than her, being the natural leader, Rachel ended up giving the orders to her two colleagues.

"Okay, give me vitals!" Ian's wet suit had been cut away with sharp angled scissors. Blood had dried on his face where it had exited his nose and clogged one nostril.

"Pressure: ninety over seventy. Beat slightly erratic."

"Thanks." Rachel pulled open an eye and shone her small pencil flashlight into the wide-open pupils.

"Damn, fixed and dilated. We need to get him to a hospital. Call the police boat and tell him to be ready for transport. Better yet, see if there is a Life Flight available in the area." The radio at her side squelched. She lifted it to her ear. "Go ahead . . . okay . . . understood, out." She placed the small radio down on the infirmary's small steel instrument table. "Brian, get a plasma IV going. We have a second patient on the back of the ship. Please see if can you get a preliminary. They said it's a gun shot wound to the neck."

"Shit, that can't be good. Will do, Rachel." She smiled at him, content he did not question her taking over the situation. A loud shriek emanated from the heart monitor whose sensors had been attached to Ian's bare chest.

"Damn! Cardiac arrest!"

7.

One of the deckhands shuffled under the dangling neck placed the animal's head on his shoulder and, with a grunt, lifted with his legs. Others moved underneath the neck to support it as the foreman directed the crane to slowly swing the sling and animal over the stern deck in preparation for lowering. Andrew offered some advice.

"You may not want to fully lower it onto the deck. Since it's young, it probably still has a lot of cartilage and may be unable to support its own weight on land. Like a whale or shark, its own unsupported weight can injure internal organs. If these really do go on land to lay eggs, they do it when they're older."

"Okay, Doc'." The foreman signaled the crane operator to stop the winch when the creature's torso almost touched the cold steel deck. The deckhand shifted his stance to better support the heavy head that rested on his shoulder. He saw the large, glazed over black eye slowly open.

"Um, it's waking up."

"Okay, get a tranquilizer ready. If it starts thrashing about it may hurt itself." The deckhand continued to nervously peer into the blinking, watery eye. "Bobby, get on the horn to the Eagle. She is going to have to wait until the sling is free. Sam, I want mattresses. Go to the staterooms and get me at least seven." The deckhand stood for a moment, looking confused. He then complied, making for the nearest door with the Explorer's interior.

"What are you up to?" Bobby stepped forward from where he had leaned with one leg up against the container that housed the Eagle control center.

"Well, I am going to put one mattress on the deck, and then stack three on each side, one on top of the other. That should form a vee that will support the weight of the thing, so I can free up the sling and get your boss on board. We are expecting some wind." He scanned the lake. "We already have a few white caps developing so I don't want to delay any longer. Getting that puppy on board in chop can be a struggle."

Bobby grunted agreement, remembering the time they had almost lost the Deep Eagle I while trying to bring it aboard in an unexpected storm in the deep waters off Andros, Greece. That was now of course irrelevant, as the first of the Eagle's was now a home for various marine life in the crushing depths of the Puerto Rico trench. Bobby decided he would quietly supervise, intervening only if necessary. He would make certain the Deep Eagle II did not meet the same fate.

8.

Rebecca watched as several mattresses were brought out onto the deck and stacked as the foreman had specified. Most still had the fresh linen that had been placed on them that morning by the ship's house keeping staff. One tightly stretched cover shot off the mattress, ending in a crumpled rust stained pile on the far deck. When a hatch opened, all attention focused on it. Rachel emerged. Once outside, her kinked and curly hair whipped her face in the stiffening breeze. She carried a triage kit and dangled a stethoscope from her clenched hand. She approached Andrew and began speaking with him.

Rebecca watched from above as Andrew crossed his arms while Rachel spoke, the blood draining from his face. He looked to the steel deck and kicked a scrap of PVC tubing. After a long moment, he looked up at Rebecca. With tightly pursed lips he slowly shook his head side-to-side. Rebecca cocked her head, not understanding what he was communicating and then, realized that he was telling her Ian had died. A tear slowly flowed down her blushed cheek. Andrew stared out to the lake for a moment and then turned for where the foreman directed the final lowering of the Plesiosaur.

"Okay, bring it down slowly. Sammy, make sure those stacked mattresses don't move when we lower it between them. Get some support on that side there." He pointed with a cigarette he had just lit and adjusted the sleeves of his blue coveralls.

"Right chief." The deckhand scrambled to comply. Slowly the sling came down. The creature seemed to have slipped into unconsciousness once again or at least had closed its eyes. When it contacted the first of the padding, a small grunt exited its slightly open mouth its weight forcing the air from its lungs. A thick saliva bubble formed on one of its two nostrils as it breathed shallow.

"S-So, that's what we have been hearing about?" Rachel paused for a moment and soaked in the scene.

A cameraman emerged from the ship interior, his eyes still half closed with sleep. He began filming despite his inability to focus and moved in on his subject until the foreman raised a halting palm and shot a warning glance. Now, joined by the rest of the team, Rachel began setting up a makeshift triage. The tackle box opened, telescoping its drawers that overflowed with supplies.

"Okay, we have a gun shot to the neck." Brian stood in awe. "C'mon, let's gape later. It might have grazed an artery. We have a lot of blood here." Brian snapped out of it and immediately applied pressure with a large sheet of gauze. "I need vitals." Both of Rachel's colleagues stopped and looked at her questioningly.

"Okay fearless leader, from where?" Brian gave his best sarcastic look. Rachel cocked her hips and locked her double-jointed leg.

"Good question."

Andrew stepped forward.

"See this breastplate here?" Andrew ran his finger along the broad, bony front of the animal. "The heart and lungs are behind this. Similar to a human, the heart is slightly off to the left of the sternum. Feel this notch here?" Rachel nodded as Andrew cupped her hand in his and ran her fingers along the rough, leathery skin. "Get your reading here."

"What kind of beat should it have and what's a normal pressure?" Andrew paused and shrugged his shoulders.

"Hey, remember, up until a few days ago we thought these were extinct. I have no idea. I'd say similar to an young elephant."

"What do I look like? I'm not a freaking zoo keeper?" *This one was feisty,* Andrew thought. He tried to smile and then looked up at Rebecca who appeared morose. He decided to join and comfort her and made for the stairs that lead to the promenade deck. "Okay guys, let's get to it. Do the best you can."

9.

"Okay, sling is away." The foreman guided the sling over the transom of the Explorer and signaled the crane operator to again lower it into the lake. Divers stood geared to assist James and the Eagle into the heavy harness. Spotlights again focused on the water at the Explorers stern, which, despite its mass, corkscrewed slightly in the erratic surface.

Once assured that the Zodiac's had secured their lines to the hard-point eye that jutted from the top and middle of the Eagle's cylindrical body, James began powering down systems. He decided to submerge the Eagle another foot to help minimize the effect of the chop the steadily increasing wind had stirred up. James watched through the nose as the Zodiacs began to slap against the surface, disturbed by the growing waves.

"NEST."

"Go ahead James." Though outside of the control center, in order to better direct the submersible recovery, Bobby donned a headset and connected it to a receptacle under a small panel in the corrugated wall.

"It's getting rough out here. Any estimate on recovery?"

"The sling is clear now and the Zodiacs will bring you in any moment."

"Okay, most systems powered down. I am going to keep one battery on the circuit and motors on standby in case this chop forces a maneuver." James switched the circuit for battery one from the open to the closed position with a resounding click. James, exhausted, rubbed his dry and red eyes. "NEST, how's Ian? Are they taking good care of him? Thought I had lost him there for a minute."

"Um, no word yet boss." Bobby looked at his shoes, feeling guilty for the lie. Although aware of Ian's fate, he was reluctant to distract James with the news.

James watched as the propellers of the Zodiac outboards began to revolve, kicking up a stream of spinning bubbles and white foam. The towline stretched for a moment, then sprung back, jerking, before the Eagle settled into a slow, forward motion.

10.

Bobby watched as the two inflatables carefully made for the transom. Their bows rose and slapped back down on the lake water as the effect of the growing waves became more pronounced. The two towlines they trailed radiated from their sterns and formed a vee where they came together, penetrating the lake surface.

James made subtle adjustments to pitch and trim controls to counter-act the uneven pulling force on the submersible. He grew concerned with the now angry chop. White capped waves careened above him. He felt their effect on the light inflatables as it was transmitted down the towlines to the submersible.

"NEST. EAGLE here. I want extra guidelines ready. Once out of the water, she's going to be swinging like mad."

"Roger EAGLE. We are ready for yah."

Captain Thomas—looking tired and, at the same time, focused—ordered the Explorers bow thruster be used. He would try and maintain the Explorer's position until operations on the fantail were complete. The chop now slapped along the ships starboard side and had started her rocking and moving out of position. A bridge crewman immediately entered commands at a keyboard, allowing a small computer to tie into the global positioning system in order to facilitate accurate station keeping. The bow immediately began to swing back to starboard as the computer and keel-mounted propeller began their task.

"Make the pivot point the stern. We want the least motion there right now. Use the rudders if you need to." Captain Thomas adjusted his hat and took a long sip of the black coffee someone had put in his hand.

"Aye sir!"

"Okay. Let's do it folks!" The Zodiac's released their towlines and immediately deployed their divers. Alfred was the first to splash into the frigid, turbulent dark waters. The dense canvas of the sling floated at the surface while its metal spars and supports clanked against the aluminum hull of the Explorer, dinging its bright white paint job. Smudges of blue anti-fouling paint from the waterline appeared on the harness as it slapped and bumped the Explorer.

The intensifying winds stirred up dust, paint chips and rust speckles from the aft deck, tossing them into a dancing cloud that burned the eyes and stung the nostrils.

Alfred and his assistant expertly secured the harness around the Eagle in moments.

James watched through the nose as they swam below, around and on top of the now bobbing Eagle. As the submersible moved in the water, the sound of the canvas rubbing on the hull and the metal fittings tapping and scraping echoed through the pilot cylinder. Alfred made for the surface and, once there, gave a thumb up to the foreman who stood on the fantail, his legs far apart to counter-act the heaving deck. Before submerging again, he watched as the foreman's blue New York Yankees baseball cap was captured and taken by the wind into the dark night. It would inevitably end up on the lonely gray silt wasteland some three hundred feet below after a long, slow descent.

"Crane, do your thing. Make it slow and gentle." The foreman climbed onto the crane cab and combed his flying hair with his thick fingers. He grabbed on to a handhold and hung by one arm. The crane's diesel engine sprang to life in a noxious puff of thick, black smoke that was quickly swept away and dissipated by the now howling wind.

James felt the first tug and the groans of the canvas sling as it began to lift the heavy machine. The divers hovered some five feet away, gently kicking to assist the partially inflated buoyancy control devices they wore in keeping them afloat. They were ready to adjust any of the sling straps that may shift position as the strain grew or steady the Eagle should it start to rotate on the steel wire.

As the Eagle rose from the grasp and suction of the water, the crest of a wave slapped it. James felt queasy as he watched the deck and horizon pitch and roll through the clear nose. A cold sweat formed on his generous forehead and his eyes rolled in their sockets. He closed them tight to prevent throwing up the late night snack of cheesy French Onion soup he had eaten shortly before the unscheduled dive.

11.

Rachel worked frantically to resuscitate the struggling Plesiosaur. She struggled to pierce the dense, rubbery skin with the relatively small needle in an attempt to get stabilizing plasma into the blood stream. Guessing from the slow pupil reactions when she directed her pocket light beam at them, she assumed the creature was in shock and perhaps comatose. Hastily attached monitors did their best to deliver vital signs to their respective computers and readouts.

"Brian, forget that! Just count the rise and fall of the abdomen as she breaths." Brian abandoned his stethoscope, shrugged his shoulders and placed the palm of his right hand on the large torso of the animal. He twitched his arm to reveal his wristwatch from underneath his windbreaker and began to count the laborious breaths.

Rachel studied the traced curve of the electrocardiogram display and then ran her finger along the lines displayed by the electrocardiograph, the record of electric potentials associated with the electric currents that traverse the heart. Brian, now done with his count, began attaching electrodes to the skullcap of the still animal. An electroencephalograph would collect the feedback from these sensors and an electroencephalogram would be produced to help them determine the status of the brain.

"Damn it! We need a veterinarian. I am taking stabs in the dark here." Rachel's frustration at her unorthodox patient grew. "Brian, what was that count?"

"Seven."

"Seven? Seven! I don't know if that is good or bad!"

"Let's assume it is slow." Brian's calm response made Rachel realize she was growing stressed and she immediately calmed herself.

"Right. Good assumption. Let's tube her and get an oxygen tank ready."

12.

James came close to loosing his snack and making an awful mess of the pilot cabin and control panels. Luckily, just as he again tasted the sweet onions and Swiss cheese, the Eagle landed firmly in its cradle.

"EAGLE. NEST. You are aboard. We'll get you out of there as quickly as possible." James did not respond but instead swallowed hard and opened one of his tightly shut eyes. He was face-to-face with the animal. The supporting mattresses hid the majority of its body. He shook his head when he saw the tubes and wires emanating from the helpless animal and the frantically working medical personnel. He fought back a tear as he began to feel partially responsible for its fate.

"Hey, Bobby. Ian. What is the word on Ian?"

"James . . . we lost Ian several minutes ago." Bobby clenched his teeth waiting for a response to come through the radio. None did. James sobbed freely, certain that no one could see through the fog and ice crystals that had formed on the nose cone. The culmination of stress, coming off an adrenaline rush and the dreadful news made it impossible not to cry. For the first time ever, he felt his age and the weariness of his body.

The clang of a wrench against the metal hull startled him, making him choke back his tears. They had begun to loosen the ring of bolts and gaskets that made the submersible watertight. Soon he would feel the cold night air rush in as the submersible was rolled apart and he was pulled leg first out of the back of the forward section.

13.

Rachel opened her coveralls to aerate her sweaty skin. The new red coveralls the company had given her were still stiff and scratchy. She sat on her supply box and let her head fall into her hands. Brian walked up to her and rested his hand on her shoulder, giving a gentle squeeze of reassurance. The red blood vessels made the blue iris of her eyes look even more pronounced. She sniffled. A look of surrender replaced the one of determination that had occupied her face.

"Okay. We might as well call it. Brian."

"I have 3:42 A.M." Brian tried the most matter-of-fact voice he could muster under the circumstances. Rachel fought back tears.

"Okay. Patient deceased at 3:42 A.M. Make a good log of all procedures used as well as medicines and quantities."

"Okay, Rachel." Brian pushed his glasses up on his sharp nose.

Above and behind them, Rebecca wept in Andrew's comforting arms. He led her to the warm interior of the Explorer and towards her cabin.

14.

"Aw, crap!" James raised his head from the blanket that enshrouded him and the chicken noodle soup that, despite his disturbed stomach, he attempted to sip. "We have company." The foreman, now crowned by a white hard hat, pointed into the night sky. The police helicopter that had been searching the general area of the pen now banked and made for the Explorer. Following as quickly and closely as possible, the blue strobes and searchlight of a police boat also changed direction and headed towards the Explorer. "I think Vermont's finest have just realized what is going on." About to order that the creature's body be covered by a tarpaulin, he cut the words off before they had a chance to form and roll off his tongue. Looking around, his crew seemed to walk about aimlessly, as if in a dream-state. Bobby and James stood mannequin-like, deep in their own thoughts.

As the Bell Jet Ranger settled over the fantail of the Explorer, the foreman waved his arms to alert them to the rigging and cables that were nearly invisible in the early morning darkness. The tips of the spinning blades, traveling faster than the speed of sound, radiated small sonic booms that echoed through the night and reverberated among the corners and turns of the Explorer's steel superstructure. The large spotlight that hung beneath the helicopter pilot scanned the Explorers deck and, once illuminating the sprawled creature, fixed its bright gaze upon it.

James and Bobby shielded their eyes from the light and dust the rhythmically thumping blades kicked up. James spilled the rest of his unappetizing soup and pulled the blanket over his nose and mouth. Bobby gestured that they enter the shelter of the control center. James followed, rolling his eyes and looking extremely tired. As they entered the shadows of the NEST, Bobby overheard the foreman speaking into his radio.

"Okay, looks like we have a police boat approaching. Inform the captain we may be boarded. He is required to be present to grant permission to the police if there is no warrant. Since no Coast Guard personnel are present, he must give the okay. *Do not* let them up the ramp until he arrives, understood? Good, thanks. Out."

Captain Thomas removed his face from the black rubber skirt of the radar screen after following the green blip it displayed.

"Yeah, I see them. Tell that chopper to *back off*. We are moving too much to mess around. Damn hot shots!" He moved for the foggy window and again raised his binoculars. Scanning for a moment, he then spotted the green and red navigational lights perched on the bow of the rapidly approaching police boat. It rose and fell in the choppy water, its two occupants standing and absorbing the impacts with their legs. As the boat drew closer, a siren came on to accompany the blue strobes. The captain lowered the glasses and nodded to the first mate. A klaxon sounded, bringing the watch to general quarters. Though usually reserved for inspections or actual emergencies, the captain wanted his ship in top shape if the law was to come aboard.

"What are you going to say sir?" The first mate stood at near attention.

"Well, the individual responsible for the animals release is no longer with us. I was merely conducting a rescue. Anyway, it is the Explorer Channel's lawyers that will have to deal with this one. When they leased my vessel and services, the company and I are absolved of any legal action resulting from their expedition. Let's have a priest brought out, okay? I want the last rites administered properly to the poor kid. Confirm his religion, it could be we need a rabbi. Who knows?"

"Yes sir, right away."

A deckhand stood on the bobbing platform, ready to receive the police boat. As it came alongside, she caught the poorly thrown line and began to wrap it around the nearest cleat in figure eight fashion. Once secured, she again stood, saluted casually and welcomed the officers.

"Sirs, kindly wait here for permission from the captain to board." The younger of the two officers looked to his partner and, when a nod was delivered, rested his hand on the butt of his holstered Glock 30 handgun and reluctantly waited.

15.

The arrival of the priest removed any denial. Ian was dead. A somber, silent mood settled over the Explorer. Even the wind seemed to slow to a quiet breeze. The priest, Father Francis Cullany, showed the fact he had been roused from a deep sleep and had hastily donned his robes. His purple and gold scapular hung from his neck. When offered some breakfast from the galley, he refused, wanting instead to deliver the sacrament as soon as possible.

"I will have something afterwards, thank you. Can you please show me to the infirmary." Though his eyes were puffy and red, his smile was broad, warm and comforting.

Making for the infirmary, Captain Thomas strolled down the central corridor of the Explorer. His stride was determined as he was still riled from the arrogance of the police officers. "Damn land loving high school dropouts." Though finally allowed to board and conduct their business, their contempt for maritime tradition was disturbing. "Stupid Gestapo wannabe's." The captain continued to mumble to himself, his eyes fixed on the carpet pattern and his shiny shoes. He almost missed the door, embroiled in his own thoughts and emotions and feeling the effects of the interrupted night of sleep. He turned and spun, facing the red and white cross of the infirmary door. He gently rapped it. A muffled, "Enter," filtered through the thin, pressed wood door. Captain Thomas removed his cap, ran his fingers through his matted hair and turned the knob.

Father Callany knelt over the bed that held Ian. He made the sign of the cross on Ian's forehead, pushing aside his still wet long matted hair. Despite the best efforts of the staff to clean him up, dried blood still crusted his nostrils and ear lobes. Ian's wet suit had been removed and his naked body placed in the bed under fresh linens and a blanket.

"Please excuse the interruption Father." Captain Thomas stood still, his head hung low and hands together. He squeezed his cap rim between two fingers. He did not speak again until the sacrament had been completed and the priest slowly turned and looked at him. "Father, the representatives of Mr. Chelsea's family have contacted me concerning the," he clears his throat, "body." Father Callany closed his eyes for a moment, acknowledging what had been said but unable to shake the ethereal feeling that came over him whenever performing his duties. "He is to be transported as soon as possible to Logan for a flight to JFK in New York. Once there, they have arranged for space on a Concorde flight to London. They have asked for divine escort. They, how did they put it, promise to be generous to your church."

"It would be my pleasure. Will you arrange for a boat and then a flight from Burlington to Logan?"

"I am sure we can do something." Captain Thomas gave a final glance at Ian lying in state before turning and leaving for the bridge. Too young, too damn young, he thought.

"Oh, my dear captain, should you need me, I will be on the back of the boat tending to the other soul that has passed tonight." Captain Thomas looked momentarily surprised and then tipped his hat.

16.

"Okay, make sure that spike is set well. This stone is a bit brittle." The spelunker hit the spike again with his hammer, driving it another inch into the rock face. "I'd say we are about two miles in. You'd better place another marker." The officer continued to rummage through the equipment they had found and then eyed the bottomless shaft that lay before them and inevitably had to be traversed. The professional spelunkers lead the way. The police officer, required to be on hand for proper logging of any evidence related to the case, would follow once the appropriate safety lines and harnesses had been established. "Looks like they shed some of their equipment here, probably to lighten the load before crossing the shaft." The team to do the same thing. The young cop gave him a Don't Tell Me My Business look, but said, "Yeah, your probably right."

17.

"Do not interfere with my duty and I shall not interfere with yours." Father Callany pushed aside the police officer that stood guard over the carcass of the dead Plesiosaur. He fiddled with the rosary beads and cross, his eyes widening with every step he took towards this . . . miracle.

James and Bobby stood silently watching from the shadows. The ship deckhand's and their foreman gathered around the now kneeling holy man. Heads bowed instinctively. A line of Hebrew could be heard from the small crowd that had encircled the animal and its attendant. An Arabic prayer sounded just like mumbled English to the untrained ear and blended in with the other whispers and the breeze. Hats came off, hands came together and heads bowed instinctively.

"Bless the passing of your child Oh Lord. Take his soul into your arms and forever keep it near." Father Callany's eyes were wide, soaking in the sight before him while trying to concentrate on the rites. He ran his fingers in the sign of the cross along the rubbery skin of the creature's head.

Rachel continued to sob on the periphery of the crowd.

On the fantail, the last of the expedition experiments was being carried out. First, a cement filled can labeled *Kalamata Olive Oil—Product of Greece* was pushed overboard and sent to the bottom. It trailed a steel cable, down which a stainless steel coring device would travel. A low-tech means of guiding and delivering a high tech device. Once at the bottom, the speed of its descent would drive the device several feet into the peaty sediment of the lake floor. This layered coring sample would yield nematodes, a millennium old worm-like segmented creature. Though usually less in fresh water, ten to twenty million of the creatures could exist in every square foot of bottom muck.

Once at the surface and analyzed, the soupy samples could yield data on climatic change and the effect of pollution on the Lake Champlain ecosystem. James turned to watch as the coring device was threaded to the now taught guide wire and allowed to begin it kamikaze dive for the bottom.

18.

The officer shone a light down the deep, water-filled shaft. Ahead lay a tunnel where scratches on its floor revealed the site of a struggle.

"Something got dragged here against its will. Hey what's this?" Utilizing tweezers and a small Zip Lock bag labeled Evidence, he picked a small collection of hair and clotted blood from a fold in the rock. "I'd say whatever happened, happened right here. Looks like we might have foul play as well. They must've run into some whacked out hobo that was using the joint as a home." He again shone the lamp down the hole, catching a glimpse of something. "Let's get a line down there. I think I see something floating. Anyone volunteer to climb down?"

"I'll do it." A wide-eyed, spidery looking individual stepped forward, adjusting the way the helmet sat on his unkempt hair.

"Okay, easy, easy. Lower him down smooth like."

The spelunker was half down the shaft when he said, "Hold on, got something here."

"Remember to use the tweezers and get it in a bag." The officer refreshed the spelunker's memory of unfamiliar police procedures.

"It looks like, like a fingernail." He turned his head, directing his helmet mounted light on the rather flush sides of the shaft. After bagging the item, he continued down towards the water, some seven feet below his dangling boots. "There is something in the water. Hold on." He lowered his head, directing the light towards the metallic looking surface of the cave water. He squinted his eyes. "My God, it's a leg." His muffled voice echoed in the confined space.

19.

Andrew rolled off of Rebecca but kept her naked body close. They both breathed heavily. Neither spoke but stared blankly at the plain ceiling and the single lamp that hung from its center. It swayed side to side as the Explorer's hull moved in the disturbed lake, almost hypnotizing them. Andrew wiped his sweaty head on the pillow and looked to Rebecca.

"Sweetheart, you okay?"

"Yeah, I'm okay. Just very tired. I don't think I have stayed up all night since college. Hell, I didn't think I even could anymore." Her smile was forced and she again looked at the pendulum-like motion of the swinging light.

"Want some water?"

"Yeah, sure." She watched him move for the small mini-bar refrigerator and remove two chilled bottles of sparkling mineral water. The whoosh of escaping bubbles got her attention when Andrew opened one and took a long draw on the bottle. The sharp bubbles cut through the cottony taste in his mouth and throat.

"What happens after this?" Andrew paused for a moment and then lowered the bottle from his mouth, handing Rebecca hers after twisting off its jagged top.

"Well, I do have to go to Australia after this for at least a few weeks. The big find I told you about. Probably stop in Los Angeles for a few days on the way. After that, it's back to Colorado."

"I meant with us silly." Andrew winked, trying to cheer her up.

"Well, you work in Denver, me in Boulder. What does that tell you?"

"I was hoping you'd say that." Andrew started to hum Rocky Mountain High as he put on his underwear and shirt.

"You hungry? I could eat a horse."

"No, I'm fine." Rebecca was surprised at how quickly Andrew could forget. Perhaps he was just better at hiding his feelings than most. She decided she had plenty of time to figure him out.

Epilogue: Carrying On

1.

"El vuelo seis cinquente dos de American Airlines desde Miami ja ha jegado en la puerta doce. American Airlines flight six five two from Miami has arrived at gate twelve." The announcement crackled and echoed through the mainly cement terminal.

Bobby passed under the illuminated sign that said, Luis Muñoz Marin International Airport. Bienvenidos-Welcome to Puerto Rico. La Isla de Ecanto—The Island of Enchantment. He looked at his dive watch. "Perfect." His barong, a light Filipino shirt, and his dark complexion blended him into the hordes of Puerto Rican's making for flights to the mainland.

The rhythmic songs of Coquís, a tiny but vocal tree frog, made the cool evening even more enticing. The warm Trade Wind breezes blew through the open airport. The smell of bacalaitos, a fried cod fish pastry, being sold from carts near the taxi line filled the air. He considered buying one but remembered the Cubano sandwich he had stopped for near the airport in Isla Verde and his ever-expanding waist. He strolled past the crowds and passed through security, having to remove his watch lest it triggers the metal detector—which it always did.

Bobby strolled up the worn carpeted corridor, heading for gate twelve. When twenty feet away, the gate door opened, releasing a stampede of people heading for the open arms of waiting family. Bobby smiled when he saw James. White hat, white shirt, white pants and sandals. The smile faded a bit when he saw James looked much older than he remembered him. Three weeks only since Vermont, Bobby thought. The toll it took on him is obvious. James looked up, his eyes magnified by his glasses, and smiled widely when he saw his trusty assistant and friend.

"Bobby!" They embraced for a quick moment and Bobby instinctively took hold of James' carried luggage.

"Hi boss."

"How has everything been going?"

"Well, I was able to rent a warehouse on the water, you know, where the Antilles Airboats took off from?" James nodded. "The Deep Eagle III has been moved there already—still working on the boat though. I was able to rent an apartment for us on Callé Washington in Condado."

"That's across from the Presbyterian Hospital, right?"

"Yup. Should be okay for a while. It's only half an hour from the docks."

"Perfect. I can't wait to get to work on the new sub. A two man version. I am so excited! Faster and deeper she'll go! It is good to see you old boy." James and Bobby made for baggage claim and, once the bags were collected, went out into the warm Caribbean night. James smiled and took a deep breath of the moist, salty air.

2.

The cold wind came off the Rocky Mountain's like a freight train, stabbing Rebecca's red cheeks and exposed hands. She wiped the magnetic strip of her access card after it failed to open the door to the Oceanographic Modeling Center of the National Oceanic and Atmospheric Association. She tried again, swiping the card in the panel slot. This time the electric motor slid the heavy dark safety glass door along its track. She immediately felt the warmth of the centers conditioned interior rush out into the frigid day. The change from the bright, thin high altitude air to the dark computer center blinded her momentarily before able to remove her sunglasses.

"Dr. McClintock! Great hunter of monsters!" She was in no

mood for the peanut gallery and made straight for her office. The familiar brass placard: *Dr. Rebecca McClintock—Director*, stared her in the face as she inserted the key in the brass doorknob. When the door opened, the air of her office smelled stagnant, like a tomb opened for the first time in ages. She immediately eyed her coffee maker and set about making a hot pot to ease her jet lag.

She powered up her personal computer and fell into her chair. As it booted up and launched Windows, she reached for her dusty green and white Cousteau Society mug. She blew into it, kicking up a cloud of grime into her face. It's going to be a long day, she thought. A beep from the computer confirmed it was done loading the operating system. She reached for the mouse, directed the cursor to the television icon and double clicked. She clicked the mouse on the graphical channel selector, changing from Star Trek to Days of Our Lives; then Oprah to CNN. She turned up the volume dial on her computers under monitor speakers.

"Ladies and gentlemen, the President of the United States." The White House Press Secretary stepped aside, giving the podium and microphone to the president.

"Good day. We have all been amazed by the recent discovery in Lake Champlain. As we all know by now, these marine reptiles, Plesiosaurs, have long been thought extinct."

Rebecca leaned back in her swivel chair and put her feet up on her desk, closing her eyes but continuing to listen intently. "I have asked the Director of the Environmental Protection Agency to list these creatures as endangered as defined under the Endangered Species Act of 1973. This would afford them the protection they deserve and preserve the environment upon which they rely, Lake Champlain. I will ask the leaders of other nations where it is suspected that these creatures may also live to follow suit and grant similar protections. This would of course apply to Loch Ness in Scotland and a long list of other suspected lakes around the globe. At this time I will take a few questions. Please just a few, I have the Prime Minister of Great Britain waiting in the Oval Office for me. If I leave him there too long, he tends to steal my cigars, something that could easily lead to war between our two great nations. So, keep it short." The room of reporters, camera operators and sound technicians erupted in laughter, relaxing with the Presidents jovial mood.

3.

Andrew took a deep breath of the carbon dioxide and monoxide laden air. The dry bright day warmed his face and body. He stood and stretched, glimpsing the Screen Actors Guild building, the Pavilion for Japanese Art, the Los Angeles County Museum of Art as well as the rest of museum row. The tall palm trees that lined Wilshire Boulevard swayed in the light morning breeze.

"You know, sometimes I think Los Angeles gets a bum wrap." Andrew removed his tee shirt, letting the rapidly warming day caress his skin. The concrete groaned and the air began to shimmy as heat built up.

"Yeah? Try living here." Gunther Landers pulled his pants up slightly and again knelt on the soft earth. "Did you get a substitute for your classes?"

"Only for the first week we're gonna be in Australia. The second and third weeks are still not filled." Andrew took the final bite of the bagel with cream cheese he had bought at the restaurant next to the George C. Page Museum of La Brea Discoveries on Fairfax Avenue. He sipped his bottle of lemon ice tea, pondered for a lazy moment and said, "How 'bout lunch on the Third Street promenade in Santa Monica? I heard a new Italian place opened up and is pretty good. We can take the 32 bus right down Wilshire from here. It'll take us right there."

"Okay." Gunther was never one to turn down an invitation for a meal. "How about helping me finish up here first?" Cleaning a gooey cluster of ancient shells, seeds, insects and pollen from Pit#9 of the La Brea Tar Pits, Gunther's pudgy hands made the delicate work all the more taxing.

"Sure big guy." Andrew stepped over a sticky hill of tar that had erupted through the soggy lawn the previous night, splattering a young tree with its viscid discharge. Andrew had overheard a tour guide state that the high levels of precipitation associated with the El Niño phenomenon had saturated the ground, increasing its weight and forcing more tar than ever to make its way up through the fissures and fractures of the bedrock below them. He poked at the mess with a stick. "I wonder if Angelinos realize they're sitting on top of a likely site for a volcanic eruption."

"Hey, it adds to the charm of the place. *Please* Andrew, give me a hand." Andrew dropped the goo-encrusted stick and reached for the small pick Gunther was handing him.

A pocket of methane gas seeped up through the tar, formed into a large bubble and then burst, spraying Andrew and James with the black muck. They both looked at the large *No Smoking* sign that hung on the small chain link fence that formed a square perimeter around the open, asphalt filled pit. They then scanned the small congregation of on lookers that had formed, looking for potentially explosive and deadly non-compliance.

4.

The old man stored the oars after reaching his favorite fishing spot in his small wooden rowboat. He scanned the somber Lake Champlain and unpacked the small lunch he had made and placed each item in an ordered row on the worn wood plank seat in front of him. First, the plaid thermos of chicken noodle soup, then the tuna fish sandwich and finally, a bright red apple. A phalarope overhead spotted the feast and began to circle the small boat.

The calm lake gently gurgled against the sides of the boat. The day was bright and the air crisp.

Choosing his favorite lure from his tackle box, a silvery spinner given to him by a Native American at a local powwow, he expertly tied it to the end of his line and, swinging the rod overboard, lowered it into the water. He would let it drop to the bottom and then slowly reel it up, jerking it every few feet to entice the cautious trout, bass or pike. When he released the drag on the reel, the lure began its descent, moving swiftly due to its weight. When almost on the bottom, it passed a shadow in the dark water.

Had the fake, plastic bead eyes of the lure been able to see, a green glow would have emanated from the shadow. The green glow became two distinct and bright orbs and finally two particular outlines.

The large female Plesiosaur and her young, smaller off spring, glided through the darkness. With its sonar abilities limited, the youngster relied on the glowing chemicals on its mother's forehead to stay close by her side.

Having fed on the abundance of fish near and in the thermocline, they headed for the lake bottom and the gaping chasm in the rocky, protective Badlands. Once there, they dove for the entrance to the underworld and the shelter and safety of their home.

-VONB

90000
9 780738 821320